TILL WE HAVE FACES

BY C. S. LEWIS

The Pilgrim's Regress
The Problem of Pain
The Screwtape Letters and *Screwtape Proposes a Toast*
Broadcast Talks
The Abolition of Man
Christian Behaviour
Beyond Personality
The Great Divorce
George MacDonald: An Anthology
Miracles
Transposition and Other Addresses
Mere Christianity
Surprised by Joy: The Shape of My Early Life
Reflections on the Psalms
The World's Last Night and Other Essays
The Four Loves
Letters to Malcolm: Chiefly on Prayer
Poems
Of Other Worlds: Essays and Stories
Letters of C. S. Lewis
Narrative Poems
A Mind Awake: An Anthology of C. S. Lewis
On Stories: And Other Essays on Literature
Spirits in Bondage: A Cycle of Lyrics
The Business of Heaven: Daily Readings from C. S. Lewis
Present Concerns
All My Road Before Me: The Diary of C. S. Lewis 1922–1927

FOR CHILDREN
THE CHRONICLES OF NARNIA:
   The Lion, the Witch and the Wardrobe
   Prince Caspian
   The Voyage of the Dawn Treader
   The Silver Chair
   The Horse and His Boy
   The Magician's Nephew
   The Last Battle

FICTION
Out of the Silent Planet
Perelandra
That Hideous Strength
Till We Have Faces: A Myth Retold
The Dark Tower and Other Stories
Boxen: The Imaginary World of the Young C. S. Lewis

TILL WE HAVE FACES A MYTH RETOLD

C. S. LEWIS

Drawings by Fritz Eichenberg

Love is too young to know what conscience is

A Harvest Book
Harcourt Brace & Company
San Diego   New York   London

Requests for permission to make copies of any part of the work should be
mailed to: Permissions Department, Harcourt Brace & Company,
6277 Sea Harbor Drive, Orlando, Florida 32887-6777.

Library of Congress Cataloging-in-Publication Data
Lewis, Clive Staples, 1898–1963.
Till we have faces.
(A Harvest book)
1. Psyche (Goddess)—Fiction. 2. Cupid—Fiction.
I. Title.
[PZ3.L58534Ti   1980]   [PR6023.E926]   823'.9'12   79-24272
ISBN 0-15-690436-5 (pbk.)

Printed in the United States of America
Y X W V U

TO JOY DAVIDMAN

ONE

I AM old now and have not much to fear from the anger of gods. I have no husband nor child, nor hardly a friend, through whom they can hurt me. My body, this lean carrion that still has to be washed and fed and have clothes hung about it daily with so many changes, they may kill as soon as they please. The succession is provided for. My crown passes to my nephew.

Being, for all these reasons, free from fear, I will write in this book what no one who has happiness would dare to write. I will accuse the gods, especially the god who lives on the Grey Mountain. That is, I will tell all he has done to me from the very beginning, as if I were making my complaint of him before a judge. But there is no judge between gods and men, and the god of the mountain will not answer me. Terrors and plagues are not an answer. I write in Greek as my old master taught it to me. It may some day happen that a traveller from the Greeklands will again lodge in this palace and read the book. Then he will talk of it among the Greeks, where there is great freedom of speech even about the

3

gods themselves. Perhaps their wise men will know whether my complaint is right or whether the god could have defended himself if he had made an answer.

I was Orual the eldest daughter of Trom, King of Glome. The city of Glome stands on the left hand of the river Shennit to a traveller who is coming up from the south-east, not more than a day's journey above Ringal, which is the last town southward that belongs to the land of Glome. The city is built about as far back from the river as a woman can walk in the third of an hour, for the Shennit overflows her banks in the spring. In summer there was then dry mud on each side of it, and reeds, and plenty of waterfowl. About as far beyond the ford of the Shennit as our city is on this side of it you come to the holy house of Ungit. And beyond the house of Ungit (going all the time east and north) you come quickly to the foothills of the Grey Mountain. The god of the Grey Mountain, who hates me, is the son of Ungit. He does not, however, live in the house of Ungit, but Ungit sits there alone. In the furthest recess of her house where she sits it is so dark that you cannot see her well, but in summer enough light may come down from the smoke-holes in the roof to show her a little. She is a black stone without head or hands or face, and a very strong goddess. My old master, whom we called the Fox, said she was the same whom the Greeks call Aphrodite; but I write all the names of people and places in our own language.

I will begin my writing with the day my mother died and they cut off my hair, as the custom is. The Fox

—but he was not with us then—said it is a custom we learned from the Greeks. Batta, the nurse, shore me and and my sister Redival outside the palace at the foot of the garden which runs steeply up the hill behind. Redival was my sister, three years younger than I, and we two were still the only children. While Batta was using the shears many other of the slave women were standing round, from time to time wailing for the Queen's death and beating their breasts; but in between they were eating nuts and joking. As the shears snipped and Redival's curls fell off, the slaves said, "Oh, what a pity! All the gold gone!" They had not said anything like that while I was being shorn. But what I remember best is the coolness of my head and the hot sun on the back of my neck when we were building mud houses, Redival and I, all that summer afternoon.

Our nurse Batta was a big-boned, fair-haired, hard-handed woman whom my father had bought from traders who got her further north. When we plagued her she would say, "Only wait till your father brings home a new queen to be your stepmother. It'll be changed times for you then. You'll have hard cheese instead of honey-cakes then and skim milk instead of red wine. Wait and see."

As things fell out, we got something else before we got a stepmother. There was a bitter frost that day. Redival and I were booted (we mostly went barefoot or sandalled) and trying to slide in the yard which is at the back of the oldest part of the palace, where the walls are wooden. There was ice enough all the way from the byre-door to the big dunghill, what with frozen spills of milk and puddles and the stale of the beasts, but too rough for sliding. And out comes Batta, with the cold reddening her nose, calling out, "Quick, quick! Ah, you filthies! Come and be cleaned and then to the King. You'll see who's waiting for you there. My word! This'll be a change for you."

"Is it the Stepmother?" said Redival.

"Oh, worse than that, worse than that; you'll see," said Batta, polishing Redival's face with the end of her apron. "Lots of whippings for the pair of you, lots of ear-pullings, lots of hard work." Then we were led off and over to the new parts of the palace, where it is built of painted brick, and there were guards in their armour, and skins and heads of animals hung up on the walls. In the Pillar Room our father was standing by the hearth, and opposite him there were three men in travelling dress whom we knew well enough—traders who came to Glome three times a year. They were just packing up their scales, so we knew they had been paid for something, and one was putting up a fetter, so we knew they must have sold our father a slave. There was a short, thick-set man standing before them, and we knew this must be the man they had sold, for you could still see the sore places on his legs where the irons had been. But he did not look like any other slave we had ever known. He was very bright-eyed, and whatever of his hair and beard was not grey was reddish.

"Now, Greekling," said my father to this man, "I trust to beget a prince one of these days and I have a

6

mind to see him brought up in all the wisdom of your people. Meanwhile practice on *them*." (He pointed at us children.) "If a man can teach a girl, he can teach anything." Then, just before he sent us away, he said, "Especially the elder. See if you can make her wise; it's about all she'll ever be good for." I didn't understand that, but I knew it was like things I had heard people say of me ever since I could remember.

I loved the Fox, as my father called him, better than anyone I had yet known. You would have thought that a man who had been free in the Greeklands, and then been taken in war and sold far away among the barbarians, would be downcast. And so he was sometimes, possibly more often than I, in my childishness, guessed. But I never heard him complain; and I never heard him boast (as all the other foreign slaves did) about the great man he had been in his own country. He had all sorts of sayings to cheer himself up with: "No man can be an exile if he remembers that all the world is one city," and, "Everything is as good or bad as our opinion makes it." But I think what really kept him cheerful was his inquisitiveness. I never knew such a man for questions. He wanted to know everything about our country and language and ancestors and gods, and even our plants and flowers.

That was how I came to tell him all about Ungit, about the girls who are kept in her house, and the presents that brides have to make to her, and how we sometimes, in a bad year, have to cut someone's throat and pour the blood over her. He shuddered when I said

7

that and muttered something under his breath; but a moment later he said, "Yes, she is undoubtedly Aphrodite, though more like the Babylonian than the Greek. But come, I'll tell you a tale of our Aphrodite."

Then he deepened and lilted his voice and told how their Aphrodite once fell in love with the prince Anchises while he kept his father's sheep on the slopes of a mountain called Ida. And as she came down the grassy slopes towards his shepherd's hut, lions and lynxes and bears and all sorts of beasts came about her fawning like dogs, and all went from her again in pairs to the delights of love. But she dimmed her glory and made herself like a mortal woman and came to Anchises and beguiled him and they went up together into his bed. I think the Fox had meant to end here, but the song now had him in its grip, and he went on to tell what followed; how Anchises woke from sleep and saw Aphrodite standing in the door of the hut, not now like a mortal but with the glory. So he knew he had lain with a goddess, and he covered his eyes and shrieked, "Kill me at once."

"Not that this ever really happened," the Fox said in haste. "It's only lies of poets, lies of poets, child. Not in accordance with nature." But he had said enough to let me see that if the goddess was more beautiful in Greece than in Glome she was equally terrible in each.

It was always like that with the Fox; he was ashamed of loving poetry ("All folly, child") and I had to work much at my reading and writing and what he called philosophy in order to get a poem out of him. But thus, little by little, he taught me many. *Virtue, sought by man*

8

with travail and toil was the one he praised most, but I was never deceived by that. The real lilt came into his voice and the real brightness into his eyes when we were off into *Take me to the apple-laden land* or

> *The Moon's gone down, but*
> *Alone I lie.*

He always sang that one very tenderly and as if he pitied me for something. He liked me better than Redival, who hated study and mocked and plagued him and set the other slaves on to play tricks on him.

We worked most often (in summer) on the little grass plot behind the pear trees, and it was there one day that the King found us. We all stood up, of course, two children and a slave with our eyes on the ground and our hands crossed on our breasts. The King smacked the Fox heartily on the back and said, "Courage, Fox. There'll be a prince for you to work on yet, please the gods. And thank them too, Fox, for it can't often have fallen to the lot of a mere Greekling to rule the grandson of so great a king as my father-in-law that is to be. Not that you'll know or care more about it than an ass. You're all pedlars and hucksters down in the Greeklands, eh?"

"Are not all men of one blood, Master?" said the Fox.

"Of one blood?" said the King with a stare and a great bull-laugh. "I'd be sorry to think so."

Thus in the end it was the King himself and not Batta who first told us that the Stepmother was really at hand. My father had made a great match. He was to have the third daughter of the King of Caphad, who is the biggest

9

king in all our part of the world. (I know now why Caphad wanted an alliance with so poor a kingdom as we are, and I have wondered how my father did not see that his father-in-law must already be a sinking man. The marriage itself was a proof of it.)

It cannot have been many weeks before the marriage took place, but in my memory the preparations seem to have lasted for almost a year. All the brick work round the great gate was painted scarlet, and there were new hangings for the Pillar Room, and a great new royal bed which cost the King far more than he was wise to give. It was made of an eastern wood which was said to have such virtue that four of every five children begotten in such a bed would be male. ("All folly, child," said the Fox, "these things come about by natural causes.") And as the day drew nearer there was nothing but driving in of beasts and slaughtering of beasts—the whole courtyard reeked with the skins of them—and baking and brewing. But we children had not much time to wander from room to room and stare and hinder, for the King suddenly took it into his head that Redival and I and twelve other girls, daughters of nobles, were to sing the bridal hymn. And nothing would do him but a Greek hymn, which was a thing no other neighbouring king could have provided. "But, Master—" said the Fox, almost with tears in his eyes. "Teach 'em, Fox, teach 'em," roared my father. "What's the use of my spending good food and drink on your Greek belly if I'm not to get a Greek song out of you on my wedding night? What's that? No one's asking you to teach them Greek. Of course they won't understand what they're singing, but they can make the noises. See to it, or your back'll be redder than ever your beard was."

It was a crazy scheme, and the Fox said afterwards that the teaching of that hymn to us barbarians was what greyed the last red hair. "I was a fox," he said, "now I am a badger."

When we had made some progress in our task the King brought the Priest of Ungit in to hear us. I had a fear of that Priest which was quite different from my fear of my father. I think that what frightened me (in those early days) was the holiness of the smell that hung about him—a temple-smell of blood (mostly pigeons' blood, but he had sacrificed men, too) and burnt fat and singed hair and wine and stale incense. It is the Ungit smell. Perhaps I was afraid of his clothes too; all the skins they were made of, and the dried bladders, and the great mask shaped like a bird's head which hung on his chest. It looked as if there were a bird growing out of his body.

He did not understand a word of the hymn, nor the music either, but he asked, "Are the young women to be veiled or unveiled?"

"Need you ask?" said the King with one of his great laughs, jerking his thumb in my direction. "Do you think I want my queen frightened out of her senses? Veils of course. And good thick veils too." One of the other girls tittered, and I think that was the first time I clearly understood that I am ugly.

This made me more afraid of the Stepmother than

ever. I thought she would be crueller to me than to Redival because of my ugliness. It wasn't only what Batta had said that frightened me; I had heard of stepmothers in plenty of stories. And when the night came and we were all in the pillared porch, nearly dazzled with the torches and trying hard to sing our hymn as the Fox had taught us to—and he kept on frowning and smiling and nodding at us while we sang, and once he held up his hands in horror—pictures of things that had been done to girls in the stories were dancing in my mind. Then came the shouts from outside, and more torches, and next moment they were lifting the bride out of the chariot. She was as thickly veiled as we, and all I could see was that she was very small; it was as if they were lifting a child. That didn't ease my fears; "the little are the spiteful," our proverb says. Then (still singing) we got her into the bridal chamber and took off her veil.

I know now that the face I saw was beautiful, but I did not think of that then. All I saw was that she was frightened, more frightened than I—indeed terrified. It made me see my father as he must have looked to her, a moment since, when she had her first sight of him standing to greet her in the porch. His was not a brow, a mouth, a girth, a stance, or a voice to quiet a girl's fear.

We took off layer after layer of her finery, making her yet smaller, and left the shivering, white body with its staring eyes in the King's bed, and filed out. We had sung very badly.

TWO

I CAN say very little about my father's second wife, for she did not live till the end of her first year in Glome. She was with child as soon as anyone could reasonably look for it, and the King was in high spirits and hardly ever ran across the Fox without saying something about the prince who was to be born. He made great sacrifices to Ungit every month after that. How it was between him and the Queen I do not know; except that once, after messengers had come from Caphad, I heard the King say to her, "It begins to look, girl, as if I had driven my sheep to a bad market. I learn now that your father has lost two towns—no, three, though he tries to mince the matter. I would thank him to have told me he was sinking before he persuaded me to embark in the same bottom." (I was leaning my head on my window-sill to dry my hair after the bath, and they were walking in the garden.) However that might be, it is certain that she was very homesick, and I think our winter was too hard for her southern body. She was soon pale and thin. I learned that I had nothing to fear from her. She was at first more afraid of me; after that, very loving in her timid way, and more like a sister than a stepmother.

Of course no one in the house went to bed on the night of the birth, for that, they say, will make the child refuse to wake into the world. We all sat in the great hall between the Pillar Room and the Bedchamber, in a red glare of birth-torches. The flames swayed and guttered terribly, for all doors must be open; the shutting of a door might shut up the mother's womb. In the middle of the hall burned a great fire. Every hour the Priest of Ungit walked round it nine times and threw in the proper things. The King sat in his chair and never moved all night, not even his head. I was sitting next to the Fox.

"Grandfather," I whispered to him, "I am terribly afraid."

"We must learn, child, not to fear anything that nature brings," he whispered back.

I must have slept after that, for the next thing I knew was the sound of women wailing and beating the breast as I had heard them do it the day my mother died. Everything had changed while I slept. I was shivering with cold. The fire had sunk low, the King's chair was empty, the door of the Bedchamber was at last shut, and the terrible sounds from within it had stopped. There must have been some sacrifice too, for there was a smell of slaughtering, and blood on the floor, and the Priest was cleaning his holy knife. I was all in a daze from my sleep, for I started up with the wildest idea; I would go and see the Queen. The Fox was after me long before I reached the door of the Bedchamber. "Daughter,

daughter," he was saying. "Not now. Are you mad? The King—"

At that moment the door was flung open and out came my father. His face shocked me full awake, for he was in his pale rage. I knew that in his red rage he would storm and threaten, and little might come of it, but when he was pale he was deadly. "Wine," he said, not very loud; and that too was a bad sign. The other slaves pushed forward a boy who was rather a favourite, as slaves do when they are afraid. The child, white as his master and in all his finery (my father dressed the younger slaves very fine) came running with the flagon and the royal cup, slipped in the blood, reeled, and dropped both. Quick as thought, my father whipped out his dagger and stabbed him in the side. The boy dropped dead in the blood and wine, and the fall of his body sent the flagon rolling over and over. It made a great noise in that silence; I hadn't thought till then that the floor of the hall was so uneven. (I have re-paved it since.)

My father stared for a moment at his own dagger; stupidly, it seemed. Then he went very gently up to the Priest.

"What have you to say for Ungit now?" he asked, still in that low voice. "You had better recover what she owes me. When are you going to pay me for my good cattle?" Then, after a pause, "Tell me, prophet, what would happen if I hammered Ungit into powder and tied you between the hammers and the stone?"

But the Priest was not in the least afraid of the King.

"Ungit hears, King, even at this moment," he said.

"And Ungit will remember. You have already said enough to call down doom upon all your descendants."

"Descendants," says the King. "You talk of descendants," still very quiet, but now he was shaking. The ice of his rage would break any moment. The body of the dead boy caught his eye. "Who did that?" he asked. Then he saw the Fox and me. All the blood rushed into his face, and now at last the voice came roaring out of his chest loud enough to lift the roof.

"Girls, girls, girls!" he bellowed. "And now one girl more. Is there no end to it? Is there a plague of girls in heaven that the gods send me this flood of them? You —you—" He caught me by the hair, shook me to and fro, and flung me from him so that I fell in a heap. There are times when even a child knows better than to cry. When the blackness passed and I could see again, he was shaking the Fox by his throat.

"Here's an old babbler who has eaten my bread long enough," he said. "It would have paid me better to buy a dog as things turn out. But I'll feed you in idleness no longer. Some of you take him to the mines tomorrow. There might be a week's work in his old bones even now."

Again there was dead silence in the hall. Suddenly the King flung up his hands, stamped, and cried, "Faces, faces, faces! What are you all gaping at? It'd make a man mad. Be off! Away! Out of my sight, the whole pack of you!"

We were out of the hall as quick as the doorways would let us.

16

The Fox and I went out of the little door by the herb-garden on the east. It was nearly daylight now and there was a small rain beginning.

"Grandfather," said I, sobbing, "you must fly at once. This moment, before they come to take you to the mines."

He shook his head. "I'm too old to run far," he said. "And you know what the King does to runaway slaves."

"But the mines, the mines! Look, I'll come with you. If we're caught I'll say I made you come. We shall be almost out of Glome once we're over *that*." I pointed to the ridge of the Grey Mountain, now dark with a white daybreak behind it, seen through the slanting rain.

"That is foolishness, daughter," said he, petting me like a small child. "They would think I was stealing you to sell. No; I must fly further. And help me you shall. Down by the river; you know the little plant with the purple spots on its stalk. It's the roots of it I need."

"The poison?"

"Why, yes. (Child, child, don't cry so.) Have I not told you often that to depart from life of a man's own will when there's good reason is one of the things that are according to nature? We are to look on life as—"

"They say that those who go that way lie wallowing in filth—down there in the land of the dead."

"Hush, hush. Are you also still a barbarian? At death we are resolved into our elements. Shall I accept birth and cavil at—"

"Oh, I know, I know. But, Grandfather, do you really in your heart believe nothing of what is said about the gods and Those Below? But you do, you do. You are trembling."

"That's my disgrace. The body is shaking. I needn't let it shake the god within me. Have I not already carried this body too long if it makes such a fool of me at the end? But we are wasting time."

"Listen!" said I. "What's that?" For I was in a state to be scared by every sound.

"Horses," said the Fox, peering through the quickhedge with his eyes screwed up to see against the rain. "They are coming to the great door. Messengers from Phars, by the look of them. And that will not sweeten the King's mood either. Will you—ah, Zeus, it is already too late." For there was a call from within-doors, "The Fox, the Fox, the Fox to the King."

"As well go as be dragged," said the Fox. "Farewell, daughter," and he kissed me, Greek fashion, on the eyes and the head. But I went in with him. I had an idea I would face the King; though whether I meant to beseech him or curse him or kill him I hardly knew. But as we came to the Pillar Room we saw many strangers within, and the King shouted through the open door, "Here, Fox, I've work for you." Then he saw me and said, "And you, curd-face, be off to the women's quarters and don't come here to sour the morning drink for the men."

I do not know that I have ever (to speak of things merely mortal) been in such dread as I was for the rest of that day—dread that feels as if there were an empty place between your belly and your chest. I didn't know whether I dared be comforted by the King's last words or not, for they sounded as if his anger had passed, but it might blaze out again. Moreover, I had known him do a cruel thing not in anger but in a kind of murderous joke, or because he remembered he had sworn to do it when he was angry. He had sent old house-slaves to the mines before. And I could not be alone with my terror, for now comes Batta to shear my head and Redival's again as they had been shorn when my mother died, and to make a great tale (clicking her tongue) of how the Queen was dead in childbed, which I had known ever since I heard the mourning, and how she had borne a daughter alive. I sat for the shearing and thought that, if the Fox must die in the mines, it was very fit I should offer my hair. Lank and dull and little it lay on the floor beside Redival's rings of gold.

In the evening the Fox came and told me that there was no more talk of the mines—for the present. A thing that had often irked me had now been our salvation. More and more, of late, the King had taken the Fox away from us girls to work for him in the Pillar Room; he had begun to find that the Fox could calculate and read and write letters (at first only in Greek but now in the speech of our parts too) and give advice better than any man in Glome. This very day the Fox had taught him to drive a better bargain with the King of Phars than he would ever have thought of for himself. The Fox was a true Greek; where my father could give only a Yes or a No to some neighbouring king or dangerous noble, he could pare the Yes to the very quick and

19

sweeten the No till it went down like wine. He could make your weak enemy believe that you were his best friend and make your strong enemy believe you were twice as strong as you really were. He was far too useful to be sent to the mines.

They burnt the dead Queen on the third day, and my father named the child Istra. "It is a good name," said the Fox, "a very good name. And you know enough now to tell me what it would be in Greek."

"It would be Psyche, Grandfather," said I.

New-born children were no rarity in the palace; the place sprawled with the slaves' babies and my father's bastards. Sometimes my father would say, "Lecherous rascals! Anyone'd think this was Ungit's house, not mine," and threaten to drown a dozen of them like blind puppies. But in his heart he thought the better of a man-slave if he could get half the maids in the place with child, especially if they bore boys. (The girls, unless they took his own fancy, were mostly sold when they were ripe; some were given to the house of Ungit.) Nevertheless, because I had (a little) loved the Queen, I went to see Psyche that very evening as soon as the Fox had set my mind at rest. And so, in one hour, I passed out of the worst anguish I had yet suffered into the beginning of all my joys.

The child was very big, not a wearish little thing as you might have expected from her mother's stature, and very fair of skin. You would have thought she made bright all the corner of the room in which she lay. She slept (tiny was the sound of her breathing). But there never was a child like Psyche for quietness in her cradle days. As I gazed at her the Fox came in on tiptoes and looked over my shoulder. "Now by all the gods," he whispered, "old fool that I am, I could almost believe that there really is divine blood in your family. Helen herself, new-hatched, must have looked so."

Batta had put her to nurse with a red-haired woman who was sullen and (like Batta herself) too fond of the wine-jar. I soon had the child out of their hands. I got for her nurse a free woman, a peasant's wife, as honest and wholesome as I could find, and after that both were in my own chamber day and night. Batta was only too pleased to have her work done for her, and the King knew and cared nothing about it. The Fox said to me, "Don't wear yourself out, daughter, with too much toil, even if the child is as beautiful as a goddess." But I laughed in his face. I think I laughed more in those days than in all my life before. Toil? I lost more sleep looking on Psyche for the joy of it than in any other way. And I laughed because she was always laughing. She laughed before the third month. She knew me for certain (though the Fox said not) before the second.

This was the beginning of my best times. The Fox's love for the child was wonderful; I guessed that long before, when he was free, he must have had a daughter of his own. He was like a true grandfather now. And it was now always we three—the Fox, and Psyche, and I—alone together. Redival had always hated our lessons

21

and, but for the fear of the King, would never have come near the Fox. Now, it seemed, the King had put all his three daughters out of his mind, and Redival had her own way. She was growing tall, her breasts rounding, her long legs getting their shape. She promised to have beauty enough, but not like Psyche's.

Of Psyche's beauty—at every age the beauty proper to that age—there is only this to be said, that there were no two opinions about it, from man or woman, once she had been seen. It was beauty that did not astonish you till afterwards when you had gone out of sight of her and reflected on it. While she was with you, you were not astonished. It seemed the most natural thing in the world. As the Fox delighted to say, she was "according to nature"; what every woman, or even every thing, ought to have been and meant to be, but had missed by some trip of chance. Indeed, when you looked at her you believed, for a moment, that they had not missed it. She made beauty all round her. When she trod on mud, the mud was beautiful; when she ran in the rain, the rain was silver. When she picked up a toad—she had the strangest and, I thought, unchanciest love for all manner of brutes—the toad became beautiful.

The years, doubtless, went round then as now, but in my memory it seems to have been all springs and summers. I think the almonds and the cherries blossomed earlier in those years and the blossoms lasted longer; how they hung on in such winds I don't know, for I see the boughs always rocking and dancing against blue-and-white skies, and their shadows flowing water-like over all the hills and valleys of Psyche's body. I wanted to be a wife so that I could have been her real mother. I wanted to be a boy so that she could be in love with me. I wanted her to be my full sister instead of my half sister. I wanted her to be a slave so that I could set her free and make her rich.

The Fox was so trusted by now that when my father did not need him he was allowed to take us anywhere, even miles from the palace. We were often out all day in summer on the hill-top to the south-west, looking down on all Glome and across to the Grey Mountain. We stared our eyes out on that jagged ridge till we knew every tooth and notch of it, for none of us had ever gone there or seen what was on the other side. Psyche, almost from the beginning (for she was a very quick, thinking child), was half in love with the Mountain. She made herself stories about it. "When I'm big," she said, "I will be a great, great queen, married to the greatest king of all, and he will build me a castle of gold and amber up there on the very top."

The Fox clapped his hands and sang, "Prettier than Andromeda, prettier than Helen, prettier than Aphrodite herself."

"Speak words of better omen, Grandfather," I said, though I knew he would scold and mock me for saying it. For at his words, though on that summer day the rocks were too hot to touch, it was as if a soft, cold hand had been laid on my left side, and I shivered.

"Babai!" said the Fox. "It is your words that are ill omened. The divine nature is not like that. It has no envy."

But whatever he said, I knew it is not good to talk that way about Ungit.

THREE

I т was Redival who ended the good time. She had always been feather-headed and now grew wanton, and what must she do but stand kissing and whispering love-talk with a young officer of the guard (one Tarin) right under Batta's window an hour after midnight. Batta had slept off her wine in the earlier part of the night and was now wakeful. Being a busybody and tattler in grain, she went off straight and woke the King, who cursed her roundly but believed her. He was up, and had a few armed men with him, and was out into the garden and surprised the lovers before they knew that anything was amiss. The whole house was raised by the noise of it. The King had the barber to make a eunuch of Tarin there and then (as soon as he was healed, they sold him down at Ringal). The boy's screams had hardly sunk to a whimper before the King turned on the Fox and me, and made us to blame for the whole thing. Why had the Fox not looked to his pupil? Why had I not looked to my sister? The end of it was a strict command that we were never to let her out of our sight. "Go where you will and do what you will," said my father. "But the salt bitch must be with you. I tell you, Fox, if she loses her maidenhead before I find her a husband, you'll yell louder for it than she. Look to your hide. And you, goblin daughter, do what you're good for, you'd best. Name of Ungit! if you with that face can't frighten the men away, it's a wonder."

Redival was utterly cowed by the King's anger and obeyed him. She was always with us. And that soon cooled any love she had for Psyche or me. She yawned and she quarrelled and she mocked. Psyche, who was a child so merry, so truthful, so obedient that in her (the Fox said) Virtue herself had put on a human form, could do no right in Redival's eyes. One day Redival hit her. Then I hardly knew myself again till I found that I was astride of Redival, she on the ground with her face a lather of blood, and my hands about her throat. It was the Fox who pulled me off and, in the end, some kind of peace was made between us.

Thus all the comfort we three had had was destroyed when Redival joined us. And after that, little by little, one by one, came the first knocks of the hammer that finally destroyed us all.

That year after I fought Redival was the first of the bad harvests. That same year my father tried to marry himself (as the Fox told me) into two royal houses among the neighbouring kings, and they would have none of him. The world was changing, the great alliance with Caphad had proved a snare. The tide was against Glome.

The same year, too, a small thing happened which

cost me many a shuddering. The Fox and I, up behind the pear trees, were deep in his philosophy. Psyche had wandered off, singing to herself, among the trees, to the edge of the royal gardens where they overlook the lane. Redival went after her. I had one eye on the pair of them, and one ear for the Fox. Then it seemed they were talking to someone in the lane, and shortly after that they came back.

Redival, sneering, bowed double before Psyche and went through the actions of pouring dust on her head. "Why don't you honour the goddess?" she said to us.

"What do you mean, Redival?" asked I, wearily, for I knew she meant some new spite.

"Did you not know our step-sister had become a goddess?"

"What does she mean, Istra?" said I. (I never called her Psyche now that Redival had joined us.)

"Come on, step-sister goddess, speak up," said Redival. "I'm sure I've been told often enough how truthful you are, so you'll not deny that you have been worshipped."

"It's not true," said Psyche. "All that happened was that a woman with child asked me to kiss her."

"Ah, but why?" said Redival.

"Because—because she said her baby would be beautiful if I did."

"*Because you are so beautiful yourself.*—Don't forget that. She said that."

"And what did you do, Istra?" asked I.

"I kissed her. She was a nice woman. I liked her."

"And don't forget that she then laid down a branch of myrtle at your feet and bowed and put dust on her head," said Redival.

"Has this happened before, Istra?" said I.

"Yes. Sometimes."

"How often?"

"I don't know."

"Twice before?"

"More than that."

"Well, ten times?"

"No, more. I don't know. I can't remember. What are you looking at me like that for? Is it wrong?"

"Oh, it's dangerous, dangerous," said I. "The gods are jealous. They can't bear—"

"Daughter, it doesn't matter a straw," said the Fox. "The divine nature is without jealousy. Those gods—the sort of gods you are always thinking about—are all folly and lies of poets. We have discussed this a hundred times."

"Heigh-ho," yawns Redival, lying flat on her back in the grass and kicking her legs in the air till you could see all there was of her (which she did purely to put the Fox out of countenance, for the old man was very modest). "Heigh-ho, a step-sister for goddess and a slave for counsellor. Who'd be a princess in Glome? I wonder what Ungit thinks of our new goddess."

"It is not very easy to find out what Ungit thinks," said the Fox.

Redival rolled round and laid her cheek on the grass. Then, looking up at him, she said softly, "But it would be easy to find out what the Priest of Ungit thinks. Shall I try?"

All my old fear of the Priest, and more fears for the future than I could put a name to, stabbed into me.

"Sister," said Redival to me, "give me your necklace with the blue stones, the one our mother gave you."

"Take it," said I. "I'll give it to you when we go in."

"And you, slave," she said to the Fox. "Mend your manners. And get my father to give me to some king in marriage; and it must be a young king, brave, yellow-bearded, and lusty. You can do what you like with my father when you're shut up with him in the Pillar Room. Everyone knows that you are the real King of Glome."

The year after that we had rebellion. It came of my father's gelding Tarin. Tarin himself was of no great lineage (to be about a king's house at all) and the King had thought his father would have no power to avenge him. But the father made common cause with bigger men than himself, and about nine strong lords in our north-west rose against us. My father took the field himself (and when I saw him ride out in his armour, I came nearer to loving him than I had been yet) and beat the rebels, but with great slaughter on both parts and, I think, more slaughter of the beaten men than was needed. The thing left a stench and a disaffection behind it; when all was done, the King was weaker than he had been.

That year was the second bad harvest and the beginning of the fever. In the autumn the Fox took it and nearly died. I could not be with him, for as soon as the

Fox fell sick the King said, "Now, girl, you can read and write and chatter Greek. I'll have work for you. You must take the Fox's place." So I was nearly always in the Pillar Room, for there was much business at the time. Though I was sick with fear for the Fox, the work with my father was far less dreadful to me than I expected. He came, for the time, to hate me less. In the end he would speak to me, not, certainly, with love, but friendly as one man might to another. I learned how desperate his affairs were. No neighbouring houses of divine blood (and ours cannot lawfully marry into any other) would take his daughters or give him theirs. The nobles were muttering about the succession. There were threats of war from every side, and no strength to meet any one of them.

It was Psyche who nursed the Fox, however often forbidden. She would fight, yes, and bite, any who stood between her and his door; for she, too, had our father's hot blood, though her angers were all the sort that come from love. The Fox won through his illness, thinner and greyer than before. Now mark the subtlety of the god who is against us. The story of his recovery and Psyche's nursing got abroad; Batta alone was conduit-pipe enough, and there were a score of other talkers. It became a story of how the beautiful princess could cure the fever by her touch; soon, that her touch was the only thing that could cure it. Within two days half the city was at the palace gate—such scarecrows, risen from their beds, old dotards as eager to save their lives as if their lives in any event were worth a year's purchase, babies, sick men half-dead and carried on beds. I stood looking at them from behind barred windows, all the pity and dread of it, the smell of sweat and fever and garlic and foul clothes.

"The Princess Istra," they cried. "Send out the Princess with her healing hands. We die! Healing, healing, healing!"

"And bread," came other voices. "The royal granaries! We are starving."

This was at first, while they stood a little way off from the gate. But they got nearer. Soon they were hammering at it. Someone was saying, "Bring fire." But, behind them, the weaker voices wailed on, "Heal us, heal us. The Princess with the healing hands!"

"She'll have to go out," said my father. "We can't hold them." (Two-thirds of our guards were down with the fever.)

"Can she heal them?" said I to the Fox. "Did she heal you?"

"It is possible," said the Fox. "It might be in accordance with nature that some hands can heal. Who knows?"

"Let me go out," said Psyche. "They are our people."

"Our rump!" said my father. "They shall smart for this day's work if ever I get the whip-hand of them again. But quick. Dress the girl. She has beauty enough, that's one thing. And spirit."

They put a queen's dress on her and a chaplet on her head and opened the door. You know how it is when you shed few tears or none, but there is a weight and pressure of weeping through your whole head. It is like that with me even now when I remember her going out, slim and straight as a sceptre, out of the darkness and cool of the hall into the hot, pestilential glare of that day. The people drew back, thrusting one another, the moment the doors opened. I think they expected a rush of spearmen. But a minute later the wailing and shouting died utterly away. Every man (and many a woman too) in that crowd was kneeling. Her beauty, which most of them had never seen, worked on them as a terror might work. Then a low murmur, almost a sob, began; swelled, broke into the gasping cry, "A goddess, a goddess." One woman's voice rang out clear. "It is Ungit herself in mortal shape."

Psyche went on, walking slowly and gravely, like a child going to say a lesson, right in among all the foulness. She touched and she touched. They fell at her feet and kissed her feet and the edge of her robe and her shadow and the ground where she had trodden. And still she touched and touched. There seemed to be no end of it; the crowd increased instead of diminishing. For hours she touched. The air was stifling even for us who stood in the shadow of the porch. The whole earth and air ached for the thunderstorm which (we knew now) would not come. I saw her growing paler and paler. Her walk had become a stagger.

"King," said I, "it will kill her."

"Then more's the pity," said the King. "They'll kill us all if she stops."

It was over in the end, somewhere about sunset. We

carried her to her bed, and next day the fever was on her. But she won through it. In her wanderings she talked most of her gold and amber castle on the ridge of the Grey Mountain. At her worst, there was no look of death upon her face. It was as if he dared not come near her. And when her strength came back she was more beautiful than before. The childishness had gone. There was a new and severer radiance. "Ah, no wonder," sang the Fox, "if the Trojans and the Achaeans suffer long woes for such a woman. Terribly does she resemble an undying spirit."

Some of the sick in the town died and some recovered. Only the gods know if those who recovered were those whom Psyche had touched, and gods do not tell. But the people had, at first, no doubts. Every morning there were offerings left for her outside the palace; myrtle branches and garlands and soon honeycakes and then pigeons, which are specially sacred to Ungit. "Can this be well?" I said to the Fox.

"I should be greatly afraid," said he, "but for one thing. The Priest of Ungit lies sick with the fever himself. I do not think he can do us much mischief at present."

About this time Redival became very pious and went often to the house of Ungit to make offerings. The Fox and I saw to it that she always had with her a trusty old slave who would let her get into no mischief. I thought she was praying for a husband (she wanted one badly since the King had, in a manner, chained her to the Fox and me) and also that she was as glad to be out of our

33

sight for an hour as we were to be out of hers. Yet I warned her to speak to no one on the way.

"Oh, make your mind easy, Sister," says Redival. "It's not me they worship, you know: I'm not the goddess. The men are as likely to look at you as at me, now they've seen Istra."

FOUR

U P TILL now I had not known what the common people are like. That was why their ador-
ings of Psyche, which in one way made me
afraid, comforted me in another. For I was confused in
my mind, sometimes thinking of what Ungit by her own
divine power might do to any mortal who thus stole her
honour, and sometimes of what the Priest and our enemies in the city (my father had many now) might do
with their tongues, or stones, or spears. Against the lat-
ter the people's love for Psyche seemed to me a protection.

It did not last long. For one thing, the mob had now
learned that a palace door can be opened by banging on
it. Before Psyche was out of her fever they were back at
our gates crying, "Corn, corn! We are starving. Open
the royal granaries." That time the King gave them a
dole. "But don't come again," he said. "I've no more to
give you. Name of Ungit! d'you think I can make corn if
the fields don't bear it?"

"And why don't they?" said a voice from the back of
the crowd.

"Where are your sons, King?" said another. "Where's the prince?"

"The King of Phars has thirteen sons," said another.

"Barren king makes barren land," said a fourth. This time the King saw who had spoken and nodded to one of the bowmen who stood beside him. Before you'd wink the arrow went through the speaker's throat and the mob took to its heels. But it was foolishly done; my father ought to have killed either none of them or nearly all. He was right enough, though, in saying we could give them no more doles. This was the second of the bad harvests and there was little in the granary but our own seedcorn. Even in the palace we were already living for the most part on leeks and bean-bread and small beer. It took me endless contrivance to get anything good for Psyche when she was mending from the fever.

The next thing was this. Shortly after Psyche was well, I left the Pillar Room where I had been working for the King (and he still kept the Fox with him after he let me go) and set out to look for Redival, that care being always on my mind. The King would have thought nothing of keeping me away from her at his own business all the day and then blaming me for not having my eyes on her. But as it happened I met her at once, just coming in from one of her visits to the house of Ungit, and Batta with her. Batta and she were as thick as thieves these days.

"You needn't come looking for me, sister-jailer," said Redival. "I'm safe enough. It isn't here the danger lies. When did you last see the little goddess? Where's your darling step-sister?"

"In the gardens most likely," said I. "And as for *little*, she's half a head taller than yourself."

"Oh mercy! Have I blasphemed? Will she smite me with thunder? Yes, she's tall enough. Tall enough to see her a long way off—half an hour ago—in a little lane near the market place. A king's daughter doesn't usually walk the back streets alone; but I suppose a goddess can."

"Istra out in the town and alone?" said I.

"Indeed she was then," chattered Batta, "scuttling along with her robe caught up. Like this . . . like this." (Batta was a bad mimic but always mimicking; I remembered that from my earliest years.) "I'd have followed her, the young boldface, but she went in at a doorway, so she did."

"Well, well," said I. "The child ought to have known better. But she'll do no harm and come to none."

"Come to no harm!" said Batta. "That's more than any of us know."

"You are mad, Nurse," said I. "The people were worshipping her not six days ago."

"I don't know anything about that," said Batta (who knew perfectly well). "But she'll get little worship to-day. I knew what would come of all that touching and blessing. Fine goings on indeed! The plague's worse than ever it was. There were a hundred died yesterday, the smith's wife's brother-in-law tells me. They say the touchings didn't heal the fever but gave it. I've spoken

37

to a woman whose old father was touched by the Princess, and he was dead before they had carried him home. And he wasn't the only one. If anyone had listened to old Batta—"

But I at least listened no more. I went out to the porch and looked towards the city a long half hour. I watched the shadows of the pillars slowly changing their position and it was then I first saw how the things we have known ever since we were weaned can look new and strange, like enemies. And at last I saw Psyche coming, very tired but in great haste. She caught me by the wrist and swallowed, like one that has a sob in the throat, and began leading me away and never stopped till we were in my own chamber. Then she put me in my chair and fell down and laid her head on my knees. I thought she was crying, but when at last she raised her face there were no tears on it.

"Sister," she said. "What is wrong? I mean, about me."

"About you, Psyche?" said I. "Nothing. What do you mean?"

"Why do they call me the Accursed?"

"Who has dared? We'll have his tongue torn out. Where have you been?"

Then it all came out. She had gone (very foolishly, I thought) into the city without a word to any of us. She had heard that her old nurse, the freewoman whom I had hired to suckle her and who now lived in town, was sick with the fever. And Psyche had gone to touch her—

"For they all said my hands cured it, and who knows? It might be. I felt as if they did."

I told her she had done very wrong, and it was then that I fully perceived how much older she had grown since her sickness. For she neither accepted the rebuke like a child nor defended herself like a child, but looked at me with a grave quietness, almost as if she were older than I. It gave me a pang at the heart.

"But who cursed you?" I asked.

"Nothing happened till I had left Nurse's house; except that no one in the streets had saluted me, and I thought that one or two women gathered their skirts together and drew away from me as I passed. Well, on the way back, first there was a boy—a lovely boy he was, not eight years old—who stared at me and spat on the ground. 'Oh, rude!' said I, and laughed and held out my hand to him. He scowled at me as black as a little fiend and then lost his courage and ran howling into a doorway. After that the street was empty for a space, but presently I had to pass a knot of men. They gave me black looks as I was passing, and as soon as my back was towards them they were all saying, 'The Accursed, the Accursed! She made herself a goddess.' And one said, 'She is the curse itself.' Then they threw stones. No, I'm not hurt. But I had to run. What does it mean? What did I do to them?"

"Do?" said I. "You healed them, and blessed them, and took their filthy disease upon yourself. And these are their thanks. Oh, I could tear them in pieces! Get up, child. Let me go. Even now—we are king's daughters still. I'll go to the King. He may beat me and drag me by the hair as he pleases, but this he shall hear. Bread for them indeed. I'll—I'll—"

"Hush, sister, hush," said Psyche. "I can't bear it when he hurts you. And I'm so tired. And I want my supper. There, don't be angry. You look just like our father when you say those things. Let us have supper here, you and I. There is some bad thing coming towards us—I have felt it a long time—but I don't think it will come tonight. I'll clap my hands to call your maids."

Though the words *You look just like our father*, and from her, had hurt me with a wound that sometimes aches still, I let go my anger and yielded. We supped together and turned our poor meal into a joke and a game and were, in a fashion, happy. One thing the gods have not taken from me—I can remember all that she said or did that night and how she looked from moment to moment.

But whatever my heart boded, our ruin (and even now I had no clear foresight what it would be) did not fall upon us the next day. A whole train of days went past in which nothing happened, except for the slow, steady worsening of everything in Glome. The Shennit was now no more than a trickle between one puddle and another amid dry mud-flats; it was the corpse of a river and stank. Her fish were dead, her birds dead or gone away. The cattle had all died or been killed or were not worth the killing. The bees were dead. Lions, which had not been heard of in the land for forty years, came over the ridge of the Grey Mountain and took most of the few

40

sheep we had left. The plague never ceased. All through these days I was waiting and listening, watching (when I could) everyone who went out of the palace or came in. It was well for me that the King found plenty of work both for the Fox and me in the Pillar Room. Messengers and letters from the neighbouring kings were coming in every day, demanding impossible things and contrary things, dragging up old quarrels or claiming old promises. They knew how things were in Glome and they clustered round us like flies and crows round a dying sheep. My father would pass in and out of his rages a dozen times in one morning. When he was in them he would slap the Fox about the face and pull me by the ears or the hair; and then, between the fits, the tears would stand in his eyes, and he would speak to us more like a child imploring help than a king asking counsel.

"Trapped!" he would say. "No way out. They will kill me by inches. What have I done that all these miseries should fall upon me? I've been a god-fearing man all my life."

The only betterment in these days was that the fever seemed to have left the palace. We had lost a good many slaves, but we had better luck with the soldiers. Only one died and all the rest were now back at duty.

Then we heard that the Priest of Ungit had recovered from his fever. His sickness had been very long, for he had taken the fever and won over it and then taken it again, so that it was a wonder he should be alive. But it was noticed for a strange and unlucky thing about this sickness that it killed the young more easily than the

41

old. On the seventh day after this news the Priest came to the palace. The King, who saw his coming (as I did, too) from the windows of the Pillar Room, said, "What does the old carrion mean by coming here with half an army?" There were indeed a good many spears behind his litter, for the house of Ungit has its own guards and he had brought a big handful with him. They grounded their spears some distance from our gates, and only the litter was carried to the porch. "They'd better come no nearer," said the King. "Is this treason or only pride?" Then he gave some order to the captain of his own guard. I don't think he expected it would come to a fight, but that was what I, being still young, looked for. I had never seen men fight and, being as big a fool in that way as most girls, I felt no dread, rather, a little tingling that I liked well enough.

The bearers set down the litter and the Priest was lifted out of it. He was very old now and blind, and he had two temple girls with him to lead him. I had seen their kind before, but only by torchlight in the house of Ungit. They looked strange under the sun, with their gilt paps and their huge flaxen wigs and their faces painted till they looked like wooden masks. Only these two and the Priest, with one hand on a shoulder of each, came into the palace. As soon as they were in, my father called out to our men to shut and bar the door. "The old wolf would hardly walk into such a trap if he meant mischief," he said. "But we'll make sure."

The temple girls led the Priest into the Pillar Room, and a chair was set for him and he was helped into it.

He was out of breath and sat for a long time before he spoke, making a chewing motion with his gums as old men do. The girls stood stiffly at each side of his chair, their meaningless eyes looking always straight ahead out of the mask of their painting. The smell of old age, and the smell of the oils and essences they put on those girls, and the Ungit smell, filled the room. It became very holy.

FIVE

Y FATHER greeted the Priest and wished him joy of his recovery and called for wine to be given him. But the Priest held up his hand and said, "No, King. I am under a strong vow, and neither food nor drink must pass my lips till I have given my message." He spoke well enough now, though weakly, and I noticed how much thinner he was since his sickness.

"As you please, servant of Ungit," said the King. "What's this of a message?"

"I am speaking to you, King, with the voice of Ungit and the voice of all the people and elders and nobles of Glome."

"Did all these, then, send you with a message?"

"Yes. We were all gathered—or those who could speak for all were gathered—last night, and even till this day's daybreak, in the house of Ungit."

"Were you, death and scabs?" said my father, frowning. "It's a new fashion to hold an assembly without the King's bidding; and newer still to hold it without bidding the King to it."

"There would have been no reason in bidding you to it, King, seeing that we came together not to hear what you would say to us but to determine what we would say to you."

My father's look grew very black.

"And being gathered together," said the Priest, "we reckoned up all the woes that have come upon us. First, the famine, which still increases. Second, the pestilence. Third, the drought. Fourth, the certain expectation of war by next spring at the latest. Fifth, the lions. And lastly, King, your own barrenness of sons which is hateful to Ungit—"

"That's enough," shouted the King. "You old fool, do you think I need you or any of the other wiseacres to tell me where my own belly aches? Hateful to Ungit, is it? Why does Ungit not mend it then? She's had bulls and rams and goats from me in plenty; blood enough to sail a ship on if all were reckoned."

The Priest jerked up his head as if, though blind, he were looking at the King. And now I saw better how his thinness had changed him. He looked like a vulture. I was more afraid of him than I had been. The King dropped his eyes.

"Bulls and rams and goats will not win Ungit's favour while the land is impure," said the Priest. "I have served Ungit these fifty—no, sixty-three—years, and I have learned one thing for certain. Her anger never comes upon us without cause, and it never ceases without expiation. I have made offerings to her for your father and your father's father, and it has always been the same.

45

We were overthrown long before your day by the King of Essur; and that was because there was a man in your grandfather's army who had lain with his sister and killed the child. He was the Accursed. We found him out and expiated his sin, and then the men of Glome chased the men of Essur like sheep. Your father himself could have told you how one woman, little more than a child, cursed Ungit's son, the god of the Mountain, in secret. For her sake the floods came. She was the Accursed. We found her out and expiated her sin, and Shennit returned into her banks. And now, by all the signs I have reckoned over to you, we know that Ungit's anger is far greater than ever within my memory. Thus we all said in her house last night. We all said: 'We must find the Accursed.' Though every man knew that he himself might be the Accursed, no man spoke against it. I too—I had not a word to say against it, though I knew that the Accursed might be I—or you, King. For we all knew (and you may hold it for certain) that there will be no mending of all our ills till the land is purged. Ungit will be avenged. It's not a bull or a ram that will quiet her now."

"You mean she wants Man?" said the King.

"Yes," said the Priest. "Or Woman."

"If they think I can get them a captive in war at present, they must be mad. The next time I take a thief you can cut his throat over Ungit if you like."

"That is not enough, King. And you know it. We must find the Accursed. And she (or he) must die by the rite of the Great Offering. What is a thief more than a bull or a ram? This is not to be a common sacrifice. We must make the Great Offering. The Brute has been seen again. And when it comes, the Great Offering must be made. That is how the Accursed must be offered."

"The Brute? It's the first I've heard of it."

"It may be so. Kings seem to hear very little. They do not know even what goes on in their own palaces. But I hear. I lie awake in the nights, very long awake, and Ungit tells me things. I hear of terrible doings in this land, mortals aping the gods and stealing the worship due to the gods—"

I looked at the Fox and said, soundlessly, by the shaping of my lips, "Redival."

The King was walking up and down the room with his hands clasped behind his back and his fingers working.

"You're doting," he said. "The Brute's a tale of my grandmother's."

"It may well be," said the Priest, "for it was in her time that the Brute was last seen. And we made the Great Offering and it went away."

"Who has ever seen this Brute?" asked my father. "What is it like, eh?"

"Those who have seen it closest can least say what it is like, King. And many have seen it of late. Your own chief shepherd on the Grey Mountain saw it the night the first lion came. He fell upon the lion with a burning torch. And in the light of the torch he saw the Brute— behind the lion—very black and big, a terrible shape."

47

As the Priest said this the King's walk had brought him close to the table where I and the Fox sat with our tablets and other tools for writing. The Fox slid along the bench and whispered something in my father's ear.

"Well said, Fox," muttered my father. "Speak up. Say it to the Priest."

"By the King's permission," said the Fox, "the shepherd's tale is very questionable. If the man had a torch, of necessity the lion would have a big black shadow behind it. The man was scared and new waked from sleep. He took a shadow for a monster."

"That is the wisdom of the Greeks," said the Priest. "But Glome does not take counsel with slaves, not even if they are kings' favourites. And if the Brute was a shadow, King, what then? Many say it *is* a shadow. But if that shadow begins coming down into the city, look to yourself. You are of divine blood and doubtless fear nothing. But the people will fear. Their fear will be so great that not even I will be able to hold them. They will burn your palace about your ears. They will bar you in before they burn it. You would be wiser to make the Great Offering."

"How is it made?" said the King. "It has never happened in my time."

"It is not done in the house of Ungit," said the Priest. "The victim must be given to the Brute. For the Brute is, in a mystery, Ungit herself or Ungit's son, the god of the Mountain; or both. The victim is led up the mountain to the Holy Tree, and bound to the Tree and left. Then the Brute comes. That is why you angered

48

Ungit just now, King, when you spoke of offering a thief. In the Great Offering, the victim must be perfect. For, in holy language, a man so offered is said to be Ungit's husband, and a woman is said to be the bride of Ungit's son. And both are called the Brute's Supper. And when the Brute is Ungit it lies with the man, and when it is her son it lies with the woman. And either way there is a devouring . . . many different things are said . . . many sacred stories . . . many great mysteries. Some say the loving and the devouring are all the same thing. For in sacred language we say that a woman who lies with a man devours the man. That is why you are so wide of the mark, King, when you think a thief, or an old worn-out slave, or a coward taken in battle, would do for the Great Offering. The best in the land is not too good for this office."

The King's forehead, I saw, was clammy now. The holiness and horror of divine things were continually thickening in that room. All at once the Fox burst out, "Master, Master, let me speak."

"Speak on," said the King.

"Do you not see, Master," said the Fox, "that the Priest is talking nonsense? A shadow is to be an animal which is also a goddess which is also a god, and loving is to be eating—a child of six would talk more sense. And a moment ago the victim of this abominable sacrifice was to be the Accursed, the wickedest person in the whole land, offered as a punishment. And now it is to be the best person in the whole land—the perfect victim—mar-

49

ried to the god as a reward. Ask him which he means. It can't be both."

If any hope had put up its head within me when the Fox began, it was killed. This sort of talk could do no good. I knew what had happened to the Fox; he had forgotten all his wiles, even, in a way, his love and fears for Psyche, simply because things such as the Priest had been saying put him beyond all patience. (I have noticed that all men, not only Greek men, if they have clear wits and ready tongues, will do the same.)

"We are hearing much Greek wisdom this morning, King," said the Priest. "And I have heard most of it before. I did not need a slave to teach it to me. It is very subtle. But it brings no rain and grows no corn; sacrifice does both. It does not even give them boldness to die. That Greek there is your slave because in some battle he threw down his arms and let them bind his hands and lead him away and sell him, rather than take a spear-thrust in his heart. Much less does it give them understanding of holy things. They demand to see such things clearly, as if the gods were no more than letters written in a book. I, King, have dealt with the gods for three generations of men, and I know that they dazzle our eyes and flow in and out of one another like eddies on a river, and nothing that is said clearly can be said truly about them. Holy places are dark places. It is life and strength, not knowledge and words, that we get in them. Holy wisdom is not clear and thin like water, but thick and dark like blood. Why should the Accursed not be both the best and the worst?"

50

The Priest looked more and more like a gaunt bird as he was speaking; not unlike the bird-mask that lay on his knees. And his voice, though not loud, was no longer shaking like an old man's. The Fox sat hunched together with his eyes fixed on the table. The taunt about being taken in war, I guessed, had been hot iron to some old ulcer in his soul. Certainly, I would that moment have hanged the Priest and made the Fox a king if power had been given me; but it was easy to see on which side the strength lay.

"Well, well," said the King, quickening his stride, "this may be all very true. I'm neither priest nor Greekling, I. They used to tell me I was the King. What's next?"

"Being determined, therefore," said the Priest, "to seek out the Accursed, we cast the holy lots. First we asked whether the Accursed was to be found among the commons. And the lots said 'no.' "

"Go on, go on," said the King.

"I cannot speak quickly," said the Priest. "I have not breath for it now. Then we asked if it was among the Elders. And the lots said 'no.' "

There was a queer mottled colour on the King's face now; his fear and his anger were just on the balance, and neither he nor anyone else knew at all which would have the victory.

"Then we asked if it were among the nobles. And the lots said 'no.' "

"And then you asked?" says the King, stepping up close to him and speaking low.

And the Priest said, "Then we asked: 'Is it in the King's house?' And the lots said 'yes.' "

"Aye," said the King, rather breathless. "Aye. I thought as much. I smelled it from the beginning. Treason in a new cloak. Treason." Then louder, "Treason." Next moment he was at the door, roaring, "Treason! Treason! Guards! Bardia! Where are my guards? Where's Bardia? Send Bardia."

There was a rush and a jingle of iron and guards came running. Bardia, their captain, a very honest man, came in.

"Bardia," said the King, "there are too many people about my door today. Take what men you think you need and fall on those rebels who are standing with spears out yonder over against the gate. Don't scatter them but kill. Kill, do you see? Don't leave one of them alive."

"Kill the temple guards, King?" said Bardia, looking from the King to the Priest and back at the King again.

"Temple rats! Temple pimps!" shouted the King. "Are you deaf? Are you afraid? I—I—" and his rage choked him.

"This is foolishness, King," said the Priest. "All Glome is in arms. There is a party of armed men at every door of the palace by now. Your guards are outnumbered ten to one. And they won't fight. Would you fight against Ungit, Bardia?"

"Will you slink away from my side, Bardia?" said the King. "After eating my bread? You were glad of my shield to cover you one day at Varin's wood."

"You saved my head that day, King," said Bardia. "I'll never say otherwise. May Ungit send me to do as much for you (there may be chance enough next spring). I'm for the King of Glome and the gods of Glome while I live. But if the King and the gods fall out, you great ones must settle it between you. I'll not fight against powers and spirits."

"You—you girl!" squealed the King, his voice shrill as a pipe. Then, "Be off! I'll talk with you presently." Bardia saluted and went out; you could see from his face that he cared no more for the insult than a great dog cares for a puppy making believe to fight him.

The moment the door was shut, the King, all quiet and white again, whipped out his dagger (the same he killed the page with the night Psyche was born), stepped up to the Priest's chair in three long cat's strides, shouldered the two girls away, and had the point of the dagger through the Priest's robes and into his skin.

"You old fool," he said. "Where is your plot now? Eh? Can you feel my bodkin? Does it tickle you? As that? Or that? I can drive it into your heart as quickly or slowly as I please. The wasps may be outside but I've got the queen wasp here. And now, what'll you do?"

I have never (to speak of things merely mortal) seen anything more wonderful than the Priest's stillness. Hardly any man can be quite still when a finger, much less a dagger, is thrust into the place between two ribs. The Priest was. Even his hands did not tighten on the arms of the chair. Never moving his head or changing his voice, he said,

"Drive it in, King, swift or slow, if it pleases you. It will make no difference. Be sure the Great Offering will be made whether I am dead or living. I am here in the strength of Ungit. While I have breath I am Ungit's voice. Perhaps longer. A priest does not wholly die. I may visit your palace more often, both by day and night, if you kill me. The others will not see me. I think you will."

This was the worst yet. The Fox had taught me to think—at any rate to speak—of the Priest as of a mere schemer and a politic man who put into the mouth of Ungit whatever might most increase his own power and lands or most harm his enemies. I saw it was not so. He was sure of Ungit. Looking at him as he sat with the dagger pricking him and his blind eyes unwinking, fixed on the King, and his face like an eagle's face, I was sure, too. Our real enemy was not a mortal. The room was full of spirits, and the horror of holiness.

With a beastly noise, all groan and snarl, my father turned away from the Priest and flung himself into his own chair and leaned back and passed his hands over his face and ruffled his hair like a man who is tired.

"Go on. Finish it," he said.

"And then," said the Priest, "we asked whether it was the King who was the Accursed, and the lots said 'no.'"

"What?" said the King. (And this is the greatest shame I have to tell of in my whole life.) His face cleared. He was only a hair's breadth from smiling. I had thought that he had seen the arrow pointed at Psyche all along, had been afraid for her, fighting for her.

He had not thought of her at all, nor of any of us. Yet I am credibly told that he was a brave enough man in a fight.

"Go on," he said. But his voice was changed, freshened, as if ten years of his age had slipped off him.

"The lot fell on your youngest daughter, King. She is the Accursed. The Princess Istra must be the Great Offering."

"It's very hard," said the King, gravely and glum enough, but I saw he was acting. He was hiding the greatness of his own relief. I went mad. In a moment I was at his feet, clinging to his knees as suppliants cling, babbling out I didn't know what, weeping, begging, calling him Father—a name I never used before. I believe he was glad of the diversion. He tried to kick me away, and when I still clung to his feet, rolling over and over, bruised in face and breast, he rose, gathered me up by my shoulders, and flung me from him with all his power.

"You!" he shouted. "You! You to raise your voice among the counsels of men? You trull, you quean, you mandrake root! Have I not woes and miseries and horrors enough heaped upon me by the gods but you also must come scrabbling and clawing me? And it would have come to biting in a trice if I'd let you. There's vixen in your face this minute. For two straws I'd have you to the guardhouse to be flogged. Name of Ungit! Are gods and priests and lions and shadowbrutes and traitors and cowards not enough unless I'm plagued with girls as well?"

I think he felt better the longer he railed. The breath had been knocked out of me so that I could neither sob nor rise nor speak. Somewhere above my head I heard them talking on, making all the plans for Psyche's death. She was to be kept prisoner in her chamber—or no, better in the room with five sides, which was more secure. The temple guards would reinforce our own; the whole house must be guarded, for the people were weathercocks—there might be a change of mood, even a rescue. They were talking soberly and prudently like men providing for a journey or a feast. Then I lost myself in darkness and a roaring noise.

SIX

SHE's coming to her mind again," said my father's
voice. "Take that side of her, Fox, and we'll get
her to the chair." The two of them were lifting
me; my father's hands were gentler than I expected. I
have found since that a soldier's hands often are. The
three of us were alone.

"Here, lass, this'll do you good," he said when they
had put me in the chair, holding a cup of wine to my lips.
"Faugh, you're spilling it like a baby. Take it easy. So,
that's better. If there's a bit of raw meat still to be had
in this dog-hole of a palace, you must lay it on your
bruises. And look, daughter, you shouldn't have crossed
me like that. A man can't have women (and his own
daughters, what's worse) meddling in business."

There was a sort of shame about him; whether for
beating me or for giving up Psyche without a struggle,
who knows? He seemed to me now a very vile, pitiable
king.

He set down the cup. "The thing has to be done," he
said. "Screaming and scrabbling won't help. Why, the
Fox here was just telling me it's done even in your dar-

57

ling Greeklands—which I begin to think I was a fool ever to let you hear of."

"Master," said the Fox, "I had not finished telling you. It is very true that a Greek king sacrificed his own daughter. But afterwards his wife murdered him, and his son murdered the wife, and Those Below drove the son mad."

At this the King scratched his head and looked very blank. "That's just like the gods," he muttered. "Drive you to do a thing and then punish you for doing it. The comfort is I've no wife or son, Fox."

I had got my voice again now. "King," I said, "you can't mean to do it. Istra is your daughter. You can't do it. You have not even tried to save her. There must be some way. Surely between now and the day—"

"Listen to her!" says the King. "You fool, it's to-morrow they offer her."

I was within an inch of fainting again. To hear this was as bad as to hear that she must be offered at all. As bad? It was worse. I felt that I had had no sorrow till now. I felt that if she could be spared only for a month—a month, why, a month was like eternity—we should all be happy.

"It's better so, dear," whispered the Fox to me in Greek. "Better for her and for us."

"What are you mumbling about, Fox?" said the King. "You both look at me as if I were some sort of two-headed giant they frighten children with, but what'd you have me do? What would you do yourself, Fox, with all your cleverness, if you were in my place?"

58

"I'd fight about the day first. I'd get a little time somehow. I'd say the Princess was at the wrong time of the month to be a bride. I'd say I'd been warned in a dream not to make the Great Offering till the new moon. I'd bribe men to swear that the Priest had cheated over the lots. There's half a dozen men across the river who hold land from him and don't love their landlord. I'd make a party. Anything to gain time. Give me ten days and I'd have a secret messenger to the King of Phars. I'd offer him all he wants without war—offer him anything if he'd come in and save the Princess—offer him Glome itself and my own crown."

"What?" snarled the King. "Be a little less free with other men's wealth, you'd best."

"But, Master, I'd lose not only my throne but my life to save the Princess, if I were a king and a father. Let us fight. Arm the slaves and promise them their freedom if they play the man. We can make a stand, we of your household, even now. At the worst, we should all die innocent. Better than going Down Yonder with a daughter's blood on your hands."

The King flung himself once more into his chair and began speaking with a desperate patience, like a teacher to a very stupid child (I had seen the Fox do it with Redival).

"I am a King. I have asked you for counsel. Those who counsel kings commonly tell them how to strengthen or save their kingship and their land. That is what counselling a king means. And your counsel is that I should throw my crown over the roof, sell my country

59

to Phars, and get my throat cut. You'll tell me next that the best way to cure a man's headache is to cut off his head."

"I see, Master," said the Fox. "I ask your pardon. I had forgotten that your own safety was the thing we must work for at all costs." I, who knew the Fox so well, could see such a look in his face that he could not have done the King much more dishonour if he had spat on him. Indeed I had often seen him look at the King like that, and the King never knew. I was determined he should know something now.

"King," said I, "the blood of the gods is in us. Can such a house as ours bear the shame? How will it sound if men say when you are dead that you took shelter behind a girl to save your own life?"

"You hear her, Fox, you hear her," said the King. "And then she wonders that I black her eyes! I'll not say mar her face, for that's impossible. Look, mistress, I'd be sorry to beat you twice in a day, but don't try me too far." He leaped up and began pacing the floor again.

"Death and scabs!" he said. "You'd make a man mad. Anyone'd think it was *your* daughter they were giving to the Brute. Sheltering behind a girl, you say. No one seems to remember whose girl she is. She's mine; fruit of my own body. My loss. It's I who have a right to rage and blubber if anyone has. What did I beget her for if I can't do what I think best with my own? What is it to you? There's some cursed cunning that I haven't yet smelled out behind all your sobbing and scolding. You're not asking me to believe that any woman, let alone such a fright as you, has much love for a pretty half-sister? It's not in nature. But I'll sift you yet."

I don't know whether he really believed this or not, but it is possible he did. He could believe anything in his moods, and everyone in the palace knew more than he about the life of us girls.

"Yes," he said, more quietly now. "It's I who should be pitied. It's I who am asked to give up part of myself. But I'll do my duty. I'll not ruin the land to save my own girl. The pair of you have talked me into making too much work about it. It has happened before. I'm sorry for the girl. But the Priest's right. Ungit must have her due. What's one girl—why, what would one man be—against the safety of us all? It's only sense that one should die for many. It happens in every battle."

Wine and passion had brought my strength back. I rose from my chair and found that I could stand.

"Father," said I. "You are right. It is fit that one should die for the people. Give me to the Brute instead of Istra."

The King, without a word, came up to me, took me (softly enough) by the wrist and led me the whole length of the room, to where his great mirror hung. You might wonder that he did not keep it in his bed-chamber, but the truth is he was too proud of it for that and wanted every stranger to see it. It had been made in some distant land and no king in our parts had one to match it. Our common mirrors were false and dull; in this you could see your perfect image. As I had never been in the Pillar Room alone, I had never looked in it.

He stood me before it and we saw our two selves, side by side.

"Ungit asked for the best in the land as her son's bride," he said. "And you'd give her *that*." He held me there a full minute in silence; perhaps he thought I would weep or turn my eyes away. At last he said, "Now be off. A man can't keep pace with your moods today. Get the beefsteak for your face. The Fox and I must be busy."

As I came out of the Pillar Room I first noticed the pain in my side; I had twisted myself somehow in my fall. But I forgot it again when I saw how, in that little time, our house had changed. It seemed crowded. All the slaves, whether they had anything to do or not, were walking about and gathering in knots, wearing looks of importance, chattering under their breath, too, with a sort of mournful cheerfulness. (They always will when there's great news in a house, and now it troubles me not at all.) There were many of the temple guard lounging in the porch; some temple girls sitting in the hall. From the courtyard came the smell of incense, and sacrifice was going on. Ungit had taken the house; the reek of holiness was everywhere.

At the foot of the staircase who should meet me but Redival, running to me all in tears, and a great babble pouring out of her mouth—"Oh Sister, Sister, how dreadful! Oh, poor Psyche! It's only Psyche, isn't it? They're not going to do it to all of us, are they? I never thought—I didn't mean any harm—it wasn't I—and oh, oh, oh. . . ."

I put my face close up to hers and said very low but distinctly, "Redival, if there is one single hour when I am queen of Glome, or even mistress of this house, I'll hang you by the thumbs at a slow fire till you die."

"Oh cruel, cruel," sobbed Redival. "How can you say such things, and when I'm so miserable already? Sister, don't be angry, comfort me—"

I pushed her away from me and passed on. I had known Redival's tears ever since I could remember. They were not wholly feigned, nor much dearer than ditchwater. I know now, as I felt sure then, that she had carried tattle about Psyche to the house of Ungit, and that with malice. It's likely enough she meant less mischief than she had done (she never knew how much she meant) and was now, in her fashion, sorry; but a new brooch, much more a new lover, would have had her drying her eyes and laughing in no time.

As I came to the top of the stairs (for we have upper rooms and even galleries in the palace; it is not like a Greek house) I was a little out of breath and the pain in my side came on me worse. I seemed to be somewhat lame in one foot too. I went on with all the haste I could to that five-sided room where they had shut Psyche up. The door was bolted on the outside (I have used that room for a courteous prison myself) and an armed man stood before it. It was Bardia.

"Bardia," I panted, "let me in. I must see the Princess Istra."

He looked at me kindly but shook his head. "It can't be done, Lady," he said.

"But, Bardia, you can lock us both in. There's no way out but the door."

"That's how all escapes begin, Lady. I am sorry for you and for the other Princess, but it can't be done. I'm under the sternest orders."

"Bardia," I said, with tears, my left hand to my side (for the pain was bad now), "it's her last night alive."

He looked away from me and said again, "I'm sorry."

I turned from him without another word. Though his was the kindest face (always excepting the Fox) I had seen that day, for the moment I hated him more than my father or the Priest or even Redival. What I did next shows how near I was to madness. I went as fast as I could to the Bedchamber. I knew the King had arms there. I took a plain, good sword, drew it, looked at it, and weighed it in my hand. It was not at all too heavy for me. I felt the edges and the point; they were what I then thought sharp, though a smart soldier would not have called them so. Quickly I was back at Psyche's door. Even in my woman's rage I had man enough about me to cry out, "Ward yourself, Bardia," before I fell on him.

It was of course the craziest attempt for a girl who had never had a weapon in her hand before. Even if I had known my work, the lame foot and the pain in my side (to breathe deep was agony) disabled me. Yet I made him use some of his skill; chiefly, of course, because he was not fighting to hurt me. In a moment he had twisted my sword out of my grip. I stood before him, with my hand pressed harder than ever to my side, all in a muck sweat and a tremble. His brow was dry and his breathing unchanged; it had been as easy as that for him. The knowledge that I was so helpless came over me like a new woe, or gathered the other woe up into itself. I burst into utterly childish weeping—like Redival.

"It's a thousand pities, Lady, that you weren't a man," said Bardia. "You've a man's reach and a quick eye. There are none of the recruits would do as well at a first attempt; I'd like to have the training of you. It's a thousand—"

"Ah, Bardia, Bardia," I sobbed, "if only you'd killed me. I'd be out of my misery now."

"No, you wouldn't," said he. "You'd be dying, not dead. It's only in tales that a man dies the moment the steel's gone in and come out. Unless of course you swap off his head."

I could talk no more at all now. The whole world seemed to me to be in my weeping.

"Curse it," said Bardia, "I can't bear this." There were tears in his own eyes now; he was a very tender man. "I wouldn't mind so much if the one weren't so brave and the other so beautiful. Here! Lady! Stop it. I'll risk my life, and Ungit's wrath too."

I gazed at him, but was still not able to speak.

"I'd give my own life for the girl in there, if it would do any good. You may have wondered why I, the captain of the guard, am standing here like a common sentry. I wouldn't let anyone else do it. I thought if the poor girl called, or if I had to go in to her for any rea-

65

son, I'd be homelier for her than a stranger. She sat on my knees when she was little. . . . I wonder do the gods know what it feels like to be a man."

"You'll let me in?" I said.

"On one condition, Lady. You must swear to come out when I knock. It's quiet up here now, but there'll be comings and goings later. There'll be two temple girls coming to her presently; I was warned of that. I'll give you as long as I can. But I must be sure of your coming out when I give the sign. Three knocks—like this."

"I'll come out at once when you do that."

"Swear it, Lady, here on my sword."

I swore it. He looked to left and right, did back the bolt, and said, "Quick. In you go. Heaven comfort you both."

SEVEN

THE window in that room is so small and high up that men need lights there at noon. That is why it can serve as a prison; it was built as the second story of a tower which my great-grandfather began and never finished.

Psyche sat upon the bed with a lamp burning beside her. Of course I was at once in her arms and saw this only in a flash; but the picture—Psyche, a bed, and a lamp—is everlasting.

Long before I could speak she said, "Sister, what have they done to you? Your face, your eye! He has been beating you again." Then I realised somewhat slowly that all this time she had been petting and comforting me as if it were I who was the child and the victim. And this, even in the midst of the great anguish, made its own little eddy of pain. It was so unlike the sort of love that used to be between us in our happy times.

She was so quick and tender that she knew at once what I was thinking, and at once she called me *Maia*, the old baby's name that the Fox had taught her. It was one of the first words she ever learned to say.

"Maia, Maia, tell me. What has he done to you?"

"Oh, Psyche," said I, "what does it matter? If only he had killed me! If only they would take me instead of you!"

But she would not be put off. She forced the whole tale out of me (how could one deny her?) wasting on it the little time we had.

"Sister, no more," I said at last. "What is it to me? What is he to either of us? I'll not shame your mother or mine to say he's not our father. If so, the name *father* is a curse. I'll believe now that he would hide behind a woman in a battle."

And then (it was a kind of terror to me) she smiled. She had wept very little, and mostly, I think, for love and pity of me. Now she sat tall and queenly and still. There was no sign about her of coming death, except that her hands were very cold.

"Orual," she said, "you make me think I have learned the Fox's lessons better than you. Have you forgotten what we are to say to ourselves every morning? 'Today I shall meet cruel men, cowards and liars, the envious and the drunken. They will be like that because they do not know what is good from what is bad. This is an evil which has fallen upon them not upon me. They are to be pitied, not—'." She was speaking with a loving mimicry of the Fox's voice; she could do this as well as Batta did it badly.

"Oh child, how can—" but I was choked again. All she was saying seemed to me so light, so far away from our sorrow. I felt we ought not to be talking that way, not now. What I thought it would be better to talk of, I did not know.

"Maia," said Psyche. "You must make me a promise. You'll not do anything outrageous? You'll not kill yourself? You mustn't, for the Fox's sake. We have been three loving friends." (Why must she say bare *friends?*) "Now it's only he and you; you must hold together and stand the closer. No, Maia, you must. Like soldiers in a hard battle."

"Oh, your heart is of iron," I said.

"As for the King, give him my duty—or whatever is proper. Bardia is a prudent and courteous man. He'll tell you what dying girls ought to say to fathers. One would not seem rude or ignorant at the last. But I can send the King no other message. The man is a stranger to me; I know the henwife's baby better than him. And for Redival—"

"Send her your curse. And if the dead can—"

"No, no. She also does what she doesn't know."

"Not even for you, Psyche, will I pity Redival, whatever the Fox says."

"Would you like to be Redival? What? No? Then she's pitiable. If I am allowed to give my jewels as I please, you must keep all the things that you and I have really loved. Let her have all that's big and costly and doesn't matter. You and the Fox take what you please."

I could bear no more for a while, so I laid my head down in her lap and wept. If only she would so have laid her head in mine!

"Look up, Maia," she said presently. "You'll break

69

my heart, and I to be a bride." She could bear to say that. I could not bear to hear it.

"Orual," she said, very softly, "we are the blood of the gods. We must not shame our lineage. Maia, it was you who taught me not to cry when I fell."

"I believe you are not afraid at all," said I, almost, though I had not meant it to sound so, as if I were rebuking her for it.

"Only of one thing," she said. "There is a cold doubt, a horrid shadow, in some corner of my soul. Supposing —supposing—how if there were no god of the Mountain and even no holy Shadowbrute, and those who are tied to the Tree only die, day by day, from thirst and hunger and wind and sun, or are eaten piecemeal by the crows and catamountains? And it is this—oh, Maia, Maia. . . ."

And now she did weep and now she was a child again. What could I do but fondle and weep with her? But this is a great shame to write; there was now (for me) a kind of sweetness in our misery for the first time. This was what I had come to her in her prison to do.

She recovered before I did. She raised her head, queenlike again, and said, "But I'll not believe it. The Priest has been with me. I never knew him before. He is not what the Fox thinks. Do you know, Sister, I have come to feel more and more that the Fox hasn't the whole truth. Oh, he has much of it. It'd be dark as a dungeon within me but for his teaching. And yet . . . I can't say it properly. He calls the whole world a city. But what's a city built on? There's earth beneath. And outside the wall? Doesn't all the food come from there as well as all the dangers? . . . things growing and rotting, strengthening and poisoning, things shining wet . . . in one way (I don't know which way) more like, yes, even more like the House of—"

"Yes, of Ungit," said I. "Doesn't the whole land smell of her? Do you and I need to flatter gods any more? They're tearing us apart . . . oh, how shall I bear it? . . . and what worse can they do? Of course the Fox is wrong. He knows nothing about her. He thought too well of the world. He thought there were no gods, or else (the fool!) that they were better than men. It never entered his mind—he was too good—to believe that the gods are real, and viler than the vilest men."

"Or else," said Psyche, "they are real gods but don't really do these things. Or even—mightn't it be—they do these things and the things are not what they seem to be? How if I am indeed to wed a god?"

She made me, in a way, angry. I would have died for her (this, at least, I know is true) and yet, the night before her death, I could feel anger. She spoke so steadily and thoughtfully, as if we had been disputing with the Fox, up behind the pear trees, with hours and days still before us. The parting between her and me seemed to cost her so little.

"Oh, Psyche," I said, almost in a shriek, "what can these things be except the cowardly murder they seem? To take you—you whom they have worshipped and who never hurt so much as a toad—to make you food for a monster. . . ."

You will say—I have said it many thousand times to myself—that, if I saw in her any readiness to dwell on the better part of the Priest's talk and to think she would be a god's bride more than a Brute's prey, I ought to have fallen in with her and encouraged it. Had I not come to her to give comfort, if I could? Surely not to take it away. But I could not rule myself. Perhaps it was a sort of pride in me, a little like her own, not to blind our eyes, not to hide terrible things; or a bitter impulse in anguish itself to say, and to keep on saying, the worst.

"I see," said Psyche in a low voice. "You think it devours the offering. I mostly think so myself. Anyway, it means death. Orual, you didn't think I was such a child as not to know that? How can I be the ransom for all Glome unless I die? And if I am to go to the god, of course it must be through death. That way, even what is strangest in the holy sayings might be true. To be eaten and to be married to the god might not be so different. We don't understand. There must be so much that neither the Priest nor the Fox knows."

This time I bit my lip and said nothing. Unspeakable foulness seethed in my mind; did she think the Brute's lust better than its hunger? To be mated with a worm, or a giant eft, or a spectre?

"And as for death," she said, "why, Bardia there (I love Bardia) will look on it six times a day and whistle a tune as he goes to find it. We have made little use of

72

the Fox's teaching if we're to be scared by death. And you know, Sister, he has sometimes let out that there were other Greek masters than those he follows himself; masters who have taught that death opens a door out of a little, dark room (that's all the life we have known before it) into a great, real place where the true sun shines and we shall meet—"

"Oh cruel, cruel!" I wailed. "Is it nothing to you that you leave me here alone? Psyche; did you ever love me at all?"

"Love you? Why, Maia, what have I ever had to love save you and our grandfather the Fox?" (But I did not want her to bring even the Fox in now.) "But, Sister, you will follow me soon. You don't think any mortal life seems a long thing to me tonight? And how would it be better if I had lived? I suppose I should have been given to some king in the end—perhaps such another as our father. And there you can see again how little difference there is between dying and being married. To leave your home—to lose you, Maia, and the Fox—to lose one's maidenhead—to bear a child—they are all deaths. Indeed, indeed, Orual, I am not sure that this which I go to is not the best."

"This!"

"Yes. What had I to look for if I lived? Is the world —this palace, this father—so much to lose? We have already had what would have been the best of our time. I must tell you something, Orual, which I never told to anyone, not even you."

I know now that this must be so even between the

lovingest hearts. But her saying it that night was like stabbing me.

"What is it?" said I, looking down at her lap where our four hands were joined.

"This," she said, "I have always—at least, ever since I can remember—had a kind of longing for death."

"Ah, Psyche," I said, "have I made you so little happy as that?"

"No, no, no," she said. "You don't understand. Not that kind of longing. It was when I was happiest that I longed most. It was on happy days when we were up there on the hills, the three of us, with the wind and the sunshine . . . where you couldn't see Glome or the palace. Do you remember? The colour and the smell, and looking across at the Grey Mountain in the distance? And because it was so beautiful, it set me longing, always longing. Somewhere else there must be more of it. Everything seemed to be saying, Psyche come! But I couldn't (not yet) come and I didn't know where I was to come to. It almost hurt me. I felt like a bird in a cage when the other birds of its kind are flying home."

She kissed both my hands, flung them free, and stood up. She had her father's trick of walking to and fro when she talked of something that moved her. And from now till the end I felt (and this horribly) that I was losing her already, that the sacrifice tomorrow would only finish something that had already begun. She was (how long had she been, and I not to know?) out of my reach, in some place of her own.

Since I write this book against the gods, it is just that

74

I should put into it whatever can be said against myself. So let me set this down: as she spoke I felt, amid all my love, a bitterness. Though the things she was saying gave her (that was plain enough) courage and comfort, I grudged her that courage and comfort. It was as if someone or something else had come in between us. If this grudging is the sin for which the gods hate me, it is one I have committed.

"Orual," she said, her eyes shining, "I am going, you see, to the Mountain. You remember how we used to look and long? And all the stories of my gold and amber house, up there against the sky, where we thought we should never really go? The greatest King of all was going to build it for me. If only you could believe it, Sister! No, listen. Do not let grief shut up your ears and harden your heart—"

"Is it *my* heart that is hardened?"

"Never to me; nor mine to you at all. But listen. Are these things so evil as they seemed? The gods will have mortal blood. But they say whose. If they had chosen any other in the land, that would have been only terror and cruel misery. But they chose me. And I am the one who has been made ready for it ever since I was a little child in your arms, Maia. The sweetest thing in all my life has been the longing—to reach the Mountain, to find the place where all the beauty came from—"

"And that was the sweetest? Oh, cruel, cruel. Your heart is not of iron—stone, rather," I sobbed. I don't think she even heard me.

"—my country, the place where I ought to have been

born. Do you think it all meant nothing, all the longing? The longing for home? For indeed it now feels not like going, but like going back. All my life the god of the Mountain has been wooing me. Oh, look up once at least before the end and wish me joy. I am going to my lover. Do you not see now—?"

"I only see that you have never loved me," said I. "It may well be you are going to the gods. You are becoming cruel like them."

"Oh Maia!" cried Psyche, tears at last coming into her eyes again. "Maia, I—"

Bardia knocked on the door. No time for better words, no time to unsay anything. Bardia knocked again, and louder. My oath on his sword, itself like a sword, was upon us.

So, the last, spoiled embrace. Those are happy who have no such in their memory. For those who have—would they endure that I should write of it?

EIGHT

As soon as I was out in the gallery my pains, which I had not perceived while I was with Psyche, came strongly back upon me. My grief, even, was deadened for a while, though my wits became very sharp and clear. I was determined to go with Psyche to the Mountain and the holy Tree, unless they bound me with chains. I even thought I might hide up there and set her free when the Priest and the King and all the rest had turned to come home. "Or if there is a real Shadowbrute," I thought, "and I cannot save her from it, I'll kill her with my own hand before I'll leave her to its clutches." To do all this I knew I must eat and drink and rest. (It was now nearly twilight and I was still fasting.) But first of all I must find out when their murder, their Offering, was to be. So I limped along the gallery, holding my side, and found an old slave, the King's butler, who was able to tell me all. The procession, he said, was to leave the palace an hour before sunrise. Then I went to my own chamber and told my women to bring me food. I sat down to wait till it came. A great dullness and heaviness crept over me; I thought and felt nothing, except that I was very cold. When the food came I could not eat though I tried to force myself to it; it was like putting cloth in my mouth. But I drank; a little of the small beer which was all they had to give me, and then (for my stomach rose against the beer) a great deal of water. I must have been almost sleeping before I finished, for I remember that I knew I was in some great sorrow but I could not recall what it was.

They lifted me into the bed (I shrank and cried out a little at their touch) and I fell at once into a dead stupidity of sleep; so that it seemed only a heartbeat later that they were waking me—two hours before sunrise, as I had bidden them. I woke screaming, for all my sore places had stiffened while I slept and it was like hot pincers when I tried to move. One eye had closed up so that I might as well have been blind on that side. When they found how much they hurt me in raising me from the bed, they begged me to lie still. Some said it was useless for me to rise, for the King had said that neither of the Princesses should go to the Offering. One asked if she should bring Batta to me. I told that one, with bitter words, to hold her tongue, and if I had had the strength I would have hit her; which would have been ill done, for she was a good girl. (I have always been fortunate with my women since first I had them to myself and out of the reach of Batta's meddling.)

They dressed me somehow and tried to make me eat. One even had a little wine for me, stolen, I guess, from a flagon intended for the King. They were all weeping; I was not.

78

Dressing me (so sore I was) had taken a great time, so that I had hardly swallowed the wine before we heard the music beginning: temple music, Ungit's music, the drums and the horns and rattles and castanets, all holy, deadly—dark, detestable, maddening noises.

"Quick!" said I. "It's time. They're going. Oh, I can't get up. Help me, girls. No, quicker! Drag me, if need be. Take no heed of my groaning and screaming."

They got me with great torture as far as the head of the staircase. I could now see down into the great hall between the Pillar Room and the Bedchamber. It was ablaze with torches and very crowded. There were many guards. There were some girls of noble blood veiled and chapleted like a bride's party. My father was there in very splendid robes. And there was a great bird-headed man. By the smell and the smoke there seemed to have been much killing already, at the altar in the courtyard. (Food for the gods must always be found somehow, even when the land starves.) The great gateway was opened. I could see cold, early dawn through it. Outside, priests and girls were singing. There must have been a great mob of the rabble too; in the pauses you could hear (who can mistake it?) their noise. No herd of other beasts, gathered together, has so ugly a voice as Man.

For a long time I could not see Psyche at all. The gods are cleverer than we and can always think of some vileness it never entered our heads to fear. When at last I saw her, that was the worst of all. She sat upright on an open litter between the King and the Priest. The reason I had not known her was that they had painted and gilded and be-wigged her like a temple girl. I could not even tell whether she saw me or not. Her eyes, peering out of the heavy, lifeless mask which they had made of her face, were utterly strange; you couldn't even see in what direction she was looking.

It is, in its way, admirable, this divine skill. It was not enough for the gods to kill her; they must make her father the murderer. It was not enough to take her from me, they must take her from me three times over, tear out my heart three times. First her sentence; then her strange, cold talk last night; and now this painted and gilded horror to poison my last sight of her. Ungit had taken the most beautiful thing that was ever born and made it into an ugly doll.

They told me afterwards that I tried to start going down the stairway and fell. They carried me to my bed.

For many days after that I was sick, and most of them I do not remember. I was not in my right mind, and slept (they tell me) not at all. My ravings—what I can recall of them—were a ceaseless torture of tangled diversity, yet also of sameness. Everything changed into something else before you could understand it, yet the new thing always stabbed you in the very same place. One thread ran through all the delusions. Now mark yet again the cruelty of the gods. There is no escape from them into sleep or madness, for they can pursue you into them with dreams. Indeed you are then most at their mercy. The nearest thing we have to a defence against them (but there is no real defence) is to be very wide awake and sober and hard at work, to hear no music, never to look at earth or sky, and (above all) to love no one. And now, finding me heart-shattered for Psyche's sake, they made it the common burden of all my fantasies that Psyche was my greatest enemy. All my sense of intolerable wrong was directed against her. It was she who hated me; it was on her that I wanted to be revenged. Sometimes she and Redival and I were all children together, and then Psyche and Redival would drive me away and put me out of the game and stand with their arms linked laughing at me. Sometimes I was beautiful and had a lover who looked (absurdly) a little like poor, eunuch'd Tarin or a little like Bardia (I suppose because his was the last man's face, almost, that I had seen before I fell ill). But on the very threshold of the bridal chamber, or from the very bedside, Psyche, wigged and masked and no bigger than my forearm, would lead him away with one finger. And when they got to the door they would turn round and mock and point at me. But these were the clearest visions. More often it was all confused and dim—Psyche throwing me down high precipices, Psyche (now very like the King, but still Psyche) kicking me and dragging me by the hair, Psyche with a torch or a sword or a whip pursuing me over vast swamps and dark mountains—I running to save my life. But always wrong, hatred, mockery, and my determination to be avenged.

The beginning of my recovery was when the visions ceased and left behind them only a settled sense of some great injury that Psyche had done me, though I could not gather my wits to think what it was. They say I lay for hours saying, "Cruel girl. Cruel Psyche. Her heart is of stone." And soon I was in my right mind again and knew how I loved her and that she had never willingly done me any wrong, though it hurt me somewhat that she should have found time, at our last meeting of all, talking so little of me, to talk so much about the god of the Mountain, and the King, and the Fox, and Redival, and even Bardia.

Soon after that I was aware of a pleasant noise that had already been going on a long time.

"What is it?" I asked (and was astonished at the weak croak of my voice).

"What is what, child?" said the voice of the Fox; and I knew somehow that he had been sitting by my bed for many hours.

"The noise, Grandfather. Above our heads."

"That is the rain, dear," he said. "Give thanks to Zeus for that and for your own recovery. And I—but you must sleep again. And drink this first." I saw the tears on his face as he gave me the cup.

I had no broken bones; the bruises were gone, and my other pains with them. But I was very weak. Weakness, and work, are two comforts the gods have not taken from us. I'd not write it (it might move them to take these also away) except that they must know it already. I was too weak now to feel much grief or anger. These days, before my strength came back, were almost happy. The Fox was very loving and tender (and much weakened himself) and so were my women. I was loved; more than I had thought. And my sleeps were sweet now and there was much rain and, betweenwhiles, the kind south-wind blowing in at the window, and sunshine. For a long time we never spoke of Psyche. We talked, when we talked at all, of common things.

They had much to tell me. The weather had changed the very day after my sickness began. The Shennit was full again. The breaking of the drought had come too late to save the crops for the most part (one or two fields put up a little); but garden stuff was growing. Above all, the grass was reviving wonderfully; we should save far more of the cattle than we had hoped. And the fever was clean gone. My own sickness had been of another kind. And birds were coming back to Glome, so that every woman whose husband could shoot with a bow or set a snare might soon have something in the pot.

These things I heard of from the women as well as from the Fox. When we were alone he told me other news. My father was now, while it lasted, the darling of his people. It seemed (this was how we first came round to the matter nearest our hearts) he had been much pitied and praised at the Great Offering. Up there at the holy Tree he had wailed and wept and torn his robes and embraced Psyche countless times (he had never done it before) but said again and again that he would not withhold his heart's dearest when the good of the people called for her death. The whole crowd was in tears, as the Fox had been told; he himself, as a slave and an alien, had not been there.

"Did you know, Grandfather," said I, "that the King

was such a mountebank?" (We were talking in Greek of course.)

"Not wholly that, child," said the Fox. "He believed it while he did it. His tears are no falser—or truer—than Redival's."

Then he went on to tell me of the great news from Phars. A fool in the crowd had said the King of Phars had thirteen sons. The truth is he had begotten eight, whereof one died in childhood. The eldest was simple and could never rule, and the King (as some said their laws allowed him) had named Argan, the third, as his successor. And now, it seemed, his second son, Trunia, taking it ill to be put out of the succession—and, doubtless, fomenting some other discontents such as are never far to seek in any land—had risen in rebellion, with a strong following, to recover what he called his right. The upshot was that all Phars was likely to be busy with civil war for a twelvemonth at least, and both parties were already as soft as butter towards Glome, so that we were safe from any threat in that quarter.

A few days later when the Fox was with me (often he could not be, for the King needed him) I said,

"Grandfather, do you still think that Ungit is only lies of poets and priests?"

"Why not, child?"

"If she were indeed a goddess what more could have followed my poor sister's death than has followed it? All the dangers and plagues that hung over us have been scattered. Why, the wind must have changed the very day after they had—" I found, now, I could not give it

84

a name. The grief was coming back with my strength. So was the Fox's.

"Cursed chance, cursed chance," he muttered, his face all screwed up, partly in anger and partly to keep back his tears (Greek men cry easily as women). "It is these chances that nourish the beliefs of barbarians."

"How often, Grandfather, you have told me there's no such thing as chance."

"You're right. It was an old trick of the tongue. I meant that all these things had no more to do with that murder than with anything else. They and it are all part of the same web, which is called Nature, or the Whole. That southwest wind came over a thousand miles of sea and land. The weather of the whole world would have to have been different from the beginning if that wind was not to blow. It's all one web; you can't pick threads out nor put them in."

"And so," said I, raising myself on my elbow, "she died to no purpose. If the King had waited a few days later we could have saved her, for all would have begun to go well of itself. And this you call comfort?"

"Not this. Their evil-doing was vain and ignorant, as all evil deeds are. This is our comfort, that the evil was theirs, not hers. They say there was not a tear in her eye, nor did so much as her hand shake, when they put her to the Tree. Not even when they turned away and left her did she cry out. She died full of all things that are really good; courage, and patience, and—and— Aiai! Aiai—oh, Psyche, oh, my little one—" Then his love got the better of his philosophy, and he pulled his mantle over his head and at last, still weeping, left me.

Next day he said, "You saw yesterday, Daughter, how little progress I have made. I began to philosophise too late. You are younger and can go further. To love, and to lose what we love, are equally things appointed for our nature. If we cannot bear the second well, that evil is ours. It did not befall Psyche. If we look at it with reason's eye and not with our passions, what good that life offers did she not win? Chastity, temperance, prudence, meekness, clemency, valour—and, though fame is froth, yet, if we should reckon it at all, a name that stands with Iphigenia's and Antigone's."

Of course he had long since told me those stories, so often that I had them by heart, mostly in the very words of the poets. Nevertheless, I asked him to tell me them again, chiefly for his sake; for I was now old enough to know that a man (above all, a Greek man) can find comfort in words coming out of his own mouth. But I was glad to hear them too. These were peaceful, familiar things and would keep at bay the great desolation which now, with my returning health, was beginning to mix itself in every thought.

Next day, being then for the first time risen, I said to him, "Grandfather, I have missed being Iphigenia. I can be Antigone."

"Antigone? How, child?"

"She gave her brother burial. I too—there may be something left. Even the Brute would not eat bones and all. I must go up to the Tree. I will bring it . . . them

. . . back if I can and burn them rightly. Or, if there's too much, I'll bury it up there."

"It would be pious," said the Fox. "It would accord with custom, if not with Nature. If you can. It's late in the year now for going up the Mountain."

"That's why it must be done speedily. I think it will be about five and twenty days before the earliest snow."

"If you can, child. You have been very sick."

"It's all I can do," said I.

NINE

I was soon able to go about the house and in the gardens again. I did it in some stealth, for the Fox told the King I was still sick. Otherwise he would have had me off to the Pillar Room to work for him. He often asked, "Where's that girl got to? Does she mean to slug abed for the rest of her life? I'll not feed drones in my hive forever." The loss of Psyche had not at all softened him to Redival and me. Rather the opposite. "To hear him talk," said the Fox, "you'd think no father ever loved a child better than he Psyche." The gods had taken his darling and left him the dross: the young whore (that was Redival) and the hobgoblin (which was I). But I could guess it all without the Fox's reports to help me.

For my own part, I was busily thinking out how I could make my journey to the Tree on the Mountain and gather whatever might remain of Psyche. I had talked lightly enough of doing this and was determined that I would do it, but the difficulties were very great. I had never been taught to ride any beast, so I must go on foot. I knew it would take a man who knew the way about six hours to go from the palace to the Tree. I, a woman, and one who had to find her way, must allow myself eight at the least. And two more for the work I went to do, and, say, six for the journey home. There were sixteen hours in all. It could not be done in one stitch. I must reckon to lie out a night on the Mountain, and must take food (water I should find) and warm clothing. It could not be done till I recovered my full strength.

And in truth (as I now see) I had the wish to put off my journey as long as I could. Not for any peril or labour it might cost; but because I could see nothing in the whole world for me to do once it was accomplished. As long as this act lay before me, there was, as it were, some barrier between me and the dead desert which the rest of my life must be. Once I had gathered Psyche's bones, then, it seemed, all that concerned her would be over and done with. Already, even with the great act still ahead, there was flowing in upon me, from the barren years beyond it, a dejection such as I had never conceived. It was not at all like the agonies I had endured before and have endured since. I did not weep nor wring my hands. I was like water put into a bottle and left in a cellar: utterly motionless, never to be drunk, poured out, spilled or shaken. The days were endless. The very shadows seemed nailed to the ground as if the sun no longer moved.

One day when this deadness was at its worst I came into the house by the little door that leads into a narrow passage between the guards' quarters and the dairy. I

89

sat down on the threshold, less weary of body (for the gods, not out of mercy, have made me strong) than unable to find a reason for going a step further in any direction or for doing anything at all. A fat fly was crawling up the doorpost. I remember thinking that its sluggish crawling, seemingly without aim, was like my life, or even the life of the whole world.

"Lady," said a voice behind me. I looked up; it was Bardia.

"Lady," he said, "I'll make free with you. I've known sorrow too. I have been as you are now; I have sat and felt the hours drawn out to the length of years. What cured me was the wars. I don't think there's any other cure."

"But I can't go to the wars, Bardia," said I.

"You can, almost," he said. "When you fought me outside the other Princess's door (peace be on her, the Blessed!) I told you you had a good eye and a good reach. You thought I was saying it to cheer you. Well, so perhaps I was. But it was true too. There's no one in the quarters, and there are blunt swords. Come in and let me give you a lesson."

"No," said I dully. "I don't want to. What would be the use?"

"Use? Try it and see. No one can be sad while they're using wrist and hand and eye and every muscle of their body. That's truth, Lady, whether you believe it or not. As well, it would be a hundred shames not to train anyone who has such a gift for the sport as you look like having."

"No," said I. "Leave me alone. Unless we can use sharps and you would kill me."

"That's women's talk, by your favour. You'd never say that again once you'd seen it done. Come. I'll not leave off till you do."

A big, kindly man, some years older than herself, can usually persuade even a sad and sullen girl. In the end I rose and went in with him.

"That shield is too heavy," he said. "Here's the one for you. Slip it on, thus. And understand from the outset; your shield is a weapon, not a wall. You're fighting with it every bit as much as your sword. Watch me, now. You see the way I twist my shield—make it flicker like a butterfly. There'd be arrows and spears and sword points flying off it in every direction if we were in a hot engagement. Now: here's your sword. No, not like that. You want to grip it firm, but light. It's not a wild animal that's trying to run away from you. That's better. Now, your left foot forward. And don't look at my face, look at my sword. It isn't my face is going to fight you. And now, I'll show you a few guards."

He kept me at it for a full half-hour. It was the hardest work I'd ever done, and, while it lasted, one could think of nothing else. I said not long before that work and weakness are comforters. But sweat is the kindest creature of the three—far better than philosophy, as a cure for ill thoughts.

"That's enough," said Bardia. "You shape very well. I'm sure now I can make a swordsman of you. You'll come again tomorrow? But your dress hampers you. It would be better if you could wear something that came only to your knee."

I was in such a heat that I went across the passage into the dairy and drank a bowl of milk. It was the first food or drink that I had really relished ever since the bad times began. While I was in there, one of the other soldiers (I suppose he had had a sight of what we were doing) came into the passage and said something to Bardia. Bardia replied, I couldn't hear what. Then he spoke louder: "Why, yes, it's a pity about her face. But she's a brave girl and honest. If a man was blind and she weren't the King's daughter, she'd make him a good wife." And that is the nearest thing to a love-speech that was ever made me.

I had my lesson with Bardia every day after that. And I knew soon that he had been a good doctor to me. My grief remained, but the numbness was gone and time moved at its right pace again.

Soon I told Bardia how I wished to go to the Grey Mountain, and why.

"That's very well thought of, Lady," he said. "I'm ashamed I have not done it myself. We all owe the Blessed Princess that much at the least. But there's no need for you to go. I'll go for you."

I said I would go.

"Then you must go with me," he said. "You'd never find the place by yourself. And you might meet a bear or wolves or a mountainy man, an outlaw, that'd be worse. Can you ride a horse, Lady?"

"No, I've never been taught."

He wrinkled up his brow, thinking. "One horse will do," he said, "I in the saddle and you behind me. And it won't take six hours getting up; there's a shorter way. But the work we have to do might take long enough. We'll need to sleep a night on the mountain."

"Will the King let you be absent so long, Bardia?"

He chuckled. "Oh, I'll spin the King a story easily enough. He isn't with us as he is with you, Lady. For all his hard words he's no bad master to soldiers, shepherds, huntsmen, and the like. He understands them and they him. You see him at his worst with women and priests and politic men. The truth is, he's half afraid of them." This was very strange to me.

Six days after that, I and Bardia set out at the milking-time of the morning, the day being so cloudy that it was almost as dark as full night. No one in the palace knew of our going except the Fox and my own women. I had on a plain black cloak with a hood, and a veil over my face. Under the mantle I wore the short smock that I used for my fencing bouts, with a man's belt and a sword, this time a sharp one, at my side. "Most likely we'll meet nothing worse than a wild cat or a fox," Bardia had said. "But no one, man or maid, ought to go weaponless up the hills." I sat with both my legs on one side of the horse, and a hand on Bardia's girdle. With the other, I held on my knees an urn.

It was all silent in the city, but for the clatter of our own beast's hoofs, though here and there you would see a light in a window. A sharp rain came on us from behind our backs as we went down from the city to the ford of the Shennit, but it ceased as we were crossing the water, and the clouds began to break. There was still no sign of dawn ahead, for it was in that direction the foul weather was packing off.

We passed the house of Ungit on our right. Its fashion is thus: great, ancient stones, twice the height of a man and four times the thickness of a man, set upright in an egg-shaped ring. These are very ancient, and no one knows who set them up or brought them into that place, or how. In between the stones it is filled up with brick to make the wall complete. The roof is thatched with rushes and not level but somewhat domed, so that the whole thing is a roundish hump, most like a huge slug lying on the field. This is a holy shape, and the priests say it resembles, or (in a mystery) that it really is, the egg from which the whole world was hatched or the womb in which the whole world once lay. Every spring the Priest is shut into it and fights, or makes believe to fight, his way out through the western door; and this means that the new year is born. There was smoke going up from it as we passed, for the fire before Ungit is always alight.

I found my mood changed as soon as we had left Ungit behind, partly because we were now going into country I had never known, and partly because I felt as if the air were sweeter as we got away from all that holiness. The Mountain, now bigger ahead of us, still shut out the brightening of the day; but when I looked back and saw, beyond the city, those hills where Psyche and I and the Fox used to wander, I perceived that it was already morning there. And further off still, the clouds in the western sky were beginning to turn pale rose.

We were going up and down little hills, but always more up than down, on a good enough road, with grasslands on each side of us. There were dark woods on our left, and presently the road bent towards them. But here Bardia left the road and took to the grass.

"That's the Holy Road," he said, pointing to the woods. "That's the way they took the Blessed (peace be on her). Our way will be steeper and shorter."

We now went for a long time over grass, gently but steadily upward, making for a ridge so high and so near that the true Mountain was quite out of sight. When we topped it, and stood for a while to let the horse breathe, everything was changed. And my struggle began.

We had come into the sunlight now, too bright to look into, and warm (I threw back my cloak). Heavy dew made the grass jewel-bright. The Mountain, far greater yet also far further off than I expected, seen with the sun hanging a hand-breadth above its topmost crags, did not look like a solid thing. Between us and it was a vast tumble of valley and hill, woods and cliffs, and more little lakes than I could count. To left and right, and behind us, the whole coloured world with all its hills was heaped up and up to the sky, with, far away, a gleam of what we call the sea (though it is not to be compared with the Great Sea of the Greeks). There was a lark singing; but for that, huge and ancient stillness.

And my struggle was this. You may well believe that I had set out sad enough; I came on a sad errand. Now, flung at me like frolic or insolence, there came as if it were a voice—no words—but if you made it into words it would be, "Why should your heart not dance?" It's the measure of my folly that my heart almost answered, "Why not?" I had to tell myself over like a lesson the infinite reasons it had not to dance. My heart to dance? Mine whose love was taken from me, I, the ugly princess who must never look for other love, the drudge of the King, the jailer of hateful Redival, perhaps to be murdered or turned out as a beggar when my father died —for who knew what Glome would do then? And yet, it was a lesson I could hardly keep in my mind. The sight of the huge world put mad ideas into me, as if I could wander away, wander forever, see strange and beautiful things, one after the other to the world's end. The freshness and wetness all about me (I had seen nothing but drought and withered things for many months before my sickness) made me feel that I had misjudged the world; it seemed kind, and laughing, as if its heart also danced. Even my ugliness I could not quite believe in. Who can *feel* ugly when the heart meets delight? It is as if, somewhere inside, within the hideous face and bony limbs, one is soft, fresh, lissom and desirable.

We had stood on the ridge only for a short time. But for hours later while we went up and down winding among great hills, often dismounting and leading the horse, sometimes on dangerous edges, the struggle went on.

Was I not right to struggle against this fool-happy mood? Mere seemliness, if nothing else, called for it.

I would not go laughing to Psyche's burial. If I did, how should I ever again believe that I had loved her? Reason called for it. I knew the world too well to believe this sudden smiling. What woman can have patience with the man who can be yet again deceived by his doxy's fawning after he has thrice proved her false? I should be just like such a man if a mere burst of fair weather, and fresh grass after a long drought, and health after sickness, could make me friends again with this god-haunted, plague-breeding, decaying, tyrannous world. I had seen. I was not a fool. I did not know then, however, as I do now, the strongest reason for distrust. The gods never send us this invitation to delight so readily or so strongly as when they are preparing some new agony. We are their bubbles; they blow us big before they prick us.

But I held my own without that knowledge. I ruled myself. Did they think I was nothing but a pipe to be played on as their moment's fancy chose?

The struggle ended when we topped the last rise before the real Mountain. We were so high now that, though the sun was very strong, the wind blew bitterly cold. At our feet, between us and the Mountain, lay a cursed black valley: dark moss, dark peat-bogs, shingle, great boulders, and screes of stone sprawling down into it from the Mountain—as if the Mountain had sores and these were the stony issue from them. The great mass of it rose up (we tilted our heads back to look at it) into huge knobbles of stone against the sky, like an old giant's back teeth. The face it showed us was really no steeper than a roof, except for certain frightful cliffs on our left, but it looked as if it went up like a wall. It, too, was now black. Here the gods ceased trying to make me glad. There was nothing here that even the merriest heart could dance for.

Bardia pointed ahead to our right. There the Mountain fell away in a smooth sweep to a saddle somewhat lower than the ground we stood on, but still with nothing behind it but the sky. Against the sky, on the saddle, stood a single leafless tree.

We went down into the black valley on our own feet, leading the horse, for the going was bad and stones slipped away from under us until, at the lowest place, we joined the sacred road (it came into the valley through the northern end, away to our left). We were so near now that we did not mount again. A few loops of the road led us up to the saddle and, once more, into the biting wind.

I was afraid, now that we were almost at the Tree. I can hardly say of what, but I know that to find the bones, or even the body, would have set my fear at rest. I believe I had a senseless child's fear that she might be neither living nor dead.

And now we were there. The iron girdle, and the chain that went from it about the gaunt trunk (there was no bark on the Tree) hung there and made a dull noise from time to time as they moved with the wind. There were no bones, nor rags of clothing, nor marks of blood, nor anything else.

"How do you read these signs, Bardia?" said I.

"The god's taken her," said he, rather pale and speaking low (he was a god-fearing man). "No natural beast would have licked his plate so clean. There'd be bones. A beast—any but the holy Shadowbrute itself—couldn't have got the whole body out of the irons. And it would have left the jewels. A man, now—but a man couldn't have freed her, unless he had tools with him."

I had not thought of our journey's being so vain, nothing to do, nothing to gather. The emptiness of my life was to begin at once.

"We can search about a bit," I said, foolishly, for I had no hope of finding anything.

"Yes, yes, Lady. We can search about," said Bardia. I knew it was only his kindness that spoke.

And so we did, working round in circles, he one way and I the other, with our eyes on the ground; very cold, one's cloak flapping till leg and cheek smarted with the blows of it.

Bardia was ahead of me now, eastward and further across the saddle, when he called out. I had to thrust back the hair that was whipping about my face before I could see him. I rushed to him; half flying, for the westwind made a sail of my cloak. He showed me what he had found—a ruby.

"I never saw her wear such a stone," said I.

"She did though, Lady. On her last journey. They had put their own holy gear on her. The straps of the sandals were red with rubies."

"Oh, Bardia! Then somebody—something—carried her thus far."

"Or maybe carried only the sandals. A jackdaw'd do it."

"We must go on; further on this line."

"Carefully, Lady. If we must, I'll do it. You'd best stay behind."

"Why, what's to fear? And anyway, I'll not stay behind."

"I don't know that anyone's been over the saddle. At the Offering, even the priests come no further than the Tree. We are very near the bad part of the Mountain— I mean the holy part. Beyond the Tree, it's all gods' country, they say."

"Then it is you must stay behind, Bardia. They can't do worse to me than they've done already."

"I'll go where you go, Lady. But let's talk less of them, or not at all. And first, I must go back and get the horse."

He went back (and for a moment out of sight—I stood alone on the edge of the perilous land) to where he had tied the horse to a little stunted bush. Then he rejoined me, leading it, very grave, and we went forward.

"Carefully," he said again. "We may find we're on the top of a cliff any moment." And indeed it looked, for the next few paces, as if we were walking straight into the empty sky. Then suddenly we found we were on the brow of a steep slope; and at the same moment the sun—which had been overcast ever since we went down into the black valley—leaped out.

It was like looking down into a new world. At our

feet, cradled amid a vast confusion of mountains, lay a small valley bright as a gem, but opening southward on our right. Through that opening there was a glimpse of warm, blue lands, hills and forests, far below us. The valley itself was like a cleft in the Mountain's southern chin. High though it was, the year seemed to have been kinder in it than down in Glome. I never saw greener turf. There was gorse in bloom, and wild vines, and many groves of flourishing trees, and great plenty of bright water—pools, streams, and little cataracts. And when, after casting about a little to find where the slope would be easiest for the horse, we began descending, the air came up to us warmer and sweeter every minute. We were out of the wind now and could hear ourselves speak; soon we could hear the very chattering of the streams and the sound of bees.

"This may well be the secret valley of the god," said Bardia, his voice hushed.

"It's secret enough," said I.

Now we were at the bottom, and so warm that I had half a mind to dip my hands and face in the swift, amber water of the stream which still divided us from the main of the valley. I had already lifted my hand to put aside my veil when I heard two voices cry out—one, Bardia's. I looked. A quivering shock of feeling that has no name (but is nearest terror) stabbed through me from head to foot. There, not six feet away, on the far side of the river, stood Psyche.

TEN

WHAT I babbled, between tears and laughter, in the first wildness of my joy (the water still between us) I don't know. I was recalled by Bardia's voice.

"Careful, Lady. It may be her wraith. It may—ai! ai! —it is the bride of the god. It is a goddess." He was deadly white, and bending down to throw earth on his forehead.

You could not blame him. She was so brightface, as we say in Greek. But I felt no holy fear. What?—I to fear the very Psyche whom I had carried in my arms and taught to speak and to walk? She was tanned by sun and wind, and clothed in rags, but laughing—her eyes like two stars, her limbs smooth and rounded, and (but for the rags) no sign of beggary or hardship about her.

"Welcome, welcome, welcome," she was saying. "Oh, Maia, I have longed for this. It was my only longing. I knew you would come. Oh, how happy I am! And good Bardia, too. It was he that brought you? Of course; I might have guessed it. Come, Orual, you must cross

the stream. I'll show you where it's easiest. But, Bardia
—I can't bid you across. Dear Bardia, it's not—"

"No, no, Blessed Istra," said Bardia (and I thought
he was very relieved). "I'm only a soldier." Then, in
a lower voice, to me, "Will you go, Lady? This is a
very dreadful place. Perhaps—"

"Go?" said I. "I'd go if the river flowed with fire
instead of water."

"Of course," said he. "It's not with you as with us.
You have gods' blood in you. I'll stay here with the
horse. We're out of the wind and there's good grass for
him here."

I was already on the edge of the river.

"A little further up, Orual," Psyche was saying.
"Here's the best ford. Go straight ahead off that big
stone. Gently! make your footing sure. No, not to your
left. It's very deep in places. This way. Now, one step
more. Reach out for my hand."

I suppose the long bed-ridden and in-doors time of
my sickness had softened me. Anyhow, the coldness of
that water shocked all the breath out of me; and the
current was so strong that, but for Psyche's hand, I think
it would have knocked me down and rolled me under. I
even thought, momentarily amid a thousand other
things, "How strong she grows. She'll be a stronger
woman than ever I was. She'll have that as well as her
beauty."

The next was all a confusion—trying to talk, to cry,
to kiss, to get my breath back, all together. But she led
me a few paces beyond the river and made me sit in the

warm heather, and sat beside me, our four hands joined in my lap, just as it had been that night in her prison.

"Why, Sister," she said merrily, "you have found my threshold cold and steep! You are breathless. But I'll refresh you."

She jumped up, went a little way off, and came back, carrying something; the little cool, dark berries of the Mountain, in a green leaf. "Eat," she said. "Is it not food fit for the gods?"

"Nothing sweeter," said I. And indeed I was both hungry and thirsty enough by now, for it was noon or later. "But oh, Psyche, tell me how——"

"Wait!" said she. "After the banquet, the wine." Close beside us a little silvery trickle came out from among stones mossed cushion-soft. She held her two hands under it till they were filled and raised them to my lips.

"Have you ever tasted a nobler wine?" she said. "Or in a fairer cup?"

"It is indeed a good drink," said I. "But the cup is better. It is the cup I love best in the world."

"Then it's yours, Sister." She said it with such a pretty air of courtesy, like a queen and hostess giving gifts, that the tears came into my eyes again. It brought back so many of her plays in childhood.

"Thank you, child," said I. "I hope it is mine indeed. But, Psyche, we must be serious; yes, and busy too. How have you lived? How did you escape? And oh—we mustn't let the joy of the moment put it out of our minds —what are we to do now?"

"Do? Why, be merry, what else? Why should our hearts not dance?"

"They do dance. Do you not think—why, I could forgive the gods themselves. I'll shortly be able to forgive Redival; perhaps. But how can—it will be winter in a month or less. You can't—Psyche, how have you kept alive till now? I thought, I thought—" but to think of what I had thought overcame me.

"Hush, Maia, hush," said Psyche (once more it was she who was comforting me). "All those fears are over. All's well. I'll make it well for you too; I'll not rest till you're as happy as I. But you haven't yet even asked me my story. Weren't you surprised to find this fair dwelling place, and me living here; like this? Have you no wonder?"

"Yes, Psyche, I am overwhelmed in it. Of course I want to hear your story. Unless we should make our plans first."

"Solemn Orual," said Psyche mockingly. "You were always one for plans. And rightly too, Maia, with such a foolish child as me to bring up. And well you did it." With one light kiss she put all those days, all of my life that I cared for, behind us and began her story.

"I wasn't in my right mind when we left the palace. Before the two temple girls began painting and dressing me they gave me a sweet, sticky stuff to drink—a drug, as I guess—for soon after I had swallowed it everything went dreamlike, and more and more so for a long time. And I think, Sister, they must always give that to those whose blood is to be poured over Ungit, and that's why we see them die so patiently. And the painting on my face helped the dreaminess too. It made my face stiff till it didn't seem to be my own face. I couldn't feel it was I who was being sacrificed. And then the music and incense and the torches made it more so. I saw you, Orual, at the top of the stairway, but I couldn't lift even a hand to wave to you; my arms were as heavy as lead. And I thought it didn't matter much, because you too would wake up presently and find it was all a dream. And in a sense it was, wasn't it? And you are nearly awake now. What? still so grave? I must wake you more.

"You'd think the cold air would have given me my mind back when we came out of the great gates, but the drug must have been still coming to its full power. I had no fear; nor joy either. Sitting there on that litter, up above the heads of all that crowd, was a strange enough thing anyway . . . and the horns and the rattles were going on all the time. I don't know whether the journey up the mountain was long or short. Each bit of it was long; I noticed every pebble on the road, I looked long, long at every tree as we passed it. Yet the whole journey seemed to take hardly any time. Yet long enough for me to get some of my wits back. I began to know that something dreadful was being done to me. Then for the first time I wanted to speak. I tried to cry out to them that there was some mistake, that I was only poor Istra and it couldn't be me they meant to kill. But nothing more than a kind of grunting or babbling came out of my mouth. Then a great bird-headed man, or a bird with a man's body—"

"That would be the Priest," said I.

"Yes. If he is still the Priest when he puts on his mask; perhaps he becomes a god while he wears it. Anyway, it said, 'Give her some more,' and one of the younger priests got on someone else's shoulders and put the sweet sticky cup to my lips again. I didn't want to take it, but, you know, Maia, it all felt so like the time you had the barber to take that thorn out of my hand long ago—you remember—you holding me tight, and telling me to be good, and that it'd all be over in a moment. Well, it was like that, so I felt sure I'd better do whatever I was told.

"The next thing I knew—really knew—was that I was off the litter and on the hot earth, and they were fastening me to the Tree with iron round my waist. It was the sound of the iron that cleared the last of the drug out of my mind. And there was the King, shrieking and wailing and tearing his hair. And do you know, Maia, he actually looked at me, really looked, and it seemed to me he was then seeing me for the first time. But all I wished was that he would stop it and then he and all the rest would go away and leave me alone to cry. I wanted to cry now. My mind was getting clearer and clearer and I was terribly afraid. I was trying to be like those girls in the Greek stories that the Fox is always telling us about, and I knew I could keep it up till they were gone, if only they would go quickly."

"Oh, Psyche, you say all's well now. Forget that terrible time. Go on quickly and tell me how you were saved. We have so much to talk about and arrange. There's no time—"

"Orual! There's all the time there is. Don't you *want* to hear my story?"

"Of course I do. I want to hear every bit. When we're safe and—"

"Where shall we ever be safe if we're not safe here? This is my home, Maia. And you won't understand the wonder and glory of my adventure unless you listen to the bad part. It wasn't very bad, you know."

"It's so bad I can hardly bear to listen to it."

"Ah, but wait. Well, at last they were gone, and there I was alone under the glare of the sky with the great baked, parched mountain all round me, and not one noise to be heard. There wasn't a breath of wind even by the Tree; you remember what the last day of the drought was like. I was already thirsty—the sticky drink had done that. Then I noticed for the first time that they had so bound me that I couldn't sit down. That was when my heart really failed me. I did cry then; oh, Maia, how badly I wanted you and the Fox! And all I could do was to pray, pray, pray to the gods that whatever was going to happen to me might happen soon. But nothing happened, except that my tears made me thirstier. Then, a very long time after that, things began gathering round me."

"Things?"

"Oh, nothing dreadful. Only the mountain cattle at first. Poor lean things they were. I was sorry for them, for I thought they were as thirsty as I. And they came nearer and nearer in a great circle, but never very near, and mooed at me. And after that there came a beast that I had never seen before, but I think it was a lynx. It came right up close. My hands were free and I wondered if I would be able to beat it off. But I had no need to. After advancing and drawing back I don't know how many times (I think it began by fearing me as much as I feared it) it came and sniffed at my feet, and then it stood up with its forepaws on me and sniffed again. Then it went away. I was sorry it had gone; it was a kind of company. And do you know what I was thinking all this time?"

"What?"

"At first I was trying to cheer myself with all that old dream of my gold and amber palace on the Mountain . . . and the god . . . trying to believe it. But I couldn't believe in it at all. I couldn't understand how I ever had. All that, all my old longings, were clean gone."

I pressed her hands and said nothing. But inwardly I rejoiced. It might have been good (I don't know) to encourage that fancy the night before the Offering, if it supported her. Now, I was glad she had got over it. It was a thing I could not like, unnatural and estranging. Perhaps this gladness of mine is one of the things the gods have against me. They never tell.

"The only thing that did me good," she continued, "was quite different. It was hardly a thought, and very hard to put into words. There was a lot of the Fox's philosophy in it—things he says about gods or 'the divine nature'—but mixed up with things the Priest said, too, about the blood and the earth and how sacrifice makes the crops grow. I'm not explaining it well. It seemed to come from somewhere deep inside me, deeper than the part that sees pictures of gold and amber palaces, deeper than fears and tears. It was shapeless, but you could just hold onto it; or just let it hold onto you. Then the change came."

"What change?" I didn't know well what she was talking about, but I saw she must have her way and tell the story in her own fashion.

"Oh, the weather of course. I couldn't see it, tied the way I was, but I could feel it. I was suddenly cool. Then I knew the sky must be filling with clouds, behind my back, over Glome, for all the colours on the Mountain went out and my own shadow vanished. And then—that was the first sweet moment—a sigh of wind—west-wind —came at my back. Then more and more wind; you could hear and smell and feel the rain drawing near. So then I knew quite well that the gods really are, and that I was bringing the rain. And then the wind was roaring (but it's too soft a sound to call it a roar) all round me, and rain. The Tree kept some of it off me; I was holding out my hands all the time and licking the rain off them, I was so thirsty. The wind got wilder and wilder. It seemed to be lifting me off the ground so that, if it hadn't been for the iron round my waist, I'd have been blown right away, up in the air. And then—at last—for a moment—I saw him."

"Saw whom?"

"The west-wind."

"*Saw* it?"

"Not it; him. The god of the wind; West-wind himself."

"Were you awake, Psyche?"

"Oh, it was no dream. One can't dream things like that, because one's never seen things like that. He was in human shape. But you couldn't mistake him for a man. Oh, Sister, you'd understand if you'd seen. How can I make you understand? You've seen lepers?"

"Well, of course."

"And you know how healthy people look beside a leper?"

"You mean—healthier, ruddier than ever?"

"Yes. Now we, beside the gods, are like lepers beside us."

"Do you mean this god was so red?"

She laughed and clapped her hands. "Oh, it's no use," she said. "I see I've not given you the idea at all. Never mind. You shall see gods for yourself, Orual. It must be so; I'll make it so. Somehow. There must be a way. Look, this may help you. When I saw West-wind I was neither glad nor afraid (at first). I felt ashamed."

"But what of? Psyche, they hadn't stripped you naked or anything?"

"No, no, Maia. Ashamed of looking like a mortal—ashamed of being a mortal."

"But how could you help that?"

"Don't you think the things people are most ashamed of are the things they can't help?"

I thought of my ugliness and said nothing.

"And he took me," said Psyche, "in his beautiful arms which seemed to burn me (though the burning didn't hurt) and pulled me right out of the iron girdle—and that didn't hurt either and I don't know how he did it —and carried me up into the air, far up above the ground, and whirled me away. Of course he was invisible again almost at once. I had seen him only as one sees a lightning flash. But that didn't matter. Now I knew it was he, not it, I wasn't in the least afraid of sailing along in the sky, even of turning head over heels in it."

"Psyche, are you sure this happened? You must have been dreaming!"

"And if it was a dream, Sister, how do you think I came here? It's more likely everything that had happened to me before this was a dream. Why, Glome and the King and old Batta seem to me very like dreams now. But you hinder my tale, Maia. So he carried me through the air and set me down softly. At first I was all out of breath and too bewildered to see where I was; for West-wind is a merry, rough god. (Sister, do you think young gods have to be taught how to handle us? A hasty touch from hands like theirs and we'd fall to pieces.) But when I came to myself—ah, can you think what a moment that was!—and saw the House before me; I lying at the threshold. And it wasn't, you see, just the gold and amber house I used to imagine. If it had been just that, I might indeed have thought I was dreaming. But I saw it wasn't. And not quite like any house in this land, nor quite like those Greek houses the Fox describes to us. Something new, never conceived of—but, there, you can see for yourself—and I'll show you over every bit of it in a moment. Why need I try to show it in words?

"You could see it was a god's house at once. I don't mean a temple where a god is worshipped. A god's House, where he lives. I would not for any wealth have gone into it. But I had to, Orual. For there came a voice—sweet? oh, sweeter than any music, yet my hair rose at it too—and do you know, Orual, what it said? It said, 'Enter your House' (yes, it called it *my* House), 'Psyche, the bride of the god.'

"I was ashamed again, ashamed of my mortality, and terribly afraid. But it would have been worse shame and worse fear to disobey. I went, cold, small, and shaking, up the steps and through the porch and into the courtyard. There was no one to be seen. But then the voices came. All round me, bidding me welcome."

"What kind of voices?"

"Like women's voices—at least, as like women's voices as the wind-god was like a man. And they said, 'Enter, Lady, enter, Mistress. Do not be afraid.' And they were moving as the speakers moved, though I could see no one, and leading me by their movements. And so they brought me into a cool parlour with an arched roof, where there was a table set out with fruit and wine. Such fruits as never—but you shall see. They said, 'Refresh yourself, Lady, before the bath; after it comes the feast.'

Oh, Orual, how can I tell you what it felt like? I knew they were all spirits and I wanted to fall at their feet. But I daren't; if they made me mistress of that house, mistress I should have to be. Yet all the time I was afraid there might be some bitter mockery in it and that at any moment terrible laughter might break out and—"

"Ah!" said I, with a long breath. How well I understood.

"Oh, but I was wrong, Sister. Utterly wrong. That's part of the mortal shame. They gave me fruit, they gave me wine—"

"The voices gave you?"

"The spirits gave them to me. I couldn't see their hands. Yet, you know, it never looked as if the plates or the cup were moving of themselves. You could see that hands were doing it. And, Orual" (her voice grew very low), "when I took the cup, I—I—*felt* the other hands, touching my own. Again, that burning, though without pain. That was terrible." She blushed suddenly and (I wondered why) laughed. "It wouldn't be terrible now," she said. "Then they had me to the bath. You shall see it. It is in the most delicate pillared court open to the sky, and the water is like crystal and smells as sweet as . . . as sweet as this whole valley. I was terribly shy when it came to taking off my clothes, but—"

"You said they were all she-spirits."

"Oh, Maia, you still don't understand. This shame has nothing to do with He or She. It's the being mortal —being, how shall I say it? . . . insufficient. Don't you

114

think a dream would feel shy if it were seen walking about in the waking world? And then" (she was speaking more and more quickly now) "they dressed me again— in the most beautiful things—and then came the banquet —and the music—and then they had me to bed—and the night came—and then—he."

"He?"

"The Bridegroom . . . the god himself. Don't look at me like that, Sister. I'm your own true Psyche still. Nothing will change that."

"Psyche," said I, leaping up, "I can't bear this any longer. You have told me so many wonders. If this is all true, I've been wrong all my life. Everything has to be begun over again. Psyche, it is true? You're not playing a game with me? Show me. Show me your palace."

"Of course I will," she said, rising. "Let us go in. And don't be afraid whatever you see or hear."

"Is it far?" said I.

She gave me a quick, astonished look. "Far to where?" she said.

"To the palace, to this god's House."

You have seen a lost child in a crowd run up to a woman whom it takes for its mother, and how the woman turns round and shows the face of a stranger, and then the look in the child's eyes, silent a moment before it begins to cry. Psyche's face was like that; checked, blank; happiest assurance suddenly dashed all to pieces.

"Orual," she said, beginning to tremble, "what do you mean?"

I too became frightened, though I had yet no notion

of the truth. "Mean?" said I. "Where is the palace? How far have we to go to reach it?"

She gave one loud cry. Then, with white face, staring hard into my eyes, she said, "But *this* is it, Orual! It is here! You are standing on the stairs of the great gate."

ELEVEN

I F ANYONE could have seen us at that moment I believe he would have thought we were two enemies met for a battle to the death. I know we stood like that, a few feet apart, every nerve taut, each with eyes fixed on the other in a terrible watchfulness.

And now we are coming to that part of my history on which my charge against the gods chiefly rests; and therefore I must try at any cost to write what is wholly true. Yet it is hard to know perfectly what I was thinking while those huge, silent moments went past. By remembering it too often I have blurred the memory itself.

I suppose my first thought must have been, "She's mad." Anyway, my whole heart leaped to shut the door against something monstrously amiss—not to be endured. And to keep it shut. Perhaps I was fighting not to be mad myself.

But what I said when I got my breath (and I know my voice came out in a whisper) was simply, "We must go away at once. This is a terrible place."

Was I believing in her invisible palace? A Greek will

laugh at the thought. But it's different in Glome. There the gods are too close to us. Up in the Mountain, in the very heart of the Mountain, where Bardia had been afraid and even the priests don't go, anything was possible. No door could be kept shut. Yes, that was it; not plain belief, but infinite misgiving—the whole world (Psyche with it) slipping out of my hands.

Whatever I meant, she misunderstood me horribly.

"So," she said, "you do see it after all."

"See what?" I asked. A fool's question. I knew what.

"Why, this, this," said Psyche. "The gates, the shining walls—"

For some strange reason, fury—my father's own fury—fell upon me when she said that. I found myself screaming (I am sure I had not meant to scream), "Stop it! Stop it at once! There's nothing there!"

Her face flushed. For once, and for the moment only, she too was angry. "Well, feel it, feel it, if you can't see," she cried. "Touch it. Slap it. Beat your head against it. Here—" she made to grab my hands. I wrenched them free.

"Stop it, stop it, I tell you! There's no such thing. You're pretending. You're trying to make yourself believe it." But I was lying. How did I know whether she really saw invisible things or spoke in madness? Either way, something hateful and strange had begun. As if I could thrust it back by brute force, I fell upon Psyche. Before I knew what I was doing I had her by the shoulders and was shaking her as one shakes a child.

She was too big for that now and far too strong

(stronger than I ever dreamt she could be) and she flung my grip off in a moment. We fell apart, both breathing hard, now more like enemies than ever. All at once a look came into her face that I had never seen there, sharp, suspicious.

"But you tasted the wine. Where do you think I got it from?"

"Wine? What wine? What are you talking about?"

"Orual! The wine I gave you. And the cup. I gave you the cup. And where is it? Where have you hidden it?"

"Oh, have done with it, child. I'm in no mood for nonsense. There was no wine."

"But I gave it to you. You drank it. And the fine honeycakes. You said—"

"You gave me water, cupped in your hands."

"But you praised the wine, and the cup. You said—"

"I praised your hands. You were playing a game (you know you were) and I fell in with it."

She gaped open-mouthed, yet beautiful even then.

"So that was all," she said slowly. "You mean you saw no cup? tasted no wine?"

I wouldn't answer. She had heard well enough what I said.

Presently her throat moved as if she were swallowing something (oh, the beauty of her throat!). She pressed down a great storm of passion and her mood changed; it was now sober sadness, mixed with pity. She struck her breast with her clenched fist as mourners do.

"Aiai!" she mourned, "so this is what he meant. You

can't see it. You can't feel it. For you, it is not there at all. Oh, Maia . . . I am very sorry."

I came almost to a full belief. She was shaking and stirring me a dozen different ways. But I had not shaken her at all. She was as certain of her palace as of the plainest thing; as certain as the Priest had been of Ungit when my father's dagger was between his ribs. I was as weak beside her as the Fox beside the Priest. This valley was indeed a dreadful place; full of the divine, sacred, no place for mortals. There might be a hundred things in it that I could not see.

Can a Greek understand the horror of that thought? Years after, I dreamed, again and again, that I was in some well-known place—most often the Pillar Room—and everything I saw was different from what I touched. I would lay my hand on the table and feel warm hair instead of smooth wood, and the corner of the table would shoot out a hot, wet tongue and lick me. And I knew, by the mere taste of them that all those dreams came from that moment when I believed I was looking at Psyche's palace and did not see it. For the horror was the same: a sickening discord, a rasping together of two worlds, like the two bits of a broken bone.

But in the reality (not in the dreams), with the horror came the inconsolable grief. For the world had broken in pieces and Psyche and I were not in the same piece. Seas, mountains, madness, death itself, could not have removed her from me to such a hopeless distance as this. Gods, and again gods, always gods . . . they had stolen her. They would leave us nothing. A thought pierced up through the crust of my mind like a crocus coming up in the early year. Was she not worthy of the gods? Ought they not to have her? But instantly great, choking, blinding waves of sorrow swept it away and, "Oh!" I cried. "It's not right. It's not right. Oh, Psyche, come back! Where are you? Come back, come back."

She had me in her arms at once. "Maia—Sister," she said. "I'm here. Maia, don't. I can't bear it. I'll—"

"Yes . . . oh, my own child—I do feel you—I hold you. But oh—it's only like holding you in a dream. You are leagues away. And I . . ."

She led me a few paces further and made me sit down on a mossy bank and sat beside me. With words and touch she comforted me all she could. And as, in the center of a storm or even of a battle, I have known sudden stillness for a moment, so now for a little I let her comfort me. Not that I took any heed of what she was saying. It was her voice, and her love in her voice, that counted. Her voice was very deep for a woman's. Sometimes even now the way she used to say this or that word comes back to me as warm and real as if she were beside me in the room—the softness of it, the richness as of corn grown from a deep soil.

What was she saying? . . . "And perhaps, Maia, you too will learn how to see. I will beg and implore him to make you able. He will understand. He warned me when I asked for this meeting that it might not turn out all as I hoped. I never thought . . . I'm only simple Psyche, as he calls me . . . never thought he meant you wouldn't even see it. So he must have known. He'll tell us . . ."

He? I'd forgotten this *him;* or, if not forgotten, left him out of account ever since she first told me we were standing at his palace gates. And now she was saying *he* every moment, no other name but *he,* the way young wives talk. Something began to grow colder and harder inside me. And this also is like what I've known in wars: when that which was only *they* or *the enemy* all at once becomes the man, two feet away, who means to kill you.

"Who are you talking of?" I asked; but I meant, "Why do you talk of him to me? What have I to do with him?"

"But, Maia," she said, "I've told you all my story. My god, of course. My lover. My husband. The master of my House."

"Oh, I can't bear it," said I, leaping up. Those last words of hers, spoken softly and with trembling, set me on fire. I could feel my rage coming back. Then (like a great light, a hope of deliverance, it came to me) I asked myself why I'd forgotten, and how long I'd forgotten, that first notion of her being mad. Madness; of course. The whole thing must be madness. I had been nearly as mad as she to think otherwise. At the very name *madness* the air of that valley seemed more breathable, seemed emptied of a little of its holiness and horror.

"Have done with it, Psyche," I said sharply. "Where is this god? Where the palace is? Nowhere—in your fancy. Where is he? Show him to me? What is he like?"

She looked a little aside and spoke, lower than ever

but very clear, and as if all that had yet passed between us were of no account beside the gravity of what she was now saying. "Oh, Orual," she said, "not even I have seen him—yet. He comes to me only in the holy darkness. He says I mustn't—not yet—see his face or know his name. I'm forbidden to bring any light into his—our —chamber."

Then she looked up, and as our eyes met for a moment I saw in hers unspeakable joy.

"There's no such thing," I said, loud and stern. "Never say these things again. Get up. It's time—"

"Orual," said she, now at her queenliest, "I have never told you a lie in my life."

I tried to soften my manner. Yet the words came out cold and stern. "No, you don't mean to lie. You're not in your right mind, Psyche. You have imagined things. It's the terror and the loneliness . . . and that drug they gave you. We'll cure you."

"Orual," said she.

"What?"

"If it's all my fancy, how do you think I have lived these many days? Do I look as if I'd fed on berries and slept under the sky? Are my arms wasted? Or my cheeks fallen in?"

I would, I believe, have lied to her myself and said they were, but it was impossible. From the top of her head to her naked feet she was bathed in life and beauty and well-being. It was as if they flowed over her or from her. It was no wonder Bardia had worshipped her as a goddess. The very rags served only to show more of her beauty; all the honey-sweetness, all the rose-red and the ivory, the warm, breathing perfection of her. She even seemed (but that's impossible, I thought) taller than before. And as my lie died unspoken she looked at me with something like mockery in her face. Her mocking looks had always been some of her loveliest.

"You see?" she said. "It's all true. And that—no, listen, Maia—that's why all will come right. We'll make —he will make you able to see, and then—"

"I don't want it!" I cried, putting my face close to hers, threatening her almost, till she drew back before my fierceness. "I don't want it. I hate it. Hate it, hate it, hate it. Do you understand?"

"But, Orual, why? What do you hate?"

"Oh, the whole—what can I call it? You know very well. Or you used to. This, this—" and then something she had said about *him* (hardly noticed till now) began to work horribly in my mind. "This thing that comes to you in the darkness . . . and you're forbidden to see it. Holy darkness, you call it. What sort of thing? Faugh! it's like living in the house of Ungit. Everything's dark about the gods . . . I think I can smell the very—" The steadiness of her gaze, the beauty of her, so full of pity yet in a way so pitiless, made me dumb for a moment. Then my tears broke out again. "Oh, Psyche," I sobbed, "you're so far away. Do you even hear me? I can't reach you. Oh, Psyche, Psyche! You loved me once . . . come back. What have we to do with gods and wonders and all these cruel, dark things? We're women, aren't we? Mortals. Oh, come back to the real world. Leave all that alone. Come back where we were happy."

"But, Orual—think. How can I go back? This is my home. I am a wife."

"Wife! Of what?" said I, shuddering.

"If you only knew him," she said.

"You like it! Oh, Psyche!"

She would not answer me. Her face flushed. Her face, and her whole body, were the answer.

"Oh, you ought to have been one of Ungit's girls," said I savagely. "You ought to have lived in there— in the dark—all blood and incense and muttering and the reek of burnt fat. To like it—living among things you can't see—dark and holy and horrible. Is it nothing to you at all that you are leaving me, going into all that . . . turning your back on all our love?"

"No, no, Maia. I can't go back to you. How could I? But you must come to me."

"Oh, it's madness," said I.

Was it madness or not? Which was true? Which would be worse? I was at that very moment when, if they meant us well, the gods would speak. Mark what they did instead.

It began to rain. It was only a light rain, but it changed everything for me.

"Here, child," said I, "come under my cloak. Your poor rags! Quick. You'll be wet through."

She gazed at me wonderingly. "How should I get wet, Maia," she said, "when we are sitting in-doors with a roof above us? And 'rags'?—but I forgot. You can't see my robes either." The rain shone on her cheeks as she spoke.

If that wise Greek who is to read this book doubts that this turned my mind right round, let him ask his mother or wife. The moment I saw her, my child whom I had cared for all her life, sitting there in the rain as if it meant no more to her than it does to cattle, the notion that her palace and her god could be anything but madness was at once unbelievable. All those wilder misgivings, all the fluttering to and fro between two opinions, was (for that time) quite over. I saw in a flash that I must choose one opinion or the other; and in the same flash knew which I had chosen.

"Psyche," I said (and my voice had changed). "This is sheer raving. You can't stay here. Winter'll be on us soon. It'll kill you."

"I cannot leave my home, Maia."

"Home! There's no home here. Get up. Here—under my cloak."

She shook her head, a little wearily.

"It's no use, Maia," she said. "I see it and you don't. Who's to judge between us?"

"I'll call Bardia."

"I'm not allowed to let him in. And he wouldn't come."

That, I knew, was true.

"Get up, girl," I said. "Do you hear me? Do as you're told. Psyche, you never disobeyed me before."

She looked up (wetter every moment) and said, very

tender in voice but hard as a stone in her determination, "Dear Maia, I am a wife now. It's no longer you that I must obey."

I learned then how one can hate those one loves. My fingers were round her wrist in an instant, my other hand on her upper arm. We were struggling.

—"You *shall* come," I panted. "We'll force you away—hide you somewhere—Bardia has a wife, I believe—lock you up—his house—bring you to your senses."

It was useless. She was far stronger than I. ("Of course," I thought, "they say mad people have double strength.") We left marks on one another's skin. There was a thick, tangled sort of wrestling. Then we were apart again; she staring with reproach and wonder, I weeping (as I had wept at her prison door), utterly broken with shame and despair. The rain had stopped. It had, I suppose, done all the gods wanted.

And now there was nothing at all left that I could do.

Psyche, as always, recovered herself first. She laid her hand—there was a smear of blood on it; was it possible I could have scratched her?—across my shoulder.

"Dear Maia," she said, "you have very seldom been angry with me in all the years I can remember. Do not begin now. Look, the shadows have already crept nearly all the way across the courtyard. I had hoped that before this we should have feasted together and been merry. But, there—you would have tasted only berries and cold water. Bread and onions with Bardia will be more comfort to you. But I must send you away before the sun sets. I promised that I would."

"Are you sending me away forever, Psyche? And with nothing?"

"Nothing, Orual, but a bidding to come again as soon as you can. I'll work for you here. There must be some way. And then—oh Maia—then we shall meet here again with no cloud between us. But now you must go."

What could I do but obey her? In body she was stronger than I; her mind I could not reach. She was already leading me back to the river, back through the desolate valley she called her palace. The valley looked hideous to me now. There was a chill in the air. Sunset flamed up behind the black mass of the saddle.

She clung to me at the very edge of the water. "You will come back soon, soon?" she said.

"If I can, Psyche. You know how it is in our house."

"I think," said she, "the King will not be much hindrance to you in the next few days. Now, there's no more time. Kiss me again. Dear Maia. And now, lean on my hand. Feel for the flat stone with your foot."

Again I endured the sword-cut of the icy water. From this side I looked back.

"Psyche, Psyche," I broke out. "There's still time. Come with me. Anywhere—I'll smuggle you out of Glome—we'll go for beggarwomen all over the world —or you can go to Bardia's house—anywhere, anything you like."

She shook her head. "How could I?" she said. "I'm not my own. You forget, Sister, that I'm a wife. Yet always yours, too. Oh if you knew, you'd be happy. Orual, don't look so sad. All will be well; all will be better than you can dream of. Come again soon. Farewell for a little."

She went away from me into her terrible valley, and out of sight finally among the trees. It was already deep twilight on my side of the river, close in under the shadow of the saddle.

"Bardia," I called. "Bardia, where are you?"

TWELVE

BARDIA, a grey shape in the twilight, came to-wards me.

"You have left the Blessed?" he said.

"Yes," said I. I could not talk to him about it, I thought.

"Then we must speak of how to spend our night. We'd never find a way for the horse up to the saddle now, and if we did, we'd have to go down again beyond the Tree into the other valley. We couldn't sleep on the saddle itself—too much wind. It'll be cold enough here, where we're sheltered, in an hour or so. I fear we must lie here. Not where a man'd choose; too near the gods."

"What does it matter?" said I. "It will do as well as anywhere else."

"Then come with me, Lady. I've gathered a few sticks."

I followed him; and in that silence (there was nothing now but the chattering of the stream, and it seemed louder than ever) we could hear, long before we came to the horse, the sound of the grass torn up by his teeth.

A man and a soldier is a wonderful creature. Bardia

had chosen a place where the bank was steepest, and two rocks close together made the next best thing to a cave. The sticks were all laid and the fire alight, though still sputtering from the late rain. And he brought out of the saddle-bags things better than bread and onions; even a flask of wine. I was still a girl (which in many matters is the same thing as a fool) and it seemed to me shameful that, in all my sorrow and care, I was so eager for the food when it came. I never tasted better. And that meal in the firelight (which had made all the rest of the world a mere darkness as soon as it blazed up) seemed to me very sweet and homelike; mortal food and warmth for mortal limbs and bellies, no need (for a space) to think of gods and riddles and wonders.

When we had ended Bardia said, somewhat shamefacedly, "Lady, you're not used to lying in the open and you might be cruelly chilled before day. So I'll make so free—for I'm no more to you, Lady, than one of your father's big dogs—as to say we'd best lie close, back to back, the way men do in the wars. And both cloaks over us."

I said yes to that, and indeed no woman in the world has so little reason as I to be chary in such matters. Yet it surprised me that he should have said it; for I did not yet know that, if you are ugly enough, all men (unless they hate you deeply) soon give up thinking of you as a woman at all.

Bardia rested as soldiers do; dead asleep in two breaths but ready (I have seen him tested since) to be wide awake in one if need were. I think I never slept at all. First there was the hardness and slope of the ground, and after that the cold. And besides these, fast and whirling thoughts, wakeful as a madman's: about Psyche and my hard riddle, and also of another thing.

At last the cold grew so bitter that I slipped from under the cloak (its outer side was wet with dew by now) and began walking to and fro. And now, let that wise Greek whom I look to as my reader and the judge of my cause, mark well what followed.

It was already twilight and there was much mist in the valley. The pools of the river as I went down to it to drink (for I was thirsty as well as cold) seemed to be dark holes in the greyness. And I got my drink, ice-cold, and I thought it steadied my mind. But would a river flowing in the gods' secret valley do that, or the clean contrary? This is another of the things to be guessed. For when I lifted my head and looked once more into the mist across the water, I saw that which brought my heart into my throat. There stood the palace, grey— as all things were grey in that hour and place—but solid and motionless, wall within wall, pillar and arch and architrave, acres of it, a labyrinthine beauty. As she had said, it was like no house ever seen in our land or age. Pinnacles and buttresses leaped up—no memories of mine, you would think, could help me to imagine them —unbelievably tall and slender, pointed and prickly as if stone were shooting out into branch and flower. No light showed from any window. It was a house asleep. And somewhere within it, asleep also, someone or something—how holy, or horrible, or beautiful or strange?—

with Psyche in its arms. And I, what had I done and said? what would it do to me for my blasphemies and unbelievings? I never doubted that I must now cross the river, or try to cross it, even if it should drown me. I must lie on the steps at the great gate of that house and make my petition. I must ask forgiveness of Psyche as well as of the god. I had dared to scold her (dared, what was worse, to try to comfort her as a child) but all the time she was far above me; herself now hardly mortal. . . . if what I saw was real. I was in great fear. Perhaps it was not real. I looked and looked to see if it would not fade or change. Then as I rose (for all this time I was still kneeling where I had drunk), almost before I stood on my feet, the whole thing was vanished. There was a tiny space of time in which I thought I could see how some swirlings of the mist had looked, for the moment, like towers and walls. But very soon, no likeness at all. I was staring simply into fog, and my eyes smarting with it.

And now, you who read, give judgement. That moment when I either saw or thought I saw the House— does it tell against the gods or against me? Would they (if they answered) make it a part of their defence? say it was a sign, a hint, beckoning me to answer the riddle one way rather than the other? I'll not grant them that. What is the use of a sign which is itself only another riddle? It might—I'll allow so much—it might have been a true seeing; the cloud over my mortal eyes may have been lifted for a moment. It might not; what would be easier than for one distraught and not, maybe, so fully waking as she seemed, gazing at a mist, in a half-light, to fancy what had filled her thoughts for so many hours? What easier, even, than for the gods themselves to send the whole ferly for a mockery? Either way, there's divine mockery in it. They set the riddle and then allow a seeming that can't be tested and can only quicken and thicken the tormenting whirlpool of your guess-work. If they had an honest intention to guide us, why is their guidance not plain? Psyche could speak plain when she was three; do you tell me the gods have not yet come so far?

When I came back to Bardia he was just awake. I did not tell him what I had seen; until I wrote it in this book, I have never told it to anyone.

Our journey down was comfortless, for there was no sun and the wind was always in our faces, with scudding showers at times. I, sitting behind Bardia, got less of it than he.

We halted somewhere about noon, under the lee of a small wood, to eat what was left of our food. Of course my riddle had been working in my mind all morning, and it was there, out of the wind for a little and somewhat warmer (was Psyche warm? and worse weather soon to come) that I made up my mind to tell him the whole story; always excepting that moment when I looked into the mist. I knew he was an honest man, and secret, and (in his own way) wise.

He listened to it all very diligently but said nothing when I had ended. I had to draw his answer out of him.

"How do you read it all, Bardia?"

"Lady," says he, "it's not my way to say more than I can help of gods and divine matters. I'm not impious. I wouldn't eat with my left hand, or lie with my wife when the moon's full, or slit open a pigeon to clean it with an iron knife, or do anything else that's unchancy and profane, even if the King himself were to bid me. And as for sacrifices, I've always done all that can be expected of a man on my pay. But for anything more—I think the less Bardia meddles with the gods, the less they'll meddle with Bardia."

But I was determined to have his counsel.

"Bardia," I said, "do you think my sister is mad?"

"Look, Lady," he answered, "there at your very first word you say what's better unsaid. Mad? The Blessed —mad? Moreover, we've seen her and anyone could tell she was in her right mind."

"Then you think there really was a palace in the valley though I couldn't see it?"

"I don't well know what's *really*, when it comes to houses of gods."

"And what of this lover who comes to her in the dark?"

"I say nothing about him."

"Oh, Bardia—and among the spears men say you're the bravest! Are you afraid even to whisper your thought to me? I am in desperate need of counsel."

"Counsel about what, Lady? What is there to do?"

"How do you read this riddle? Does anyone really come to her?"

"She says so, Lady. Who am I to give the Blessed One the lie?"

"Who is he?"

"She knows that best."

"She knows nothing. She confesses she has never seen him. Bardia, what kind of a lover must this be who forbids his bride to see his face?"

Bardia was silent. He had a pebble between his thumb and forefinger and was drawing little scratches in the earth.

"Well?" said I.

"There doesn't seem to be much of a riddle about it," he said at last.

"Then what's your answer?"

"I should say—speaking as mortal man, and likely enough the gods know better—I should say it was one whose face and form would give her little pleasure if she saw them."

"Some frightful thing?"

"They called her the Bride of the Brute, Lady. But it's time we were riding again. We're not much better than half way home." He got up as he spoke.

His thought was not new to me; it was only the most horrible of the guesses which had been jostling and wrangling in my head. But the shock of hearing it from his lips lay in this, that I knew he had no doubt of it. I had come to know Bardia very well by now, and I could clearly see that all my difficulty in drawing out his answer came from his fear to say the thing and not from any uncertainty. As he had said, my riddle was

136

no riddle to him. And it was as though all the people of Glome had spoken to me through him. As he thought, so, doubtless, every prudent, god-fearing man of our nation and our time would think too. My other guesses would not even come into their minds; here was the plain answer, clear as noon-day. Why seek further? The god and the Shadowbrute were all one. She had been given to it. We had got our rain and water and (as seemed likely) peace with Phars. The gods, for their share, had her away into their secret places where something, so foul it would not show itself, some holy and sickening thing, ghostly or demonlike or bestial—or all three (there's no telling, with gods)—enjoyed her at its will.

I was so dashed that, as we continued our journey, nothing in me even fought against this answer of Bardia's. I felt as, I suppose, a tortured prisoner feels when they dash water in his face to rouse him from his faint, and the truth, worse than all his fantasies, becomes clear and hard and unmistakable again around him. It now seemed to me that all my other guesses had been only self-pleasing dreams spun out of my wishes, but now I was awake. There never had been any riddle; the worst was the truth, and truth as plain as the nose on a man's face. Only terror would have blinded me to it so long.

My hand stole to the sword-hilt under my cloak. Before my sickness, I had sworn that, if there were no other way, I would have killed Psyche rather than leave her to the heat or hunger of a monster. Now again I made a deep resolve. I was half frightened when I perceived

137

what I was resolving. "So it might come even to that," my heart said; even to killing her (Bardia had already taught me the straight thrust, and where to strike). Then my tenderness came over me again, and I cried, never more bitterly, till I could not tell whether it was tears or rain that had most drenched my veil. (It was settling down to steadier rain as the day went on.) And in that tenderness I even asked myself why I should save her from the Brute, or warn her against the Brute, or meddle with the matter at all. "She is happy," said my heart. "Whether it's madness or a god or a monster, or whatever it is, she is happy. You have seen that for yourself. She is ten times happier, there in the Mountain, than you could ever make her. Leave her alone. Don't spoil it. Don't mar what you've learnt you can't make."

We were down in the foothills now, almost (if one could have seen through the rain) in sight of the house of Ungit. My heart did not conquer me. I perceived now that there is a love deeper than theirs who seek only the happiness of their beloved. Would a father see his daughter happy as a whore? Would a woman see her lover happy as a coward? My hand went back to the sword. "She shall not," I thought. Come what might, she should not. However things might go, whatever the price, by her death or mine or a thousand deaths, by fronting the gods "beard to beard" as the soldiers say, Psyche should not—least of all, contentedly—make sport for a demon.

"We are king's daughters still," I said.

I had hardly said it when I had good cause to remember, in a different fashion, that I was a king's daughter, and what king's. For now we were fording the Shennit again and Bardia (whose mind was ever on next things) was saying that when we had passed the city, and before we had reached the palace, I had best slip off the horse and go up that little lane—where Redival first saw Psyche being worshipped—and so through the gardens and into the women's quarters by the back way. For it was easy to guess how my father would take it if he found that I (supposed too sick to work with him in the Pillar Room) had journeyed to the Holy Tree.

THIRTEEN

IT was nearly dark in the palace, and as I came to my chamber door a voice said in Greek, "Well?" It was the Fox, who had been squatting there, as my women told me, like a cat at a mouse-hole.

"Alive, Grandfather," said I, and kissed him. Then, "Come back as soon as you can. I am wet as a fish and must wash and change and eat. I'll tell you all when you come."

When I was reclothed and finishing my supper, his knock came at the door. I made him come and sit with me at table and poured him drink. There was no one with us but little Poobi, my dark-skinned maid, who was faithful and loving and knew no Greek.

"You said *alive*," the Fox began, raising his cup. "See. I make a libation to Zeus the Saviour." He did it Greek-fashion with a clever twist of the cup that lets fall just one drop.

"Yes, Grandfather, alive and well and says she's happy."

"I feel as if my heart would crack for joy, child," said he. "You tell me things almost beyond belief."

"You've had the sweet, Grandfather. There's sour to follow."

"Let me hear it. All is to be borne."

Then I told him the whole story, always excepting that one glimpse in the fog. It was dreadful to me to see the light die out of his face as I went on, and to feel that I was darkening it. And I asked myself, "If you can hardly bear to do this, how will you bear to wipe out Psyche's happiness?"

"Alas, alas, poor Psyche!" said the Fox. "Our little child! And how she must have suffered! Hellebore's the right medicine, with rest, and peace, and loving care . . . oh, we'd bring her into frame again, I don't doubt it, if we could nurse her well. But how are we to give her all or any of the things she needs? My wits are dry, daughter. We must think, though, contrive. I wish I were Odysseus, aye, or Hermes."

"You think, then, she's mad, for certain?"

He darted a quick glance at me. "Why, daughter, what then have you been thinking?"

"You'll call it folly, I suppose. But you weren't with her, Grandfather. She talked so calmly. There was nothing disordered in her speech. She could laugh merrily. Her glance wasn't wild. If I'd had my eyes shut, I would have believed her palace was as real as this."

"But, your eyes being open, you saw no such thing."

"You don't think—not possibly—not as a mere hundredth chance—there might be things that are real though we can't see them?"

"Certainly I do. Such things as Justice, Equality, the Soul, or musical notes."

"Oh, Grandfather, I don't mean things like that. If there are souls, could there not be soul-houses?"

He ran his hands through his hair with an old, familiar gesture of teacher's dismay.

"Child," he said, "you make me believe that, after all these years, you have never even begun to understand what the word *soul* means."

"I know well enough what you mean by it, Grandfather. But do you, even you, know all? Are there no things—I mean *things*—but what we see?"

"Plenty. Things behind our backs. Things too far away. And all things, if it's dark enough." He leaned forward and put his hand on mine. "I begin to think, daughter, that if I can get that hellebore, yours had better be the first dose," he said.

I had had half a thought, at the outset, of telling him about the ferly, my glimpse of the palace. But I couldn't bring myself to it; he was the worst hearer in the world for such a story. Already he was making me ashamed of half the things I had been thinking. And now a more cheering thought came to me.

"Then, perhaps," said I, "this lover who comes to her in darkness is also part of the madness."

"I wish I could believe it," said the Fox.

"Why not, Grandfather?"

"You say she's plump and rosy? not starveling?"

"Never better."

"Then who's fed her all this time?"

I was silenced.

"And who took her out of the irons?"

I had never thought of this question at all. "Grandfather!" I said. "What is in your mind? You—you of all men—are not hinting that it is the god. You'd laugh at me if I said so."

"I'd be more likely to weep. Oh, child, child, child, when shall I have washed the nurse and the grandam and the priest and the soothsayer out of your soul? Do you think the Divine Nature—why, it's profane, ridiculous. You might as well say the universe itched or the Nature of Things sometimes tippled in the wine cellar."

"I haven't said it was a god, Grandfather," said I. "I am asking who you think it was."

"A man, a man, of course," said the Fox, beating his hands on the table. "What? Are you still a child? Didn't you know there were men on the Mountain?"

"Men!" I gasped.

"Yes. Vagabonds, broken men, outlaws, thieves. Where are your wits?"

Indignation came burning into my cheeks and I sprang up. For any daughter of our house to mix, even in lawful marriage, with those who have not (at least by one grandparent) divine descent, is an utter abomination. The Fox's thought was unendurable.

"What are you saying?" I asked him. "Psyche would die on sharp stakes sooner than—"

"Peace, daughter," said the Fox. "Psyche doesn't know. As I read it, some robber or runaway has found the poor child, half-crazed with terror and loneliness,

143

and with thirst, too (likely enough), and got her out of her irons. And if she were not in her right mind, what would she most probably babble of in her ravings? Her gold and amber house on the Mountain, of course. She has had that fantasy from her childhood. The fellow would fall in with it. He'd be the god's messenger . . . why, that's where her god of the Westwind comes from. It would be the man himself. He'd take her to this valley. He'd whisper to her that the god, the bridegroom, would come to her that night. And after dark, he'd come back."

"But the palace?"

"Her old fantasy, raised up by her madness and taken by her for reality. And whatever she tells the rascal about her fine house, he echoes it all. Perhaps adds more of his own. And so the delusion is built up stronger and stronger."

For the second time that day I was utterly aghast. The Fox's explanation seemed too plain and evident to allow me any hope of doubt. While Bardia was speaking, his had seemed the same.

"It looks, Grandfather," said I dully, "as if you had read the riddle right."

"It needed no Oedipus. But the real riddle's still to guess. What must we do? Oh, I'm barren, barren. I think your father has addled my brains with beating me about the ears. There must be some way . . . yet we've so little time."

"And so little freedom. I can't pretend to be on my

sickbed much longer. And once the King knows I'm whole, how shall I ever get to the Mountain again?"

"Oh, for that—but I'd forgotten. There's been news today. The lions have been seen again."

"What?" I cried in terror. "On the Mountain?"

"No, no, not so bad as that. Indeed, rather good than bad. Somewhere down south, and west of Ringal. The King will have a great lion hunt."

"The lions back . . . so Ungit has played us false after all. Perhaps he'll sacrifice Redival this time. Is the King in a great rage?"

"Rage? No. Why, you'd think the loss of a herdsman and (what he values far more) some of the best dogs, and I don't know how many bullocks, was the best news he'd ever heard! I never saw him in better spirits. There's been nothing in his mouth all day but dogs and beaters and weather . . . and such rummage and bustle—messages to this lord and that lord—deep talks with the Huntsman—inspecting of kennels—shoeing of horses—beer flowing like water—even I have been slapped on the back in pure good fellowship till my ribs ache with it. But what concerns us is that he'll be out at the hunting the next two days at least. With luck it might be five or six."

"Then that's the time we have to work in."

"No more than that. He goes at daybreak tomorrow. And anyway, we'd have little longer. She'll die if winter catches her on the Mountain. Living without a roof. And she'll be with child, no doubt, before we've time to look about us."

It was as if I'd been hit about the heart. "Leprosy and scabs on the man!" I gasped. "Curse him, curse him! Psyche to carry a beggar's brat? We'll have him impaled if ever we catch him. He shall die for days. Oh, I could tear his body with my bare teeth."

"You darken our counsels—and your own soul—with these passions," said the Fox. "If there were anywhere she could lie hidden (if we could get her)!"

"I had thought," said I, "we could hide her in Bardia's house."

"Bardia! He'd never take one who's been sacrificed into his house. He's afraid of his own shadow where gods and old wives' tales are concerned. He's a fool."

"That he is not," said I, sharply enough, for the Fox often nettled me with his contempt for very brave and honest people if they had no tincture of his Greek wisdom.

"And if Bardia would," the Fox added, "that wife of his wouldn't let him. And everyone knows that Bardia's tied to his wife's apron-strings."

"Bardia! And such a man. I couldn't have believed—"

"Pah! He's as amorous as Alcibiades. Why, the fellow married her undowered—for her beauty, if you please. The whole town knows of it. And she rules him like her slave."

"She must be a very vile woman, Grandfather."

"What does it matter to us whether she is or no? But you needn't think to find refuge for our darling in that house. I'll go further, daughter. There's nothing

146

for it but to send her right out of Glome. If anyone in Glome knew that she had not died, they would seek her out and sacrifice her again. If we could get her to her mother's family . . . but I see no way of doing it. Oh Zeus, Zeus, Zeus, if I had ten hoplites and a sane man to command them!"

"I can't see," said I, "even how to get her to leave the Mountain. She was obstinate, Grandfather. She obeys me no more. I think we must use force."

"And we have no force. I am a slave and you are a woman. We can't lead a dozen spears up the Mountain. And if we could, the secret would never be kept."

After that we sat silent for a long time, the fire flickering, Poobi sitting cross-legged by the hearth, feeding the logs into it, and playing a strange game of her own people's with beads (she once tried to teach it to me, but I could never learn). The Fox made as if to speak a dozen times but always checked himself. He was quick to devise plans, but no less quick to see the faults in them.

At last I said, "It all comes to this, Grandfather. I must go back to Psyche. I must overrule her somehow. Once she is on our side, once she knows her shame and danger, then the three of us must devise as best we can. It may be that she and I must go out into the wide world together—wander like Oedipus."

"And I with you," said the Fox. "You once bade me run away. This time I'll do it"

"One thing's certain," said I. "She shall not be left

to the felon who has abused her. I will choose any way
—any way—rather than that. It rests on me. Her mother's dead. (What mother but me has she ever known?)
Her father's nothing, nothing for a father, and nothing
for a king either. The honour of our house—the very
being of Psyche—only I am left to care for them. She
shall not be left. I'll—I'll"

"What, child? You are pale! Are you fainting?"

"If there is no other way, I will kill her."

"Babai!" said the Fox, so loud that Poobi stopped her
game and stared at him. "Daughter, daughter. You are
transported beyond all reason and nature. Do you know
what it is? There's one part love in your heart, and five
parts anger, and seven parts pride. The gods know I love
Psyche, too. And you know it; you know I love her as
well as you do. It's a bitter grief that our child—our very
Artemis and Aphrodite all in one—should live a beggar's life and lie in a beggar's arms. Yet even this . . .
it is not to be named beside such detested impieties as
you speak of. Why, look at it squarely, as reason and
nature have made it, not as passion would paint it. To
be poor and in hardship, to be a poor man's wife—"

"Wife! You mean his trull, his drab, his whore, his
slut."

"Nature knows nothing of these names. What you call
marriage is by law and custom not nature. Nature's marriage is but the union of the man who persuades with the
woman who consents. And so—"

"The man who persuades—or, more likely, forces or

148

deceives—being some murderer, alien, traitor, runaway slave or other filth?"

"Filth? Perhaps I do not see it as you do. I am an alien and a slave myself; and ready to be a runaway—to risk the flogging and impaling—for your love and hers."

"You are ten times my father," said I, raising his hand to my lips. "I meant no such thing. But, Grandfather, there are matters you don't understand. Psyche said so herself."

"Sweet Psyche," he said. "I have often told her so. I am glad she has mastered the lesson. She was ever a good pupil."

"You don't believe in the divine blood of our house," I said.

"Oh yes. Of all houses. All men are of divine blood, for there is the god in every man. We are all one. Even the man who has taken Psyche. I have called him rascal and villain. Too likely he is. But it may not be. A good man might be an outlaw and a runaway."

I was silent. All this meant nothing to me.

"Daughter," said the Fox suddenly (I think no woman, at least no woman who loved you, would have done it). "Sleep comes early to old men. I can hardly keep my eyes open. Let me go. Perhaps we shall see more clearly in the morning."

What could I do but send him away? This is where men, even the trustiest, fail us. Their heart is never so wholly given to any matter but that some trifle of a meal, or a drink, or a sleep, or a joke, or a girl, may come in between them and it, and then (even if you are a queen) you'll get no more good out of them till they've had their way. In those days I had not yet understood this. Great desolation came over me.

"Everyone goes from me," I said. "None of them cares for Psyche. She lives at the very outskirts of their thoughts. She is less to them, far less, than Poobi is to me. They think of her a little and then get tired and go to something else, the Fox to his sleep, and Bardia to his doll or scold of a wife. You are alone, Orual. Whatever is to be done, you must devise and do it. No help will come. All gods and mortals have drawn away from you. You must guess the riddle. Not a word will come to you until you have guessed wrong and they all come crowding back to accuse and mock and punish you for it."

I sent Poobi to bed. Then I did a thing which I think few have done. I spoke to the gods myself, alone, in such words as came to me, not in a temple, and without a sacrifice. I stretched myself face downward on the floor and called upon them with my whole heart. I took back every word I had said against them. I promised anything they might ask of me, if only they would send me a sign. They gave me none. When I began there was red firelight in the room and rain on the roof; when I rose up again the fire had sunk a little lower, and the rain drummed on as before.

Now, when I knew that I was left utterly to myself, I said, "I must do it . . . whatever I do . . . tomorrow. I must, then, rest tonight." I lay down on the bed.

I was in that state when the body is so tired that sleep comes soon, but the mind is in such anguish that it will wake you the moment the body's sated. It woke me a few hours past midnight, with no least possibility of further sleep in me. The fire was out; the rain had stopped. I went to my window and stood looking out into the gusty blackness, twisting my hair in my fists with my knuckles against my temples, and thought.

My mind was much clearer. I now saw that I had, strangely, taken both Bardia's explanation and the Fox's (each while it lasted) for certain truth. Yet one must be false. And I could not find out which, for each was well-rooted in its own soil. If the things believed in Glome were true, then what Bardia said stood; if the Fox's philosophy were true, what the Fox said stood. But I could not find out whether the doctrines of Glome or the wisdom of Greece were right. I was the child of Glome and the pupil of the Fox; I saw that for years my life had been lived in two halves, never fitted together.

I must give up, then, trying to judge between Bardia and my master. And as soon as I said that, I saw (and wondered I had not seen before) that it made no difference. For there was one point on which both agreed. Both thought that some evil or shameful thing had taken Psyche for its own. Murdering thief or spectral Shadow-brute—did it matter which? The one thing neither of them believed was that anything good or fair came to her in the night. No one but myself had dallied with that thought even for a moment. Why should they? Only my desperate wishes could have made it seem possible. The thing came in darkness and forbade itself to be seen. What lover would shun his bride's eyes unless he had some terrible reason for it?

Even I had thought the opposite only for an instant, while I looked at that likeness of a house across the river.

"It shall not have her," I said. "She shall not lie in those detestable embraces. Tonight must be the last night of that."

Suddenly there rose up before me the memory of Psyche in the mountain valley, brightface, brimming over with joy. My terrible temptation came back; to leave her to that fool-happy dream, whatever came of it, to spare her, not to bring her down from it into misery. Must I be to her an avenging fury, not a gentle mother? And part of my mind now was saying, "Do not meddle. Anything might be true. You are among marvels that you do not understand. Carefully, carefully. Who knows what ruin you might pull down on her head and yours?" But with the other part of me I answered that I was indeed her mother and her father, too (all she had of either), that my love must be grave and provident, not slip-shod and indulgent, that there is a time for love to be stern. After all, what was she but a child? If the present case were beyond my understanding, how much more must it be beyond hers? Children must obey. It had hurt me, long ago, when I made the barber pull out the thorn. Had I not none the less done well?

I hardened my resolution. I knew now what (which of two things) I must do, and no later than on the day which would soon be breaking—provided only that Bardia were not going on the lion hunt and that I could get him clear of that wife of his. As a man, even in great pain or sorrow, can still be fretted by a fly that buzzes in his face, I was fretted by the thought of this wife, this petted thing, suddenly starting up to delay or to hinder.

I lay down on my bed to wait for morning, calmed and quiet in a way now that I knew what I would do.

FOURTEEN

I T SEEMED long to me before the palace was stirring, though it stirred early because of the King's
hunting. I waited till that noise was well begun.
Then I rose and dressed in such clothes as I had worn the
day before, and took the same urn. This time I put in it a
lamp and a little pitcher of oil and a long band of linen
about a span and a half broad, such as bridesmaids wear
in Glome, wrapped over and over round them. Mine
had lain in my chest ever since the marriage night of
Psyche's mother. Then I called up Poobi and had food
brought to me, of which I ate some and some I put in
the urn under the band. When I knew by the horse-hoofs
and horns and shoutings that the King's party was gone,
I put on my veil and a cloak and went down. I sent the
first slave I met to find whether Bardia were gone to the
hunting, and if he were in the palace, to send him to me.
I waited for him in the Pillar Room. It was a strange
freedom to be in there alone; and indeed, amid all my
cares, I could not help perceiving how the house was, as
it were, lightened and set at liberty by the absence of

the King. I thought, from their looks, that all the family felt it.

Bardia came to me.

"Bardia," said I, "I must go again to the Mountain."

"It's impossible you should go with me, Lady," he said. "I was left out of the hunting (ill-luck for me) for one purpose only; to watch over the house. I must even lie here at nights till the King's back."

This dashed me very much. "Oh, Bardia," said I, "what shall we do? I am in great straits. It's on my sister's business."

Bardia rubbed his forefinger across his upper lip in a way he had when he was graveled. "And you can't ride," he said. "I wonder now—but no, that's foolishness. There's no horse to be trusted with a rider that can't ride. And a few days hence won't serve? The best would be to give you another man."

"But, Bardia, it must be you. No one else would be able . . . it's a very secret errand."

"I could let Gram off with you for two days and a night."

"Who is Gram?"

"The small dark one. He's a good man."

"But can he hold his tongue?"

"It's more a question if he can ever loosen it. We get hardly ten words from him in as many days. But he's a true man, true to me, above all, for I once had the chance to do him a good turn."

"It will not be like going with you, Bardia."

"It's the best you can do, Lady, unless you can wait."

But I said I could not wait, and Bardia had Gram called. He was a thin-faced man, very black-eyed, and (I thought) looked at me as if he feared me. Bardia told him to get his horse and await me where the little lane meets the road into the city.

As soon as he was gone, I said, "Now, Bardia, get me a dagger."

"A dagger, Lady? And for what?"

"To use as a dagger. Come, Bardia, you know I mean no ill."

He looked strangely at me, but got it. I put it on at my belt where the sword had hung yesterday. "Farewell, Bardia," said I.

"*Farewell*, Lady? Do you go for longer than a night?"

"I don't know, I don't know," said I. Then, all in haste, and leaving him to wonder, I went out and went on foot by the lane and joined Gram. He set me up on the horse (touching me, unless it was my fantasy, as one who touched a snake or a witch) and we began.

Nothing could be less like that day's journey and the last. I never got more than, "Yes, Lady," or, "No, Lady," out of Gram all day. There was much rain and even between the showers the wind was wet. There was a grey driving sky and the little hills and valleys, which had been so distinct with brightness and shade for Bardia and me the other day, were all sunk into one piece. We had started many hours later, and it was nearer evening than noon when we came down from the saddle into that secret valley. And there at last, as if by some trick of the gods (which perhaps it was), the weather cleared so that it was hard not to think the valley had a sunlight of its own and the blustering rains merely ringed it about as the mountains did.

I brought Gram to the place where Bardia and I had passed the night and told him to await me there, and not to cross the river. "I must go over it myself. It may be I shall recross it to your side by nightfall, or in the night. But I think that whatever time I spend on this side I will spend over yonder, near the ford. Do not come to me there unless I call you."

He said, as always, "Yes, Lady," and looked as if he liked this adventure very little.

I went to the ford—about a long bow-shot from Gram. My heart was still as ice, heavy as lead, cold as earth, but I was free now from all doubting and deliberating. I set my foot on the first stone of the crossing and called Psyche's name. She must have been very close, for almost at once I saw her coming down to the bank. We might have been two images of love, the happy and the stern—she so young, so brightface, joy in her eye and limbs—I, burdened and resolute, bringing pain in my hand.

"So I spoke truly, Maia," she said as soon as I had crossed the water and we had embraced. "The King has been no hindrance to you, has he? Salute me for a prophetess!"

This startled me a moment, for I had forgotten her foretelling. But I put it aside to be thought of later.

Now, I had my work to do; I must not, now of all times, begin doubting and pondering again.

She brought me a little way from the water—I don't know into what part of her phantom palace—and we sat down. I threw back my hood and put off my veil and set down the urn beside me.

"Oh, Orual," said Psyche, "what a storm-cloud in your face! That's how you looked when you were most angry with me as a child."

"Was I ever angry? Ah, Psyche, do you think I ever scolded or denied you without grieving my heart ten times more than yours?"

"Sister, I meant to find no fault with you."

"Then find no fault with me today either. For indeed we must talk very gravely. Now listen, Psyche. Our father is no father. Your mother (peace upon her!) is dead, and you have never seen her kindred. I have been—I have tried to be and still I must be—all the father and mother and kin you have. And all the King too."

"Maia, you have been all this and more since the day I was born. You and the dear Fox are all I ever had."

"Yes, the Fox. I'll have something to say of him, too. And so, Psyche, if anyone is to care for you or counsel you or shield you, or if anyone is to tell you what belongs to the honour of our blood, it can be only I."

"But why are you saying all this, Orual? You do not think I have left off loving you because I now have a husband to love as well? If you would understand it, that makes me love you—why, it makes me love everyone and everything—more."

This made me shudder but I hid it and went on. "I know you love me, Psyche," said I. "And I think I should not live if you didn't. But you must trust me too."

She said nothing. And now I was right on top of the terrible thing, and it almost struck me dumb. I cast about for ways to begin it.

"You spoke last time," I said, "of the day we got the thorn out of your hand. We hurt you that time, Psyche. But we did right. Those who love must hurt. I must hurt you again today. And, Psyche, you are still little more than a child. You cannot go your own way. You will let me rule and guide you."

"Orual, I have a husband to guide me now."

It was difficult not to be angered or terrified by her harping on it. I bit my lip, then said, "Alas, child, it is about that very husband (as you call him) that I must grieve you." I looked straight at her eyes and said sharply, "Who is he? What is he?"

"A god," she said, low and quivering. "And, I think, the god of the Mountain."

"Alas, Psyche, you are deceived. If you knew the truth, you would die rather than lie in his bed."

"The truth?"

"We must face it, child. Be very brave. Let me pull out this thorn. What sort of god would he be who dares not show his face?"

"*Dares not!* You come near to making me angry, Orual."

159

"But think, Psyche. Nothing that's beautiful hides its face. Nothing that's honest hides its name. No, no, listen. In your heart you must see the truth, however you try to brazen it out with words. Think. Whose bride were you called? The Brute's. And think again. If it's not the Brute, who else dwells in these mountains? Thieves and murderers, men worse than brutes, and lecherous as goats we may be sure. Are you a prize they'd let pass if you fell in their way? There's your lover, child. Either a monster—shadow and monster in one, maybe, a ghostly, un-dead thing—or a salt villain whose lips, even on your feet or the hem of your robe, would be a stain to our blood."

She was silent a long time, her eyes on her lap.

"And so, Psyche," I began at last, tenderly as I could —but she tossed away the hand that I had laid on hers.

"You mistake me, Orual. If I am pale, it is with anger. There, Sister, I have conquered it. I'll forgive you. You mean—I'll believe you mean—nothing but good. Yet how—or why—you can have blackened and tormented your soul with such thoughts . . . but no more of that. if ever you loved me, put them away now."

"Blackened my thoughts. They're not only mine. Tell me, Psyche, who are the two wisest men we know?"

"Why, the Fox for one. For the second—I know so few. I suppose Bardia is wise, in his own way."

"You said yourself, that night in the five-walled room, that he was a prudent man. Now, Psyche, these two—so wise and so different—are both agreed with each other and with me concerning this lover of yours.

Agreed without doubt. All three of us are certain. Either Shadowbrute or felon."

"You have told them my story, Orual? It was ill done. I gave you no leave. My lord gave no leave. Oh, Orual! It was more like Batta than you."

I could not help it if my face reddened with anger, but I would not be turned aside. "Doubtless," I said. "There is no end to the secrecy of this—this *husband* as you call him. Child, has his vile love so turned your brain that you can't see the plainest thing? A god? Yet on your own showing he hides and slinks and whispers, 'Mum,' and 'Keep counsel,' and 'Don't betray me,' like a runaway slave."

I am not certain that she had listened to this. What she said was: "The Fox too! That is very strange. I never thought he would have believed in the Brute at all."

I had not said he did. But if that was what she took out of my words, I thought it no part of my duty to set her right. It was an error helping her towards the main truth. I had need of all help to drive her thither. "Neither he nor I nor Bardia," said I, "believes for one moment in your fancy that it is the god; no more than that this wild heath is a palace. And be sure, Psyche, that if we could ask every man and woman in Glome, all would say the same. The truth is too clear."

"But what is all this to me? How should they know? I am his wife. I know."

"How can you know if you have never seen him?"

"Orual, how can you be so simple? I—how could I
not know?"

"But how, Psyche?"

"What am I to answer to such a question? It's not
fitting . . . it is . . . and especially to you, Sister, who
are a virgin."

That matronly primness, from the child she was, went
near to ending my patience. It was almost (but I think
now she did not mean it so) as if she taunted me. Yet
I ruled myself.

"Well, if you are so sure, Psyche, you will not refuse to put it to the test."

"What test? Though I need none myself."

"I have brought a lamp, and oil. See. Here they are."
(I set them down beside her.) "Wait till he—or it—
sleeps. Then look."

"I cannot do that."

"Ah! . . . You see! You will abide no test. And
why? Because you are not sure yourself. If you were,
you'd be eager to do it. If he is, as you say, a god, one
glimpse will set all our doubts at rest. What you call
our dark thoughts will be put to flight. But you daren't."

"Oh, Orual, what evil you think! The reason I cannot look at him—least of all by such trickery as you'd
have me do—is that he has forbidden me."

"I can think—Bardia and the Fox can think—of one
reason only for such a forbidding. And of one only for
your obeying it."

"Then you know little of love."

"You fling my virginity in my face again, do you?

Better it than the sty you're in. So be it. Of what you now call love, I do know nothing. You can whisper about it to Redival better than to me—or to Ungit's girls, maybe, or the King's doxies. I know another sort of love. You shall find what it's like. You shall not—"

"Orual, Orual, you are raving," said Psyche; herself unangered, gazing at me large-eyed, sorrowful, but nothing humble about her sorrow. You would have thought she was my mother, not I (almost) hers. I had known this long time that the old meek, biddable Psyche was gone forever; yet it shocked me afresh.

"Yes," I said. "I was raving. You had made me angry. But I had thought (you will set me right, I don't doubt, if I am mistaken) that all loves alike were eager to clear the thing they loved of vile charges brought against it, if they could. Tell a mother her child is hideous. If it's beautiful she'll show it. No forbidding would stop her. If she keeps it hidden, the charge is true. You're afraid of the test, Psyche."

"I am afraid—no, I am ashamed—to disobey him."

"Then, even at the best, look what you make of him! Something worse than our father. Who that loved you could be angry at your breaking so unreasonable a command—and for so good a reason?"

"Foolishness, Orual," she answered, shaking her head. "He is a god. He has good grounds for what he does, be sure. How should I know of them? I am only his simple Psyche."

"Then you will not do it? You think—you say you think—that you can prove him a god and set me free from the fears that sicken my heart. But you will not do it."

"I would if I could, Orual."

I looked about me. The sun was almost setting behind the saddle. In a little while she would send me away. I rose up.

"An end of this must be made," I said. "You shall do it. Psyche, I command you."

"Dear Maia, my duty is no longer to you."

"Then my life shall end with it," said I. I flung back my cloak further, thrust out my bare left arm, and struck the dagger into it till the point pricked out on the other side. Pulling the iron back through the wound was the worse pain; but I can hardly believe now how little I felt it.

"Orual! Are you mad?" cried Psyche, leaping up.

"You'll find linen in that urn. Tie up my wound," said I, sitting down and holding my arm out to let the blood fall on the heather.

I had thought she might scream and wring her hands or faint. But I was deceived. She was pale enough but had all her wits about her. She bound my arm. The blood came seeping through fold after fold, but she staunched it in the end. (My stroke had been lucky enough. If I had known as much then as I do now about the inside of an arm, I might not—who knows? —have had the resolution to do it.)

The bandaging could not be done in a moment. The sun was lower and the air colder when we were able to talk again.

"Maia," said Psyche, "what did you do that for?"

"To show you I'm in earnest, girl. Listen. You have driven me to desperate courses. I give you your choice. Swear on this edge, with my blood still wet on it, that you will this very night do as I have commanded you; or else I'll first kill you and then myself."

"Orual," said she, very queenlike, raising her head, "you might have spared that threat of killing me. All your power over me lies in the other."

"Then swear, girl. You never knew me break my word."

The look in her face now was one I did not understand. I think a lover—I mean, a man who loved—might look so on a woman who had been false to him. And at last she said,

"You are indeed teaching me about kinds of love I did not know. It is like looking into a deep pit. I am not sure whether I like your kind better than hatred. Oh, Orual—to take my love for you, because you know it goes down to my very roots and cannot be diminished by any other newer love, and then to make of it a tool, a weapon, a thing of policy and mastery, an instrument of torture—I begin to think I never knew you. Whatever comes after, something that was between us dies here."

"Enough of your subtleties," said I. "Both of us die here, in plainest truth and blood, unless you swear."

"If I do," said she hotly, "it will not be for any doubt of my husband or his love. It will only be because I think better of him than of you. He cannot be cruel like you. I'll not believe it. He will know how I was tortured into my disobedience. He will forgive me."

"He need never know," said I.

The look of scorn she gave me flayed my soul. And yet, this very nobleness in her—had I not taught it to her? What was there in her that was not my work? And now she used it to look at me as if I were base beneath all baseness.

"You thought I would hide it? Thought I would not tell him?" she said, each word like the rubbing of a file across raw flesh. "Well. It's all of a piece. Let us, as you say, make an end. You grow more and more a stranger to me at each word. And I had loved you so—loved, honoured, trusted, and (while it was fit) obeyed. And now—but I can't have your blood on my threshold. You chose your threat well. I'll swear. Where's your dagger?"

So I had won my victory and my heart was in torment. I had a terrible longing to unsay all my words and beg her forgiveness. But I held out the dagger. (The "oath on edge," as we call it, is our strongest in Glome.)

"And even now," said Psyche, "I know what I do. I know that I am betraying the best of lovers and that perhaps, before sunrise, all my happiness may be destroyed forever. This is the price you have put upon your life. Well, I must pay it."

She took her oath. My tears burst out, and I tried to speak, but she turned her face away.

"The sun is almost down," she said. "Go. You have saved your life; go and live it as you can."

I found I was becoming afraid of her. I made my way back to the stream, crossed it somehow. And the shadow of the saddle leaped across the whole valley as the sun set.

FIFTEEN

I THINK I must have fainted when I got to this side of the water, for there seems to be some gap in my memory between the fording and being fully aware again of three things: cold, and the pain in my arm, and thirst. I drank ravenously. Then I wanted food, and now first remembered that I had left it in the urn with the lamp. My soul rose up against calling Gram, who was very irksome to me. I felt (though I saw it to be folly even at the time) that if Bardia had come with me instead, all might have been different and better. And away my thoughts wandered to imagine all he would be doing and saying now if he had, till suddenly I remembered what business had brought me there. I was ashamed that I had thought, even for a moment, of anything else.

My purpose was to sit by the ford, watching till I should see a light (which would be Psyche lighting her lamp). It would vanish when she covered and hid it. Then, most likely far later, there would be a light again; she would be looking at her vile master in its sleep. And after that—very, very soon after it, I hoped

—there would be Psyche creeping through the darkness and sending a sort of whispered call ("Maia, Maia") across the stream. And I would be half-way over it in an instant. This time it would be I who helped her at the ford. She would be all weeping and dismayed as I folded her in my arms and comforted her; for now she would know who were her true friends, and would love me again, and would thank me, shuddering, for saving her from the thing the lamp had shown. These were dear thoughts to me when they came and while they lasted.

But there were other thoughts too. Try as I would, I could not quite put out of my head the fear that I had been wrong. A real god . . . was it impossible? But I could never dwell on that part of it. What came back and back to my mind was the thought of Psyche herself somehow (I never knew well how) ruined, lost, robbed of all joy, a wailing, wandering shape, for whom I had wrecked everything. More times than I could count that night, I had the wish, tyrannously strong, to re-cross the cold water, to shout out that I forgave her her promise, that she was not to light the lamp, that I had advised her wrongly. But I governed it.

Neither the one sort of thoughts nor the other was more than the surface of my mind. Beneath them, deep as the deep ocean-sea whereof the Fox spoke, was the cold, hopeless abyss of her scorn, her un-love, her very hatred.

How could she hate me, when my arm throbbed and burned with the wound I had given it for her love?

169

"Cruel Psyche, cruel Psyche," I sobbed. But then I saw that I was falling back to the dreams of my sickness. So I set my wits against it and bestirred myself. Whatever happened I must watch and be sane.

The first light came soon enough; and vanished again. I said to myself (though indeed once I had her oath I never doubted her faith to it), "So. All's well this far." It made me wonder, as at a new question, what I meant by *well*. But the thought passed.

The cold grew bitter. My arm was a bar of fire, the rest of me an icicle, chained to that bar but never melted. I began to see that I was doing a perilous thing. I might die, thus wounded and fasting, or at least get such a chill as would bring my death soon after. And out of that seed there grew up, in one moment, a huge, foolish flower of fancies. For at once (leaping over all question of how it should come about) I saw myself laid on the pyre, and Psyche—she knew now, she loved me again now—beating her breast and weeping and repenting all her cruelties. The Fox and Bardia were there too; Bardia wept fast. Everyone loved me once I was dead. But I am ashamed to write all these follies.

What checked them was the next appearing of the light. To my eyes, long swilled with darkness, it seemed brighter than you would have thought possible. Bright and still, a homelike thing in that wild place. And for a time longer than I had expected, it shone and was still, and the whole world was still around it. Then the stillness broke.

The great voice, which rose up from somewhere close to the light, went through my whole body in such a swift wave of terror that it blotted out even the pain in my arm. It was no ugly sound; even in its implacable sternness it was golden. My terror was the salute that mortal flesh gives to immortal things. And after— barely after—the strong soaring of its incomprehensible speech, came the sound of weeping. I think (if those old words have a meaning) my heart broke then. But neither the immortal sound nor the tears of her who wept lasted for more than two heartbeats. Heartbeats, I say; but I think my heart did not beat till they were over.

A great flash laid the valley bare to my eyes. Then it thundered as if the sky broke in two, straight above my head. Lightnings, thick-following one another, pricked the valley, left, right, near and far, everywhere. Each flash showed falling trees; the imagined pillars of Psyche's house were going down. They seemed to fall silently, for the thunder hid their crashing. But there was another noise it could not hide. Somewhere away on my left the walls of the Mountain itself were breaking. I saw (or I thought I saw) fragments of rock hurled about and striking on other rocks and rising into the air again like a child's ball that bounces. The river rose, so quickly that I was overtaken by its rush before I could stumble back from it, wet to my middle; but that made little odds, for with the storm there had come a tyrannous pelting rain. Hair and clothes were already a mere sponge.

But, beaten and blinded though I was, I took these things for a good sign. They showed (so it seemed to me) that I was right. Psyche had roused some dreadful thing and these were its ragings. It had waked, she had not hidden her light soon enough; or else—yes, that was most likely—it had only feigned to be sleeping; it might be a thing that never needed sleep. It might, no doubt, destroy both her and me. But she would know. She would, at worst, die undeceived, disenchanted, reconciled to me. Even now, we might escape. Failing that, we could die together. I rose up, bent double under the battery of the rain, to cross the stream.

I believe I could never have crossed it—the deep, foaming death-race it had now become—even if I had been left free to try. I was not left free. There came as if it were a lightning that endured. That is, the look of it was the look of lightning, pale, dazzling, without warmth or comfort, showing each smallest thing with fierce distinctness, but it did not go away. This great light stood over me as still as a candle burning in a curtained and shuttered room. In the center of the light was something like a man. It is strange that I cannot tell you its size. Its face was far above me, yet memory does not show the shape as a giant's. And I do not know whether it stood, or seemed to stand, on the far side of the water or on the water itself.

Though this light stood motionless, my glimpse of the face was as swift as a true flash of lightning. I could not bear it for longer. Not my eyes only, but my heart and blood and very brain were too weak for that. A monster—the Shadowbrute that I and all Glome had imagined—would have subdued me less than the beauty this face wore. And I think anger (what men call anger) would have been more supportable than the passionless and measureless rejection with which it looked upon me. Though my body crouched where I could almost have touched his feet, his eyes seemed to send me from him to an endless distance. He rejected, denied, answered, and (worst of all) he knew, all I had thought, done or been. A Greek verse says that even the gods cannot change the past. But is this true? He made it to be as if, from the beginning, I had known that Psyche's lover was a god, and as if all my doubtings, fears, guessings, debatings, questionings of Bardia, questionings of the Fox, all the rummage and business of it, had been trumped-up foolery, dust blown in my own eyes by myself. You, who read my book, judge. Was it so? Or, at least, had it been so in the very past, before this god changed the past? And if they can indeed change the past, why do they never do so in mercy?

The thunder had ceased, I think, the moment the still light came. There was great silence when the god spoke to me. And as there was no anger (what men call anger) in his face, so there was none in his voice. It was unmoved and sweet; like a bird singing on the branch above a hanged man.

"Now Psyche goes out in exile. Now she must hunger and thirst and tread hard roads. Those against whom

I cannot fight must do their will upon her. You, woman, shall know yourself and your work. You also shall be Psyche."

The voice and the light both ended together as if one knife had cut them short. Then, in the silence, I heard again the noise of the weeping.

I never heard weeping like that before or after, not from a child, nor a man wounded in the palm, nor a tortured man, nor a girl dragged off to slavery from a taken city. If you heard the woman you most hate in the world weep so, you would go to comfort her. You would fight your way through fire and spears to reach her. And I knew who wept, and what had been done to her, and who had done it.

I rose to go to her. But already the weeping was further away. She went wailing far off to my right, down to the end of the valley where I had never been, where doubtless it fell away or dropped in sheer cliffs toward the south. And I could not cross the stream. It would not even drown me. It would bruise and freeze and bemire me, but somehow whenever I grasped a rock—earth was no use now, for great slabs of the bank were slipping into the current every moment—I found I was still on this side. Sometimes I could not even find the river—I was so bewildered in the dark, and all the ground was now little better than a swamp, so that pools and new-formed brooks lured me now this way, now that.

I cannot remember more of that night. When day began to break, I could see what the god's anger had done to the valley. It was all bare rock, raw earth, and foul water; trees, bushes, sheep, and here and there a deer, floated in it. If I could have crossed the first river in the night it would not have profited me; I should have reached only the narrow bank of mud between it and the next. Even now I could not help calling out Psyche's name, calling till my voice was gone, but I knew it was foolishness. I had heard her leaving the valley. She had already gone into the exile which the god foretold. She had begun to wander, weeping, from land to land; weeping for her lover, not (I mustn't so cheat myself) for me.

I went and found Gram; a wet, shivering wretch he was, who gave one scared glance at my bandaged arm, and no more, and asked no questions. We ate food from the saddle-bags and began our journey. The weather was fair enough.

I looked on the things about me with a new eye. Now that I'd proved for certain that the gods are and that they hated me, it seemed that I had nothing to do but to wait for my punishment. I wondered on which dangerous edge the horse would slip and fling us down a few hundred feet into a gulley; or what tree would drop a branch on my neck as we rode under it; or whether my wound would corrupt and I should die that way. Often, remembering that it is sometimes the gods' way to turn us into beasts, I put my hand up under my veil to see if I could feel cat's fur, or dog's muzzle, or hog's tusks beginning to grow there. Yet with it all I was not afraid, never less. It is a strange, yet somehow a quiet and steady thing, to look round on earth and grass and the sky and say in one's heart to each, "You are all my enemies now. None of you will ever do me good again. I see now only executioners."

But I thought it most likely those words *You also shall be Psyche* meant that if she went into exile and wandering, I must do the same. And this, I had thought before, might very easily come about, if the men of Glome had no will to be ruled by a woman. But the god had been wide of the mark—so then they don't know all things?—if he thought he could grieve me most by making my punishment the same as Psyche's. If I could have borne hers as well as my own . . . but next best was to share. And with this I felt a sort of hard and cheerless strength rising in me. I would make a good beggarwoman. I was ugly; and Bardia had taught me how to fight.

Bardia . . . that set me thinking how much of my story I would tell him. Then, how much I would tell the Fox. I had not thought of this at all.

SIXTEEN

I CREPT in by the back parts of the palace and soon learned that my father had not yet come home from the hunting. But I went as soft and slinking to my place as if he had. When it became clear to my own mind (it did not at first) that I was hiding now not from the King but from the Fox, it was a trouble to me. Always before he had been my refuge and comforter.

Poobi cried over my wound and when she had the bandage off—that part was bad—laid good dressings on it. That was hardly done, and I was eating (hungrily enough) when the Fox came.

"Daughter, daughter," he said. "Praise the gods who have sent you back. I have been in pain for you all day. Where have you been?"

"To the Mountain, Grandfather," said I, keeping my left arm out of sight. This was the first of my difficulties. I could not tell him of the self-wounding. I knew, now I saw him (I had not thought of it before), that he would rebuke me for putting that kind of force upon Psyche. One of his maxims was that if we cannot persuade our friends by reasons we must be content "and not bring a mercenary army to our aid." (He meant passions.)

"Oh, child, that was sudden," he said. "I thought we parted that night to talk it over again in the morning."

"We parted to let you sleep," said I. The words came fiercely, without my will and in my father's own voice. Then I was ashamed.

"So that's my sin," said the Fox, smiling sadly. "Well, Lady, you have punished it. But what's your news? Would Psyche hear you?"

I said nothing to that question but told him of the storm and the flood and how that mountain valley was now a mere swamp, and how I had tried to cross the stream and could not, and how I had heard Psyche go weeping away, on the south side of it, out of Glome altogether. There was no use in telling him about the god; he would have thought I had been mad or dreaming.

"Do you mean, child, you never came to speech with her at all?" said the Fox, looking very haggard.

"Yes," I said. "We did talk a little—earlier."

"Child, what is wrong? Was there a quarrel? What passed between you?"

This was harder to answer. In the end, when he questioned me closely, I told him about my plan of the lamp.

"Daughter, daughter!" cried the Fox, "what daemon put such a device in your thoughts? What did

178

you hope to do? Would not the villain by her side—he, a hunted man and an outlaw—be certain to wake? And what would he do then but snatch her up and drag her away to some other lair? Unless he stabbed her to the heart for fear she'd betray him to his pursuers. Why, the light alone would convince him she'd betrayed him already. How if it were a wound that made her weep? Oh, if you'd only taken counsel!"

I could say nothing. For now I wondered why indeed I had not thought of any of these things and whether I had never at all believed her lover was a mountainy man.

The Fox stared at me, wondering more and more, I saw, at my silence. At last he said, "Did you find it easy to make her do this?"

"No," said I. I had taken off, while I ate, the veil I had worn all day; now I greatly wished I had it on.

"And how did you persuade her?" he asked.

This was the worst of all. I could not tell him what I had really done. Nor much of what I'd said. For when I told Psyche that he and Bardia were both agreed about her lover I meant what was very true; both agreed it was some shameful or dreadful thing. But if I said this to the Fox, he would say that Bardia's belief and his were sheer contraries, the one all old wives' tales and the other plain workaday probabilities. He would make it seem that I had lied. I could never make him understand how different it had looked on the Mountain.

"I—I spoke with her," said I at last. "I persuaded her."

He looked long and searchingly at me, but never so tenderly since those old days when he used to sing *"The Moon's Gone Down,"* I on his knee.

"Well. You have a secret from me," he said in the end. "No, don't turn away from me. Did you think I would try to press or conjure it out of you? Never that. Friends must be free. My tormenting you to find it would build a worse barrier between us than your hiding it. Some day—but you must obey the god within you, not the god within me. There, do not weep. I shall not cease to love you if you have a hundred secrets. I'm an old tree and my best branches were lopped off me the day I became a slave. You and Psyche were all that remained. Now—alas, poor Psyche! I see no way to her now. But I'll not lose you."

He embraced me (I bit my lip not to scream when his arm touched the wound) and went away. I had hardly ever before been glad of his going. But I thought, too, how much kinder he was than Psyche.

I never told Bardia the story of that night at all.

I made one resolve before I slept, which, though it seems a small matter, made much difference to me in the years that followed. Hitherto, like all my country-women, I had gone bareface; on those two journeys up the Mountain I had worn a veil because I wished to be secret. I now determined that I would go always veiled. I have kept this rule, within doors and without, ever since. It is a sort of treaty made with my ugliness. There had been a time in childhood when I didn't yet know I was ugly. Then there was a time (for in this book I must hide none of my shames or follies) when I believed, as girls do—and as Batta was always telling me—that I could make it more tolerable by this or that done to my clothes or my hair. Now, I chose to be veiled. The Fox, that night, was the last man who ever saw my face; and not many women have seen it either.

My arm healed well (and so all wounds have done in my body) and when the King returned, about seven days later, I no longer pretended to be ill. He came home very drunk, for there'd been as much feasting as hunting on that party, and very out of humour, for they had killed only two lions and he'd killed neither and a favourite dog had been ripped up.

A few days later he sent for the Fox and me again to the Pillar Room. As soon as he saw me veiled, he shouted, "Now, girl, what's this? Hung your curtains up, eh? Were you afraid we'd be dazzled by your beauty? Take off that frippery!"

It was then I first found what that night on the Mountain had done for me. No one who had seen and heard the god could much fear this roaring old King.

"It's hard if I'm to be scolded both for my face and for hiding it," said I, putting no hand to the veil.

"Come here," he said, not at all aloud this time. I went up and stood so close to his chair that my knees almost touched his, still as a stone. To see his face while he could not see mine seemed to give me a kind of power. He was working himself into one of those white rages.

"Do you begin to set your wits against mine?" he said almost in a whisper.

"Yes," said I, no louder than he, but very clearly. I had not known a moment before what I would do or say; that one little word came out of itself.

He stared at me while you could count seven and I half thought he might stab me dead. Then he shrugged, and snarled out, "Oh, you're like all women. Talk, talk, talk . . . you'd talk the moon out of the sky if a man'd listen to you. Here, Fox, are those lies you've been writing ready for her to copy?"

He never struck me, and I never feared him again. And from that day I never gave back an inch before him. Rather I pressed on—so well that I told him not long after how impossible it was that I and the Fox should guard Redival if we were to work for him in the Pillar Room. He growled and cursed, yet henceforth he made Batta her jailer. Batta had grown very familiar with him of late and spent many hours in the Bedchamber. Not, I suppose, that he had her to his bed—even in the best of her days she had scarcely been what he called "savoury"—but she tattled and whispered and flattered him and stirred his possets, for he began to show his years. She was equally thick, for the most part, with Redival; but those were a pair who could be ready to scratch each other's eyes out one moment, and snuggling up for gossip and bawdy the next.

This, and all other things that were happening in the palace, mattered to me not at all. I was like a condemned man waiting for his executioner, for I believed that some sudden stroke of the gods would fall on me very soon. But as day came after day and nothing happened, I began to see, at first very unwillingly, that I might be doomed to live, and even to live an unchanged life, some while longer.

When I understood this I went to Psyche's room, alone, and put everything in it as it had been before all our sorrows began. I found some verses in Greek which seemed to be a hymn to the god of the Mountain. These I burned. I did not choose that any of that part of her should remain. Even the clothes that she had worn in the last year I burned also; but those she had worn earlier, and especially what were left of those she wore in childhood, and any jewels she had loved as a child, I hung in their proper places. I wished all to be so ordered that if she could come back she would find all as it had been when she was still happy, and still mine. Then I locked the door and put a seal on it. And, as well as I could, I locked a door in my mind. Unless I were to go mad I must put away all thoughts of her save those that went back to her first, happy years. I never spoke of her. If my women mentioned her name I bade them be silent. If the Fox mentioned it I was silent myself and led him to other things. There was less comfort than of old in being with the Fox.

Yet I questioned him much about what he called the physical parts of philosophy, about the seminal fire, and how soul arises from blood, and the periods of the universe; and also about plants and animals, and the positions, soils, airs, and governments of cities. I wanted hard things now, and to pile up knowledge.

As soon as my wound was well enough I returned very diligently to my fencing lessons with Bardia. I did it even before my left arm could bear a shield, for he said that fighting without shields was also a skill that ought to be learned. He said (and I now know it was true) that I made very good progress.

My aim was to build up more and more that strength, hard and joyless, which had come to me when I heard the god's sentence; by learning, fighting, and labouring, to drive all the woman out of me. Sometimes at night, if the wind howled or the rain fell, there would leap upon me, like water from a bursting dam, a great and anguished wonder—whether Psyche was alive, and where she was on such a night, and whether hard wives of peasants were turning her, cold and famished, from their door. But then, after an hour or so of weeping and writhing and calling out upon the gods, I would set to and rebuild the dam.

Soon Bardia was teaching me to ride on horseback as well as to fence with the sword. He used me, and talked to me, more and more like a man. And this both grieved and pleased me.

So things went on till the Midwinter, which is a great feast in our country. On the day after it the King came home from some revels he had been at in a lord's house, about three hours after noon, and in mounting the steps that go up into the porch he fell. It was so cold that day that the water the houseboys had used for scouring the steps had frozen on them. He fell with his right leg under him across the edge of a step, and when men ran to help him up he roared out with pain and was ready to set his teeth in the hands of anyone who touched him. Next minute he was cursing them for leaving him to lie there and freeze. As soon as I came I nodded to the slaves to lift him up and carry him in, whatever he said or did. We got him to his bed, with great agony, and had the barber to him, who said (as we all guessed) that his thigh was broken. "But I've no skill to set it, Lady, even if the King would let my fingers near it." I sent a messenger over to the house of Ungit to the Second Priest, who had the name of a good surgeon. Before he came the King had filled himself up with enough strong wine to throw a sound man into a fever, and as soon as the Second Priest got his clothes out of the way and began handling the leg, he started screaming like a beast and tried to pluck out his dagger. Then Bardia and I whispered to one another, and we got in six of the guards and held the King down. Between his screams he kept on pointing at me with his eyes (they had his hands fast) and crying out,

"Take her away! Take away that one with the veil. Don't let her torture me. I know who she is. I know."

He had no sleep that night or the day and night after (on top of the pain from his leg, he coughed as if his chest would burst), and whenever our backs were turned Batta would be taking him in more wine. I was not much in the Bedchamber myself, for the sight of me made him frantic. He kept on saying he knew who I was for all my veil.

"Master," said the Fox, "it is only the Princess Orual, your daughter."

"Aye, so she tells you," the King would say. "But I know better. Wasn't she using red hot iron on my leg all night? I know who she is. . . . Aiai! Aiai! Guards! Bardia! Orual! Batta! Take her away!"

On the third night the Second Priest and Bardia and the Fox and I all stood just outside his door and talked in whispers. The Second Priest's name was Arnom; he was a dark man, no older than I, smooth-cheeked as a eunuch (which he cannot have been, for though Ungit has eunuchs, only a weaponed man can hold the full priesthood).

"It's likely," said Arnom, "that this will end in the King's death."

"So," thought I. "This is how it will begin. There'll be a new world in Glome, and if I get off with my life, I shall be driven out. I too shall be a Psyche."

"I think the same," said the Fox. "And it comes at a ticklish time. There's much business before us."

"More than you think, Lysias," said Arnom (I had never heard the Fox called by his real name before). "The house of Ungit is in the very same plight as the King's house."

"What do you mean, Arnom?" said Bardia.

"The Priest is dying at last. If I have any skill, he'll not last five days."

"And you to succeed him?" said Bardia. The priest bowed his head.

"Unless the King forbids," added the Fox. This was good law in Glome.

"It's very necessary," said Bardia, "that Ungit and the palace should be of one mind at such a moment. There are those who'd see their chance of setting Glome by the ears otherwise."

"Yes, very necessary," said Arnom. "No one will rise against us both."

"It's our good fortune," said Bardia, "that there's no cause of quarrel between the Queen and Ungit."

"The Queen?" said Arnom.

"The Queen," said Bardia and the Fox now both together.

"If only the Princess were married, now!" said Arnom, bowing very courteously. "A woman cannot lead the armies of Glome in war."

"This Queen can," said Bardia; and the way he thrust out his lower jaw made him seem a whole army himself. I saw Arnom looking at me hard, and I think my veil served me better than the boldest countenance in the world, maybe better than beauty would have done.

"There is only one difference between Ungit and the King's house," he said, "and that concerns the Crumbles. But for the King's sickness and the Priest's I would have been here before now to speak of it."

I knew all about this and saw now where we were. The Crumbles was good land on the far side of the river, and it had been a cat-and-dog quarrel ever since I started working for my father as to whether it belonged, or how much of it belonged, to the King or to Ungit. I had always thought (little cause as I had to love Ungit) that it should belong to her house, which was indeed poorly provided for the charge of continual sacrifices. And I thought too that if once Ungit were reasonably furnished with land, the priests could be stopped from wringing so much out of the common people by way of gifts.

"The King still lives," said I; I had not spoken before, and my voice surprised them all. "But because of his sickness I am now the King's mouth. It is his wish to give the Crumbles to Ungit, free and forever, and the covenant to be cut in stone, upon one condition."

Bardia and the Fox looked at me with wonder. But Arnom said, "What is that, Lady?"

"That Ungit's guards be henceforward under the Captain of the King's guard, and chosen by the King (or his successor), and under his obedience."

"And paid by the King (or his successors) too?" said Arnom quick as lightning.

I had not thought of this stroke, but I judged any resolute answer better than the wisest pondering. "That," said I, "must be according to the hours of duty they spend in Ungit's house and here."

"You drive—that is, the King drives—a hard bar-

188

gain, Lady," said the priest. But I knew he would take it, for I knew that Ungit had more need of good land than of spears. Also, it would be hard for Arnom to succeed to the Priesthood if the palace was against him. Then my father began roaring out from within and the priest went back to him.

"Well done, daughter," whispered the Fox.

"Long live the Queen," whispered Bardia. Then they both followed Arnom.

I stood outside in the great hall, which was empty, and the fire low. It was as strange a moment as any in my life. To be a queen—that would not sweeten the bitter water against which I had been building the dam in my soul. It might strengthen the dam, though. Then, as a quite different thing, came the thought that my father would be dead. That struck me dizzy. The largeness of a world in which he was not . . . the clear light of a sky in which that cloud would no longer hang . . . freedom. I drew in a long breath, one way, the sweetest I had ever drawn. I came near to forgetting my great central sorrow.

But only for a moment. It was very still, and most of the household was in bed. I thought I heard a sound of weeping—a girl's weeping—the sound for which always, with or without my will, I was listening. It seemed to come from without, from behind the palace. Instantly crowns and policies and my father were a thousand leagues from my mind. In a torture of hope I went swiftly to the other end of the hall and then out by the little door between the dairy and the guard's quarters.

189

The moon was shining, but the air was not so still as I thought. And where now was the weeping? Then I thought I heard it again. "Psyche," I called. "Istra! Psyche!" I went to the sound. Now I was less sure what it was. I remembered that when the chains of the well swung a little (and there had been breeze enough to sway them just now) they could make a noise something like that. Oh, the cheat of it, the bitterness!

I stood and listened. There was no more weeping. But something was moving somewhere. Then I saw a cloaked form dart across a patch of moonlight and bury itself in some bushes. I was after it, quick as I could. Next moment I plunged my hand in among the branches. Another hand met it.

"Softly, sweetheart," said a voice. "Take me to the King's threshold."

It was a wholly strange voice, and a man's.

SEVENTEEN

W HO are you?" said I, wrenching my hand
free and leaping back as if I had touched a
snake. "Come out and show yourself." My
thought was that it must be a lover of Redival's, and
that Batta was playing bawd as well as jailer.

A slender, tall man stepped out. "A suppliant," he
said, but with a merriment in his voice that did not
sound like supplication. "And one who never let a
pretty girl go without a kiss."

He'd have had an arm around my neck in a moment if I hadn't avoided him. Then he saw my dagger
point twinkle in the moonlight, and laughed.

"You've good eyes if you can see beauty in this
face," said I, turning it on him to make sure he saw
the blank wall of the veil.

"Only good ears, sister," said he. "I'll bet a girl
with a voice like yours is beautiful."

The whole adventure was, for such a woman as I,
so unusual that I almost had a fool's wish to lengthen
it. The very world was strange that night. But I came
to my senses.

"Who are you?" I said. "Tell me quick, or I'll call the guards."

"I'm no thief, pretty one," said he, "though I confess you caught me slinking in a thief's fashion. I thought there might already be some kindred of my own in your garden whom I had no mind to meet. I am a suppliant to the King. Can you bring me to him?" He let me hear a couple of coins jingle in his hand.

"Unless the King's health mends suddenly, I am the Queen," said I.

He gave a low whistle and laughed. "If that's so, Queen," he said, "I've played the fool to admiration. Then it's your suppliant I am, suppliant for a few nights'—it might be only one—lodging and protection. I am Trunia of Phars."

The news struck me almost stupid. I have written before how this prince was at war with his brother Argan and the old king their father.

"Defeated, then?" I said.

"Beaten in a cavalry skirmish," he said, "and had to ride for it, which would be little odds but that I missed my way and blundered into Glome. And then my horse went lame not three miles back. The worst of it is, my brother's strength lies all along the border. If you can hide me for a day or so—his messengers will be at your door by daybreak, no doubt—so that I can get into Essur and so round to my main army in Phars, I'll soon show him and all the world whether I'm defeated."

"This is all very well, Prince," said I. "But if we

192

receive you as a suppliant we must, by all law, defend you. I'm not so young a queen as to think I can go to war with Phars at this time."

"It's a cold night to lie out," he said.

"You'd be very welcome if you were not a suppliant, Prince. But in that character you're too dangerous. I can give you lodging only as a prisoner."

"Prisoner?" said he. "Then, Queen, good night."

He darted away as if he were not weary at all (though I had heard weariness in his voice) and ran as one who is used to it. But that flight was his undoing. I could have told him where the old millstone lay. He fell sprawling, made to leap up again with wonderful quickness, then gave a sharp hiss of pain, struggled, cursed, and was still.

"Sprained, if not broken," he said. "Plague on the god that invented man's ankle. Well, you may call your spears, Queen. Prisoner it is. And that prison leads to my brother's hangman?"

"We'll save you if we can," said I. "If we can do it any way without full war against Phars, we'll do it."

The guards' quarters were on that side of the house, as I have said, and it was easy enough to go within calling distance of the men and yet keep my eye on the Prince. As soon as I heard them turning out I said, "Pull your hood over your face. The fewer who know my prisoner's name, the freer my hands will be."

They got him up and brought him hobbling into the hall and put him on the settle by the hearth, and I called for wine and victuals to be brought him, and

193

for the barber to bind up his ankle. Then I went into the Bedchamber. Arnom had gone. The King was worse, his face a darker red, his breathing hoarse. It seemed he could not speak; but I wondered, as his eyes wandered from one to another of us three, what he thought and felt.

"Where have you been, daughter?" said the Fox. "Here's terribly weighty news. A post has just ridden in to tell us that Argan of Phars with three—or maybe four—score of horse has crossed the border and now lies but ten miles away. He gives out that he is seeking his brother Trunia."

How quickly we learn to queen or king it! Yesterday I should have cared little how many aliens in arms crossed our borders; tonight, it was as if someone had struck me in the face.

"And," said Bardia, "whether he really believes that we have Trunia here—or whether he's crossed the border of a crippled land only to make a cheap show of valour and mend his mouldy reputation—either way—"

"Trunia is here," said I. Before their surprise let them speak, I made them come into the Pillar Room, for I found I could not bear my father's eyes on us. The others seemed to make no more account of him than of a dead man. I ordered lights and fire in the tower room, Psyche's old prison, and that the Prince should be taken there when he had eaten. Then we three went busily to our talking.

On three things we were all of one mind. First, that if Trunia weathered his present misfortune, he was

194

likely enough to beat Argan in the end and rule Phars. The old king was in his dotage and counted for nothing. The longer the broils lasted, the more Trunia's party would probably increase, for Argan was false, cruel, and hated by many, and had, moreover, from his first battle (long before these troubles) an old slur of cowardice upon him which made him contemptible. Second, that Trunia as king of Phars would be a far better neighbour to us than Argan, especially if we had befriended him when he was lowest. But thirdly, that we were in no plight to take on a war with Phars, nor even with Argan's party in Phars; the pestilence had killed too many of our young men and we still had almost no corn.

Then a new thought, as if from nowhere, came scalding hot into my head.

"Bardia," said I, "what is Prince Argan worth as a swordsman?"

"There are two better at this table, Queen."

"And he'd be very chary of doing anything that would revive the old story against his courage?"

"It's to be supposed so."

"Then if we offered him a champion to fight against him for Trunia—pawned Trunia's head on the single combat—he'd be in a manner bound to take it up."

Bardia thought for a time. "Why," he said, "it sounds like something out of an old song. Yet, by the gods, the longer I look at it the better I like it. Weak though we are, he'll not want war with us while he has war at home. Not if we leave him any other choice. And his hope hangs on keeping or getting his people's favour. He has none of it to spare even now. And it's an odious thing to be pursuing his brother at our gates as if he were digging out a fox. That won't have made him more loved. If on top of it all he refuses the combat, his name will stink worse still. I think your plan has life in it, Queen."

"This is very wise," said the Fox. "Even if our man's killed and we have to hand Trunia over, no man can say we've treated him ill. We save our good name and yet have no war with Phars."

"And if our champion kills Argan," said Bardia, "then we've done the next thing to setting Trunia on the throne and earned a good friend; for all say Trunia's a right-minded man."

"To make it surer still, friends," said I, "let our champion be one so contemptible that it would be shame beneath all shame for Argan to draw back."

"That's too subtle, daughter," said the Fox. "And hard on Trunia. We don't want our man beaten."

"What are you thinking of, Queen?" said Bardia, teasing his moustache in the old way. "We can't ask him to fight a slave, if that's what you mean."

"No. A woman," said I.

The Fox stared in bewilderment. I had never told him of my exercises with the sword, partly because I had a tenderness about mentioning Bardia to him at all, for to hear Bardia called fool or barbarian angered me. (Bardia called the Fox Greekling and "word-weaver" in return, but that never fretted me in the same way.)

"A woman?" said the Fox. "Am I mad, or are you?"

And now a great smile that would do any heart good to see it broke over Bardia's face. But he shook his head.

"I've played chess too long to hazard my Queen," he said.

"What, Bardia?" said I, steadying my voice as best I could. "Were you only flattering when you said I was a better swordsman than Argan?"

"Not so. I'd lay my money on you if it came to a wager. But there's always luck as well as skill in these things."

"And courage too, you'd say."

"I've no fear of you for that, Queen."

"I have no idea what you are both talking about," said the Fox.

"The Queen wants to fight for Trunia herself, Fox," said Bardia. "And she could do it, too. We've had scores of matches together. The gods never made anyone—man or woman—with a better natural gift for it. Oh, Lady, Lady, it's a thousand pities they didn't make you a man." (He spoke it as kindly and heartily as could be; as if a man dashed a gallon of cold water in your broth and never doubted you'd like it all the better.)

"Monstrous—against all custom—and nature—and modesty," said the Fox. On such matters he was a true Greek; he still thought it barbarous and scandalous that the women in our land go bareface. I had sometimes said to him when we were merry that I ought to call him not Grandfather but Grandam. That was another reason why I had never told him of the fencing.

"Nature's hand slipped when she made me anyway," said I. "If I'm to be hard-featured as a man, why shouldn't I fight like a man too?"

"Daughter, daughter," said the Fox. "In mercy to me, if for nothing else, put this horrible thought out of your head. The plan of a champion and a combat was good. How would this folly make it better?"

"It makes it far better," said I. "Do you think I'm so simple as to fancy I'm safe on my father's throne yet? Arnom is with me. Bardia is with me. But what of the nobles and the people? I know nothing of them nor they of me. If either of the King's wives had lived, I suppose I might have known the lords' wives and daughters. My father never let us see them, much less the lords themselves. I have no friends. Is this combat not the very thing to catch their fancy? Won't they like a woman for their ruler better if she has fought for Glome and killed her man?"

"Oh, for that," said Bardia, "it'd be incomparable. There'll be no one but you in their mouths and hearts for a twelvemonth."

"Child, child," said the Fox, his eyes full of tears, "it's your life. Your life. First my home and freedom gone; then Psyche; now you. Will you not leave one leaf on this old tree?"

I could see right into his heart, for I knew he now implored me with the same anguish I had felt when I implored Psyche. The tears that stood in my eyes behind my veil were tears of pity for myself more than for him. I did not let them fall.

"My mind's made up," I said. "And none of you can think of a better way out of our dangers. Do we know where Argan lies, Bardia?"

"At the Red Ford, the post said."

"Then let our herald be sent at once. The fields between the City and the Shennit to be the place of the combat. The time, the third day from now. The terms, these: If I fall, we deliver Trunia to him and condone his unlawful entering into our land. If he falls, Trunia is a free man and has a safe conduct to go over the border to his own people in Phars or where he will. Either way, all the aliens to be out of the land of Glome in two days."

They both stared and said nothing.

"I'll go to bed now," said I. "See to the sending, Bardia, and then to bed yourself. A good night to you both."

I knew from Bardia's face that he would obey, though he could not bring himself to assent in words. I turned quickly away and went to my own room.

To be alone there and in the silence was like coming suddenly under the lee of a wall on a wild, windy day, so that one can breathe and collect oneself again. Ever since Arnom had said hours ago that the King was dying, there seemed to have been another woman acting and speaking in my place. Call her the Queen; but Orual was someone different and now I was Orual again. (I wondered if this was how all princes felt.)

I looked back on the things the Queen had done and wondered at them. Did that Queen truly think she would kill Argan? I, Orual, as I now saw, did not believe it. I was not even sure that I could fight him. I had never used sharps before; nothing hung on my sham battles but the hope of pleasing my teacher (not that that was a small thing to me either). How would it be if, when the day came, and the trumpets had blown, and the swords were out, my courage failed me? I'd be the mockery of the whole world; I could see the shamed look on the Fox's face, on Bardia's. I could hear them saying, "And yet how bravely her sister went to the offering! How strange that she, who was so meek and gentle, should have been the brave one after all!" And so she would be far above me in everything: in courage as well as in beauty and in those eyes which the gods favoured with sight of things invisible, and even in strength (I remembered her grip when we had wrestled). "She shall not," I said with my whole soul. "Psyche? She's never had a sword in her hand in her life, never done man's work in the Pillar Room, never understood (hardly heard of) affairs of state . . . a girl's life, a child's life. . . ."

I asked myself suddenly what I was thinking. "Can it be my sickness coming back?" I thought. For it began to be like those vile dreams I had had in my ravings when the cruel gods put into my mind the horrible, mad fancy that it was Psyche who was my enemy. Psyche my enemy? She, my child, the very heart of my heart, whom I had wronged and ruined, for whose sake the gods were right to kill me? And now I saw my challenge to the Prince quite differently. Of course he would kill me. He was the gods' executioner. And this would be the best thing in the world; far better than some of the dooms I had looked for. All my life must now be a sandy waste; who could have dared to hope it would be so short? And this accorded so well with all my daily thoughts since the god's sentence, that I now wondered how I could have forgotten that sandy waste for the past few hours.

It was queenship that had done it—all those decisions to make, coming pell-mell upon me without a breathing space, and so much hanging on each; all the speed, skill, peril, and dash of the game. I resolved that for the two days left to me I'd queen it with the best of them; and if by any chance Argan didn't kill me, I'd queen it as long as the gods let me. It was not pride—the glitter of the name—that moved me; or not much. I was taking to queenship as a stricken man takes to the wine-pot or as a stricken woman, if she had beauty, might take to lovers. It was an art that left you no time to mope. If Orual could vanish altogether into the Queen, the gods would almost be cheated.

But had Arnom said my father was dying? No; not quite that.

I rose up and went back to his Bedchamber, without a taper, feeling my way along the walls, for I would have been ashamed if anyone saw me. There were still lights in the Bedchamber. They had left Batta to be with him. She sat in his own chair, close to the fire, sleeping the noisy sleep of a sodden old woman. I went over to the bedside. He was seemingly wide awake. Whether the noises he was making were an attempt at speech, who knows? But the look in his eyes, when he saw me, was not to be mistaken. It was terror. Did he know me and think I came to murder him? Did he think I was Psyche come back from the deadlands to bring him down there?

Some will say (perhaps the gods will say) that if I had murdered him indeed, I should have been no less impious than I was. For as he looked at me with fear, so I looked at him; but all my fear was lest he should live.

What do the gods expect of us? My deliverance was now so near. A prisoner may come to bear his dungeon with patience; but if he has almost escaped, tasted his first draught of the free air . . . to be retaken then, to go back to the clanking of that fetter, the smell of that straw?

I looked again at his face—terrified, idiotic, almost an animal's face. A thought of comfort came to me: "Even if he lives, he will never have his mind again."

I went back and slept soundly.

EIGHTEEN

NEXT day I went as soon as I was risen to the Bedchamber to take my first look at the King; for indeed no lover nor doctor ever watched each change of a sick man's breath and pulse so closely as I. While I was still at his bedside (I could see no difference in him) in came Redival, all in a flurry and her face blubbered, and "Oh, Orual," she said, "is the King dying? And what was going on all last night? And who's the young stranger? They say he's a wonderful, handsome man and looks as brave as a lion. Is he a prince? And oh, Sister, what will happen to us if the King dies?"

"I shall be Queen, Redival. Your treatment shall be according to your behaviour."

Almost before the words were out of my mouth she was fawning upon me and kissing my hand and wishing me joy and saying she had always loved me better than anyone in the world. It sickened me. None of the slaves would cringe to me like that. Even when I was angry and they feared me, all knew better than to put on a beggar's whine; there's nothing moves my pity less.

"Don't be a fool, Redival," said I, shoving her away from my hand. "I'm not going to kill you. But if you put your nose out of the house without my leave, I'll have you whipped. Now be off."

At the door she turned and said, "But you'll get me a husband, Queen, won't you?"

"Yes; probably two," said I. "I've a dozen sons of kings hanging in my wardrobe. But go."

Then came the Fox, who looked at the King, muttered, "He might last for days yet," and then said, "Daughter, I did badly last night. I think this offer to fight the Prince yourself is foolish and, what's more, unseemly. But I was wrong to weep and beg and try to force you by your love. Love is not a thing to be so used."

He broke off because just then Bardia came to the door. "Here's a herald back from Argan already, Queen," he said. "Our man met the Prince (curse his insolence) a great deal nearer than ten miles."

We went into the Pillar Room (my father's eyes followed me terribly) and had the herald in. He was a great, tall man, dressed as fine as a peacock. His message, stripped of many high words, was that his master accepted the combat. But he said his sword should not be stained with woman's blood, so he'd bring a rope with him to hang me when he'd disarmed me.

"That's a weapon in which I profess no skill," said I. "And therefore it's barely justice that your master should bring it. But then he's older than I (his first battle was, I think, long ago), so we'll concede it to make up for his years."

"I can't say that to the Prince, Queen," said the herald.

Then I thought I had done enough (I knew others would hear my jibe even if Argan didn't) and we went orderly to work on all the conditions of the fight and the hundred small things that had to be agreed on. It was the best part of an hour before the herald was gone. The Fox, I could see, was in great pain while all these provisions were being made, the thing growing more real and more irrevocable at each word. I was mostly the Queen now, but Orual would whisper a cold word in the Queen's ear at times.

After that came Arnom, and even before he spoke we knew the old Priest was dead and Arnom had succeeded him. He wore the skins and the bladders, the bird-mask hung at his chest. The sight of all that gave me a sudden shock, like a vile dream, forgotten on waking but suddenly remembered at noon. But my second glance braced me. He would never be terrible like the old Priest. He was only Arnom, with whom I had driven a very good bargain yesterday; there was no feeling that Ungit came into the room with him. And that started strange thoughts in my mind.

But I had no time to follow them. Arnom and the Fox went to the Bedchamber and fell into talk about the King's condition (those two seemed to understand each other well) and Bardia beckoned me out of the room. We went out by the little eastern door, where the

Fox and I had gone on the morning Psyche was born, and there paced up and down between the herb-beds while we talked.

"Now, Queen," said he, "this is your first battle."

"And you doubt my courage?"

"Not your courage to be killed, Queen. But you've never killed; and this must be a killing matter."

"What then?"

"Why, just this. Women and boys talk easily about killing a man. Yet, believe me, it's a hard thing to do; I mean, the first time. There's something in a man that goes against it."

"You think I'd pity him?"

"I don't know if it's pity. But the first time I did it—it was the hardest thing in the world to make my own hand plunge the sword into all that live flesh."

"But you did."

"Yes; my enemy was a bungler. But how if he'd been quick? That's the danger, you see. There's a moment when one pause—the fifth part of the time it takes to wink your eye—may lose a chance. And it might be your only chance, and then you'd have lost the battle."

"I don't think my hand would delay, Bardia," said I. I was trying to test it in my mind. I pictured my father, well again, and coming at me in one of his old rages; I felt sure my hand would not fail me to stab him. It had not failed when I stabbed myself.

"We'll hope not," said Bardia. "But you must go through the exercise. I make all the recruits do it."

"The exercise?"

"Yes. You know they're to kill a pig this morning. You must be the butcher, Queen."

I saw in a flash that if I shrank from this there would at once be less Queen and more Orual in me.

"I am ready," said I. I understood the work pretty well, for of course we had seen the slaughtering of beasts ever since we were children. Redival had always watched and always screamed; I had watched less often and held my tongue. So now I went and killed my pig. (We kill pigs without sacrifice, for these beasts are an abomination to Ungit; there is a sacred story that explains why.) And I swore that if I came back alive from the combat, Bardia and the Fox and Trunia and I should eat the choicest parts of it for our supper. Then, when I had taken off my butcher's apron and washed, I went back to the Pillar Room; for I had thought of something that must be done, now that my life might be only two days. The Fox was already there; I called Bardia and Arnom for witnesses and declared the Fox free.

Next moment I was plunged in despair. I cannot now understand how I had been so blind as not to foresee it. My only thought had been to save him from being mocked and neglected and perhaps sold by Redival if I were dead. But now, as soon as the other two were done wishing him joy and kissing him on the cheeks, it all broke on me. "You'll be a loss to our councils—" "There are many in Glome who'll be sorry to see you go—" "Don't make your journey in winter—" what were they saying?

"Grandfather!" I cried, no Queen now; all Orual,

207

even all child. "Do they mean you'll leave me? Go away?"

The Fox raised towards me a face full of infinite trouble, twitching. "Free?" he muttered. "You mean I could . . . I can . . . it wouldn't matter much even if I died on the way. Not if I could get down to the sea. There'd be tunnies, olives. No, it'd be too early in the year for olives. But the smell of the harbours. And walking about the market talking, real talk. But you don't know, this is all foolishness, none of you know. I should be thanking you, daughter. But if ever you loved me, don't speak to me now. Tomorrow. Let me go." He pulled his cloak over his head and groped his way out of the room.

And now this game of queenship, which had buoyed me up and kept me busy ever since I woke that morning, failed me utterly. We had made all our preparations for the combat. There was the rest of the day, and the whole of the next, to wait; and hanging over it, this new desolation, that if I lived I might have to live without the Fox.

I went out into the gardens. I would not go up to that plot behind the pear trees; that was where he, and Psyche, and I had often been happiest. I wandered miserably out on the other side, on the west of the apple-orchard, till the cold drove me in; it was a bitter, black frost that day, with no sun. I am both ashamed and afraid to revive, by writing of them, the thoughts I had. In my ignorance I could not understand the strength of the desire which must be drawing my old master to his own land. I had lived in one place all my life; everything in Glome was to me stale, common, and taken for granted, even filled with memories of dread, sorrow, and humiliation. I had no notion how the remembered home looks to an exile. It embittered me that the Fox should even desire to leave me. He had been the central pillar of my whole life, something (I thought) as sure and established, and indeed as little thanked, as sunrise and the mere earth. In my folly I had thought I was to him as he was to me. "Fool!" said I to myself. "Have you not yet learned that you are that to no one? What are you to Bardia? as much perhaps as the old King was. His heart lies at home with his wife and her brats. If you mattered to him he'd never have let you fight. What are you to the Fox? His heart was always in the Greeklands. You were, maybe, the solace of his captivity. They say a prisoner will tame a rat. He comes to love the rat—after a fashion. But throw the door open, strike off his fetters, and how much'll he care for the rat then?" And yet, how could he leave us, after so much love? I saw him again with Psyche on his knees; "Prettier than Aphrodite," he had said. "Yes, but that was Psyche," said my heart. "If she were still with us, he would stay. It was Psyche he loved. Never me." I knew while I said it that it was false, yet I would not, or could not, put it out of my head.

But the Fox sought me out before I slept, his face very grey, and his manner very quiet. But that he did not limp, you would have thought he had been in the hands of the torturers. "Wish me well, daughter," he

said. "For I have won a battle. What's best for his fel-
lows must be best for a man. I am but a limb of the
Whole and must work in the socket where I'm put. I'll
stay, and—"

"Oh, Grandfather!" said I, and wept.

"Peace, peace," he said, embracing me. "What would
I have done in Greece? My father is dead. My sons
have, no doubt, forgotten me. My daughter . . .
should I not be only a trouble—*a dream strayed into
daylight* as the verse says? Anyhow, it's a long journey
and beset with dangers. I might never have reached the
sea."

And so he went on, making little of his deed, as if he
feared I would dissuade him from it. But I, with my
face on his breast, felt only the joy.

I went to look at my father many times that day, but
could see no change in him.

That night I slept ill. It was not fear of the combat,
but a restlessness that came from the manifold changes
which the gods were sending upon me. The old Priest's
death, by itself, would have been matter for a week's
thought. I had hoped it before (and then, if he had
died, it might have saved Psyche) but never really
reckoned to see him go more than to wake one morning and find the Grey Mountain gone. The freeing of
the Fox, though I had done it myself, felt to me like
another impossible change. It was as if my father's sickness had drawn away some prop and the whole world—
all the world I knew—had fallen to pieces. I was journeying into a strange new land. It was so new and

strange that I could not, that night, even feel my great sorrow. This astonished me. One part of me made to snatch that sorrow back; it said, "Orual dies if she ceases to love Psyche." But the other said, "Let Orual die. She would never have made a queen."

The last day, the eve of the battle, shows like a dream. Every hour made it more unbelievable. The noise and fame of my combat had got abroad (it was no part of our policy to be secret) and there were crowds of the common people at the palace gates. Though I valued their favour no more than it deserved—I remembered how they had turned against Psyche—yet, willy-nilly, their cheering quickened my pulse and sent a kind of madness into my brain. Some of the better sort, lords and elders, came to wait upon me. They all accepted me for Queen, and I spoke little but, I think, well— Bardia and the Fox praised it—and I watched their eyes staring at my veil, manifestly wondering what it hid. Then I went to Prince Trunia in the tower room and told him we had found a champion (I did not say whom) to fight for him and how he would be brought in honourable custody to see the fight. Though this must have been uneasy news for him, he was too just a man not to see that we were using him as well as our weakness would bear. Then I called for wine that we might drink together. But when the door opened—this angered me for the moment—instead of my father's butler it was Redival who came in bearing the flagon and the cup. I was a fool not to have foreseen it. I knew her well enough to guess that once there was a strange man in the house she'd eat her way through stone walls in order to be seen. Yet even I was astonished to see what a meek, shy, modest, dutiful younger sister (perhaps even a somewhat down-trodden and spirit-broken sister) she could make of herself carrying that wine, with her downcast eyes (which missed nothing from Trunia's bandaged foot to the hair of his head) and her child's gravity.

"Who's that beauty?" said Trunia as soon as she was gone.

"That's my sister, the Princess Redival," said I.

"Glome is a rose-garden, even in winter," said he. "But why, cruel Queen, do you hide your own face?"

"If you become better known to my sister, she'll doubtless tell you," said I more sharply than I had intended.

"Why, that might be," said the Prince, "if your champion wins tomorrow, otherwise death's my wife. But if I live, Queen, I wouldn't let this friendship between our houses die away. Why should I not marry into your line? Perhaps yourself, Queen?"

"There's no room for two on my throne, Prince."

"Your sister then?"

It was of course an offer to be seized. Yet for a moment, saying yes to it irked me; most likely because I thought this prince twenty times too good for her.

"For all I can see," said I, "this marriage can be made. I must speak to my wise men first. For my own part, I like it well."

The day ended more strangely than it began. Bardia

had had me into the quarters for my last practice. "There's that old fault of yours, Queen," he said, "in the feint reverse. I think we've conquered it; but I must see you perfect." We went at it for half an hour and when we stopped to breathe he said, "That's as perfect as skill can go. It's my belief that if you and I were to fight with sharps you'd kill me. But there are two things more to say. This first. If it should happen, Queen—and most likely it won't happen to you, because of your divine blood—but if it should happen that when your cloak's off and the crowd's hushed and you're walking out into the empty space to meet your man— if you should then feel fear, never heed it. We've all felt it at our first fight. I feel it myself before every fight. And the second's this. That hauberk you've been wearing is excellent for weight and fit. But it's a poor thing to look at. A trace of gilding would suit a queen and a champion better. Let's see what the Bedchamber has."

I have said before that the King kept all manner of arms and armours in there. So in we went. The Fox was sitting by the bedside—why, or with what thoughts, I don't know. It was not possible he should love his old master. "Still no change," he said. Bardia and I fell to rummaging among the mail, and soon to disputing; for I thought I'd be safer and more limber in the chain-shirt which I knew than in any other, and he kept on saying, "But wait—wait—now here's a better." And it was when we were most busied that the Fox's voice from behind said, "It's finished." We turned and looked. The thing on the bed which had been half-alive for so long was dead; had died (if he understood it) seeing a girl ransacking his armoury.

"Peace be upon him," said Bardia. "We'll be done here very shortly. Then the women can come and wash the body." And we turned again at once to settle the matter of the hauberks.

And so the thing that I had thought of for so many years at last slipped by in a huddle of business which was, at that moment, of more consequence. An hour later, when I looked back, it astonished me. Yet I have often noticed since how much less stir nearly everyone's death makes than you might expect. Men better loved and more worth loving than my father go down making only a small eddy.

I kept to my old hauberk, but we told the armourer to scour it well, so that it might pass for silver.

NINETEEN

O N A great day the thing that makes it great
may fill the least part of it—as a meal takes
little time to eat, but the killing, baking and
dressing, and the swilling and scraping after it, take
long enough. My fight with the Prince took about the
sixth part of an hour; yet the business about it more
than twelve.

First of all, now that the Fox was a freeman and the
Queen's Lantern (so we call it, though my father had
let the office sleep) I would have him at the fight and
splendidly dressed. But you never had more trouble
with a peevish girl going to her first feast. He said all
barbarians' clothes were barbarous and the finer the
worse. He would go in his old motheaten gown. And
when we had brought him into some kind of order, then
Bardia wanted me to fight without my veil. He thought
it would blind me and did not see how it could well be
worn either over or under my helmet. But I refused
altogether to fight bareface. In the end I had Poobi to
stitch me up a hood or mask of fine stuff, but such as
could not be seen through; it had two eye-holes and

covered the whole helmet. All this was needless, for
I had fought Bardia himself in my old veil a dozen
times; but the mask made me look very dreadful, as
a ghost might look. "If he's the coward they'd make
him," said Bardia, "that'll cool his stomach." And then
we had to start very early, it seemed, for the crowd in
the streets would make us ride slowly. So we had Trunia
down and were all presently on horseback. There was
some talk of dressing him fine too, but he refused this.

"Whether your champion kills or is killed," he said,
"I'll fare no better in purple than in my old battle order.
But where is your champion, Queen?"

"You shall see when we come to the field, Prince,"
said I.

Trunia had started when he first saw me shrouded
like a ghost; neither throat nor helmet to be seen, but
two eye-holes in a white hummock; scarecrow or leper.
I thought his starting boded well how it would taste to
Argan.

Several lords and elders waited for us at the gate to
bring us through the city. It's easy to guess what I was
thinking. So Psyche had gone out that day to heal the
people; and so she had gone out that other day to be
offered to the Brute. Perhaps, thought I, this is what
the god meant when he said *You also shall be Psyche.*
I also might be an offering. That was a good, firm
thought to lay hold of. But the thing was so near now
that I could think very little of my own death or life.
With all those eyes upon me, my only care was to make
a brave show both now and in the fight. I'd have given

ten talents to any prophet who would have foretold me that I'd fight well for five minutes and then be killed.

The lords who rode nearest me were very grave. I supposed (and indeed one or two confessed as much to me afterwards when I came to know them) they thought Argan would soon have me disarmed, but that my mad challenge was as good a way as any of getting him and Trunia both out of our country. But if the lords were glum, the common people in the streets were huzzaing and throwing caps in the air. It would have puffed me up if I had not looked in their faces. There I could read their mind easily enough. Neither I nor Glome was in their thoughts. Any fight was a free show for them; and a fight of a woman with a man better still because an oddity—as those who can't tell one tune from another will crowd to hear the harp if a man plays it with his toes.

When at last we got down to the open field by the river there had to be more delays. Arnom was there in his bird mask and there was a bull to be sacrificed; so well the gods have wound themselves into our affairs that nothing can be done but they have their bit. And opposite us, on the far side of the field, were the horsemen of Phars, and Argan sitting on his horse in the midst of them. It was the strangest thing in the world to look upon him, a man like any other man, and think that one of us presently would kill the other. *Kill*; it seemed like a word I'd never spoken before. He was a man with straw-coloured hair and beard, thin, yet somehow bloated, with pouting lips; a very unpleasing person.

Then he and I dismounted and came close and each had to taste a tiny morsel of the bull's flesh, and take oaths on behalf of our peoples that all the agreements would be kept.

And now, I thought, surely now they'll let us begin. (There was a pale white sun in a grey sky that day, and a biting wind; "Do they want us to freeze before we fight?" I thought.) But now the people had to be pressed back with the butt-ends of spears, and the field cleared, and Bardia must go across and whisper something to Argan's chief man, and both of them must go and whisper to Arnom, and Argan's trumpeter and mine must be placed side by side.

"Now, Queen," said Bardia suddenly, when I had half despaired of ever getting to the end of the preparations, "the gods guard you."

The Fox was standing with his face set like iron; he would have wept if he had tried to speak. I saw a great shock of surprise come over Trunia (and I never blamed him for turning pale) when I flung off my cloak, drew my sword, and stepped out onto the open grass.

The men from Phars roared with laughter. Our mob cheered. Argan was within ten paces of me, then five; then we were at it.

I know he began despising me; there was a lazy insolence in his first passes. But I took the skin off his knuckles with one lucky stroke (and maybe numbed his hand a little) and that brought him to his senses. Though my eye never left his sword, yet I somehow saw his face as well. "Cross-patch," thought I. He had a puckered brow and a sort of blackguardly fretfulness about his lip, which perhaps already masked some fear. For my part, I felt no fear because, now that we were really at it, I did not believe in the combat at all. It was so like all my sham fights with Bardia: the same strokes, feints, deadlocks. Even the blood on his knuckles made no difference; a blunt sword or the flat of a sword could have done as much.

You, the Greek for whom I write, may never have fought; or if you did, you fought, most likely, as a hoplite. Unless I were with you and had a sword, or at least a stick, in my hand I could not make you understand the course of it. I soon felt sure he could not kill me. But I was less sure I could kill him. I was very afraid lest the thing should last too long and his greater strength would grind me down. What I shall remember forever is the change that presently came over his face. It was to me an utter astonishment. I did not understand it. I should now. I have since seen the faces of other men as they began to believe, "This is death." You will know it if you have seen it; life more alive than ever, a raging, tortured intensity of life. Then he made his first bad mistake, and I missed my chance. It seemed a long time (it was a few minutes really) before he made it again. That time I was ready for it. I gave the straight thrust and then, all in one motion, wheeled my sword round and cut him deeply in the inner leg where no surgery will stop the bleeding. I jumped back of course, lest his fall should bear me down with him; so my first man-killing bespattered me less than my first pig-killing.

People ran to him, but there was no possibility of saving his life. The shouting of the mob dinned in my ears, sounding strange as all things sound when you're in your helmet. I was scarcely out of breath even; most of my bouts with Bardia had been far longer. Yet I felt of a sudden very weak and my legs were shaking; and I felt myself changed too, as if something had been taken away from me. I have often wondered if women feel like that when they lose their virginity.

Bardia (the Fox close behind him) came running up to me, with tears in his eyes and joy all over his face. "Blessed! Blessed!" he cried. "Queen! Warrior! My best scholar! Gods, how prettily you did it! A stroke to remember all one's days." And he raised my left hand to his lips. I wept hard and kept my head well down so that he should not see the tears dropping from under the mask. But long before I had my voice back they were all about me (Trunia still on horseback because he could not walk) with praises and thanks, till I was almost pestered with it, though a little sweet-sharp prickle of pride thrust up inside me. There was no peace. I must speak to the people, and to the men of Phars. I must, it seemed, do a score of things. And I thought, "Oh for that bowl of milk, drunk alone in the cool dairy, the first day I ever used a sword!"

As soon as I had any voice I called for my horse, mounted, brought it alongside Trunia's, and held out my hand to him. Thus we rode forward a few paces and faced the horsemen of Phars.

"Strangers," said I, "you have seen Prince Argan

killed in clean combat. Is there any more debate concerning the succession of Phars?"

About half a dozen of them, who had no doubt been Argan's chief partisans, made no other answer than to wheel about and gallop off. The rest all raised their helmets on their spears and shouted for Trunia and peace. Then I let go his hand, and he rode forward and in among them and was soon talking with their captains.

"Now, Queen," said Bardia in my ear, "it's an absolute necessity that you should bid some of our notables and some of those from Phars (the Prince will tell us which) to a feast in the palace. And Arnom too."

"A feast, Bardia? Of bean-bread? You know we've bare larders in Glome."

"There's the pig, Queen. And Ungit must let us have a share of the bull; I'll speak to Arnom of it. You must let the King's cellar blood to some purpose tonight, and then the bread will be less noticed." Thus my fancy of a snug supper with Bardia and the Fox was dashed, and my sword not yet wiped from the blood of my first battle before I found myself all woman again and caught up in housewife's cares. If only I could have ridden away from them all and got to the butler before they reached the palace and learned what wine we really had! My father (and doubtless Batta) had had enough to swim in during his last few days.

In the end there were five and twenty of us (counting myself) who rode back from that field to the palace. The Prince was at my side, saying all manner of fine

221

things about me (as indeed he had some reason) and always begging me to let him see my face. It was only a kind of courteous banter and would have been nothing to any other woman. To me it was so new and (I must confess this also) so sweet that I could not choose but keep the sport up a little. I had been happy, far happier than I could hope to be again, with Psyche and the Fox, long ago before our troubles. Now, for the first time in all my life (and the last) I was gay. A new world, very bright, seemed to be opening all round me.

It was of course the gods' old trick; blow the bubble up big before you prick it.

They pricked it a moment after I had crossed the threshold of my house. A little girl whom I'd never seen before, a slave, came out from some corner where she'd been lurking and whispered in Bardia's ear. He had been very merry up till now; the sunlight went out of his face. Then he came up to me and said half shamefacedly, "Queen, the day's work is over. You'll not need me now. I'd take it very kindly if you'll let me go home. My wife's taken with her pains. We had thought it could not be so soon. I'd be glad to be with her tonight."

I understood in that moment all my father's rages. I put terrible constraint on myself and said, "Why, Bardia, it is very fit you should. Commend me to your wife. And offer this ring to Ungit for her safe delivery." The ring which I took off my finger was the choicest I had.

His thanks were hearty yet he had hardly time to utter

them before he was speeding away. I suppose he never dreamed what he had done to me with those words *The day's work is over*. Yes, that was it—the day's work. I was his work; he earned his bread by being my soldier When his tale of work for the day was done, he went home like other hired men and took up his true life.

That night's banquet was the first I had ever been at and the last I ever sat through (we do not lie at table like Greeks but sit on chairs or benches). After this, though I gave many feasts, I never did more than to come in three times and pledge the most notable guests and speak to all and then out again, always with two of my women attending me. This has saved me much weariness, besides putting about a great notion either of my pride or my modesty which has been useful enough. That night I sat nearly to the end, the only woman in the whole mob of them. Three parts of me was a shamed and frightened Orual who looked forward to a scolding from the Fox for being there at all, and was bitterly lonely; the fourth part was Queen, proud (though dazed too) amid the heat and clamour, sometimes dreaming she could laugh loud and drink deep like a man and a warrior, next moment, more madly, answering to Trunia's daffing, as if her veil hid the face of a pretty woman.

When I got away and up into the cold and stillness of the gallery my head reeled and ached. And "Faugh!" I thought. "What vile things men are!" They were all drunk by now (except the Fox, who had gone early), but their drinking had sickened me less than their eating. I had never seen men at their pleasures before: the

223

gobbling, snatching, belching, hiccuping, the greasiness of it all, the bones thrown on the floor, the dogs quarrelling under our feet. Were all men such? Would Bardia —? then back came my loneliness. My double loneliness, for Bardia, for Psyche. Not separable. The picture, the impossible fool's dream, was that all should have been different from the very beginning and he would have been my husband and Psyche our daughter. Then I would have been in labour . . . with Psyche . . . and to me he would have been coming home. But now I discovered the wonderful power of wine. I understand why men become drunkards. For the way it worked on me was—not at all that it blotted out these sorrows —but that it made them seem glorious and noble, like sad music, and I somehow great and reverend for feeling them. I was a great, sad queen in a song. I did not check the big tears that rose in my eyes. I enjoyed them. To say all, I was drunk; I played the fool.

And so to my fool's bed. What was that? No, no, not a girl crying in the garden. No one, cold, hungry, and banished, was shivering there, longing and not daring to come in. It was the chains swinging at the well. It would be folly to get up and go out and call again: Psyche, Psyche, my only love. I am a great queen. I have killed a man. I am drunk like a man. All warriors drink deep after the battle. Bardia's lips on my hand were like the touch of lightning. All great princes have mistresses or lovers. There's the crying again. No, it's only the buckets at the well. "Shut the window, Poobi. To your bed, child. Do you love me, Poobi? Kiss me good night. Good night." The King's dead. He'll never pull my hair again. A straight thrust and then a cut in the leg. That would have killed him. I am the Queen; I'll kill Orual too.

TWENTY

O N THE next day we burnt the old King. On
the day after that we betrothed Redival to
Trunia (and the wedding was made a month
later). The third day all the strangers rode off and we
had the house to ourselves. My real reign began.

I must now pass quickly over many years (though
they made up the longest part of my life) during which
the Queen of Glome had more and more part in me and
Orual had less and less. I locked Orual up or laid her
asleep as best I could somewhere deep down inside me;
she lay curled there. It was like being with child, but re-
versed; the thing I carried in me grew slowly smaller
and less alive.

It may happen that someone who reads this book will
have heard tales and songs about my reign and my wars
and great deeds. Let him be sure that most of it is false,
for I know already that the common talk, and especially
in neighbouring lands, has doubled and trebled the truth,
and my deeds, such as they were, have been mixed up
with those of some great fighting queen who lived longer
ago and (I think) further north, and a fine patchwork

of wonders and impossibilities made out of both. But the truth is that after my battle with Argan there were only three wars that I fought, and one of them, the last, against the Wagon Men who live beyond the Grey Mountain, was a very slight thing. And though I rode out with my men in all these wars, I was never such a fool as to think myself a great captain. All that part of it was Bardia's and Penuan's. (I met him first the night after I fought Argan, and he became the trustiest of my nobles.) I will also say this: I was never yet at any battle but that, when the lines were drawn up and the first enemy arrows came flashing in among us, and the grass and trees about me suddenly became a place, a Field, a thing to be put in chronicles, I wished very heartily that I had stayed at home. Nor did I ever do any notable deed with my own arm but once. That was in the war with Essur, when some of their horse came out of an ambush and Bardia, riding to his position, was surrounded all in a moment. Then I galloped in and hardly knew what I was doing till the matter was over, and they say I had killed seven men with my own strokes. (I was wounded that day.) But to hear the common rumour you would think I had planned every war and every battle and killed more enemies than all the rest of our army put together.

My real strength lay in two things. The first was that I had, and especially for the first years, two very good counsellors. You couldn't have had better yokefellows, for the Fox understood what Bardia did not, and neither cared a straw for his own dignity or advancement when my needs were in question. And I came to understand (what my girl's ignorance had once hidden from me) that their girding and mocking at one another was little more than a sort of game. They were no flatterers either. In this way I had some profit of my ugliness; they did not think of me as a woman. If they had, it is impossible that we three, alone, by the hearth in the Pillar Room (as we were often) should have talked with such freedom. I learned from them a thousand things about men.

My second strength lay in my veil. I could never have believed, till I had proof of it, what it would do for me. From the very first (it began that night in the garden with Trunia) as soon as my face was invisible, people began to discover all manner of beauties in my voice. At first it was "deep as a man's, but nothing in the world less mannish;" later, and until it grew cracked with age, it was the voice of a spirit, a Siren, Orpheus, what you will. And as years passed and there were fewer in the city (and none beyond it) who remembered my face, the wildest stories got about as to what that veil hid. No one believed it was anything so common as the face of an ugly woman. Some said (nearly all the younger women said) that it was frightful beyond endurance; a pig's, bear's, cat's or elephant's face. The best story was that I had no face at all; if you stripped off my veil you'd find emptiness. But another sort (there were more of the men among these) said that I wore a veil because I was of a beauty so dazzling that if I let it be seen all men in the world would run mad; or else that Ungit was jealous of my beauty and had promised to blast me if I went bareface. The upshot of all this nonsense was that I became something very mysterious and awful. I have seen ambassadors who were brave men in battle turn white like scared children in my Pillar Room when I turned and looked at them (and they couldn't see whether I was looking or not) and was silent. I have made the most seasoned liars turn red and blurt out the truth with the same weapon.

The first thing I did was to shift my own quarters over to the north side of the palace, in order to be out of that sound the chains made in the well. For though, by daylight, I knew well enough what made it, at night nothing I could do would cure me of taking it for the weeping of a girl. But the change of my quarters, and later changes (for I tried every side of the house) did no good. I discovered that there was no part of the palace from which the swinging of those chains could not be heard; at night, I mean, when the silence grows deep. It is a thing no one would have found out who was not always afraid of hearing one sound; and at the same time (that was Orual, Orual refusing to die) terribly afraid of not hearing it if for once—if possibly, at last, after ten thousand mockeries—it should be real, if Psyche had come back. But I knew this was foolishness. If Psyche were alive and able to come back, and wanted to come back, she would have done it long ago. She must be dead by now; or caught by someone and sold into slavery. . . . When that thought came, my only resource was to rise, however late and cold it was, and go to my

Pillar Room and find some work. I have read and written there till I could hardly see out of my eyes—my head on fire, my feet aching with cold.

Of course I had my bidders in every slave-market, and my seekers in every land that I could reach, and listened to every traveller's tale that might put us on Psyche's tracks. I did these things for years, but they were infinitely irksome to me, for I knew it was all hopeless.

Before I had reigned for a year (I remember the time well, for the men were picking the figs) I had Batta hanged. Following up a chance word which one of the horseboys said in my hearing, I found that she had long been the pest of the whole palace. No trifle could be given to any of the other slaves, and hardly a good bit could come on their trenchers, but Batta must have her share of it; otherwise she'd tell such tales of them as would lead to the whipping post or the mines. And after Batta was hanged I went on and reduced the household to better order. There were far too many slaves. Some thieves and sluts I sold. Many of the good ones, both men and women, if they were sturdy and prudent (for otherwise to free a slave is but to have a new beggar at your door) I set free, and gave them land and cottages for their livelihood. I coupled them off in pairs and married them. Sometimes I even let them choose their own wives or husbands, which is a strange, unusual way of making even slaves' marriages, and yet it often turned out well enough. Though it was a great loss to me I set Poobi free, and she chose a very good man. Some of my happiest hours have been beside the fire in her cottage. And most of these freed people have become very thriving husbandmen, all living near the palace, and very faithful to me. It was like having a second body of guards.

I set the mines (they are silver mines) on a better footing. My father had never, it seems, thought of them save as a punishment. "Take him to the mines!" he'd say. "I'll teach him. Work him to death." But there was more death than work in the mines, and the yield was light. As soon as I could get an honest overseer (Bardia was incomparable for finding out such men) I bought strong, young slaves for the mines, saw that they had dry lodging and good feeding, and let every man know that he should go free when he had, adding day to day, dug so much ore. The tale was such that a steady man could hope for his freedom in ten years; later we brought it down to seven. This lowered the yield for the first year, but had raised it by a tenth in the third; now, it is half as great again as in my father's day. Ours is the best silver in all this part of the world, and a great root of our wealth.

I took the Fox out of the wretched dog-hole in which he had slept all these years and gave him noble apartments on the south side of the palace and land for his living, so that he should not seem to hang by my bounties. I also put money into his hands for the buying (if it should prove possible) of books. It took a long time for traders, perhaps twenty kingdoms away, to learn that there was a vent for books in Glome, and longer still for the books to come up, changing hands many times and often delayed for a year or more on the journey. The Fox tore his hair at the cost of them. "An obol's worth for a talent," he said. We had to take what we could get, not what we chose. In this way we built up what was, for a barbarous land, a noble library—eighteen works in all. We had Homer's poetry about Troy, imperfect, coming down to that place where he brings in Patroclus weeping. We had two tragedies of Euripides, one about Andromeda and another where Dionysus says the prologue and the chorus is the wild women. Also a very good, useful book (without metre) about the breeding and drenching of horses and cattle, the worming of dogs, and such matters. Also, some of the conversations of Socrates; a poem in honour of Helen by Hesias Stesichorus; a book of Heraclitus; and a very long, hard book (without metre) which begins *All men by nature desire knowledge.* As soon as the books began to come in, Arnom would often be with the Fox learning to read in them; and presently other men, mostly younger sons of nobles, came too.

And now I began to live as a Queen should, and to know my own nobles, and to show courtesies to the great ladies of the land. In this way, of necessity, I came to meet Bardia's wife, Ansit. I had thought she would be of dazzling beauty; but the truth is she was very short, and now, having borne eight children, very fat and unshapely. All the women of Glome splay out like that, pretty early in their lives. (That was one thing, perhaps, which helped the fantasy that I had a lovely face behind my veil. Being a virgin, I had kept my shape, and that—if you didn't see my face—was for a long time very tolerable.) I put great force upon myself to be courteous to Ansit—more than courteous, even loving. More than that, I would have loved her indeed, for Bardia's sake, if I could have done it. But she was mute as a mouse in my presence; afraid of me, I thought. When we tried to talk together, her eyes would wander round the room as if she were asking, "Who will deliver me from this?" In a sudden flash, not without joy in it, the thought came to me, "Can she be jealous?" And so it was, through all those years, whenever we met. Sometimes I would say to myself, "She has lain in his bed, and that's bad. She has borne his children, and that's worse. But has she ever crouched beside him in the ambush? Ever ridden knee to knee with him in the charge? Or shared a stinking water-bottle with him at the thirsty day's end? For all the dove's eyes they've made at one another, was there ever such a glance between them as well-proved comrades exchange in farewell when they ride different ways and both into desperate danger? I have known, I have had, so much of him that she could never dream of. She's his toy, his recreation, his leisure, his solace. I'm in his man's life."

It's strange to think how Bardia went to and fro daily between Queen and wife, well assured he did his duty by both (as he did) and without a thought, doubtless, of the pother he made between them. This is what it is to be a man. The one sin the gods never forgive us is that of being born women.

The duty of queenship that irked me most was going

often to the house of Ungit and sacrificing. It would have been worse but that Ungit herself (or my pride made me think so) was now weakened. Arnom had opened new windows in the walls and her house was not so dark. He also kept it differently, scouring away the blood after each slaughter and sprinkling fresh water; it smelled cleaner and less holy. And Arnom was learning from the Fox to talk like a philosopher about the gods. The great change came when he proposed to set up an image of her—a woman-shaped image in the Greek fashion—in front of the old shapeless stone. I think he would like to have got rid of the stone altogether, but it is, in a manner, Ungit herself and the people would have gone mad if she were moved. It was a prodigious charge to get such an image as he wanted, for no one in Glome could make it; it had to be brought, not indeed from the Greeklands themselves, but from lands where men had learned of the Greeks. I was rich now and helped him with silver. I was not quite certain why I did this; I think I felt that an image of this sort would be somehow a defeat for the old, hungry, faceless Ungit whose terror had been over me in childhood. The new image, when at last it came, seemed to us barbarians wonderfully beautiful and lifelike, even when we brought her white and naked into her house; and when we had painted her and put her robes on, she was a marvel to all the lands about and pilgrims came to see her. The Fox, who had seen greater and more beautiful works at home, laughed at her.

I gave up trying to find a room where I should not

hear that noise which was sometimes chains swinging in the wind and sometimes lost and beggared Psyche weeping at my door. Instead, I built stone walls round the well and put a thatched roof over it and added a door. The walls were very thick; my mason told me they were madly thick. "You're wasting enough good stone, Queen," he said, "to have made ten new pigsties." For a while after that an ugly fancy used to come to me in my dreams, or between sleeping and waking, that I had walled up, gagged with stone, not a well but Psyche (or Orual) herself. But that also passed. I heard Psyche weeping no more. The year after that I defeated Essur.

The Fox was growing old now and needed rest; we had him less and less in my Pillar Room. He was very busy writing a history of Glome. He wrote it twice, in Greek and in our own tongue, which he now saw was capable of eloquence. It was strange for me to see our own speech written out in the Greek letters. I never told the Fox that he knew less of it than he believed, so that what he wrote in it was often laughable and most so where he thought it most eloquent. As he grew older he seemed to be ever less and less a philosopher, and to talk more of eloquence and figures and poetry. His voice grew always shriller and he talked more and more. He often mistook me for Psyche now; sometimes he called me Crethis, and sometimes even by boys' names like Charmides or Glaucon.

But I was too busy to be with him much. What did I not do? I had all the laws revised and cut in stone in the center of the city. I narrowed and deepened the Shennit till barges could come up to our gates. I made a bridge where the old ford had been. I made cisterns so that we should not go thirsty whenever there was a dry year. I became wise about stock and bought in good bulls and rams and bettered our breeds. I did and I did and I did—and what does it matter what I did? I cared for all these things only as a man cares for a hunt or a game, which fills the mind and seems of some moment while it lasts, but then the beast's killed or the king's mated, and now who cares? It was so with me almost every evening of my life; one little stairway led me from feast or council, all the bustle and skill and glory of queenship, to my own chamber to be alone with myself —that is, with a nothingness. Going to bed and waking in the morning (I woke, most often, too early) were bad times—so many hundreds of evenings and mornings. Sometimes I wondered who or what sends us this senseless repetition of days and nights and seasons and years; is it not like hearing a stupid boy whistle the same tune over and over, till you wonder how he can bear it himself?

The Fox died and I gave him a kingly funeral and made four Greek verses which were cut on his tomb; I will not write them here lest a true Greek should laugh at them. This happened about the end of harvest. The tomb is up behind the pear-trees where he used to teach Psyche and me in summer. Then the days and months and years went on again as before, round and round like a wheel, till there came a day when I looked about me at the gardens and the palace and the ridge of the Grey Mountain out eastward, and thought I could no longer endure to see these same things every day till I died. The very blisters of the pitch on the wooden walls of the byres seemed to be the same ones I had seen before the Fox himself came to Glome. I resolved to go on a progress and travel in other lands. We were at peace with everyone. Bardia and Penuan and Arnom could do all that was needed while I was away; for indeed Glome had now been nursed and trained till it almost ruled itself.

I took with me Bardia's son Ilerdia, and Poobi's daughter Alit, and two of my women and a plump of spears (all honest men) and a cook and a groom with pack animals for the tents and victual, and rode out of Glome three days later.

TWENTY-ONE

THE thing for whose sake I tell this journey happened at the very end of it, and even when I had thought it was finished. We had gone first into Phars, where they harvest later than we, so that it was like having that piece of the year twice over; we found what we had just left at home—the sound of the whetting, the singing of the reapers, the flats of stubble widening and the squares of standing corn diminishing, the piled wagons in the lanes, all the sweat and sunburn and merriment. We had lain ten nights or more in Trunia's palace, where I was astonished to see how Redival had grown fat and lost her beauty. She talked, as of old, everlastingly, but all about her children, and asked after no one in Glome except Batta. Trunia never listened to a word she said, but he and I had much talk together. I had already settled with my council that his second son, Daaran, was to be King of Glome after my day. This Daaran was (for the son of so silly a mother) a right-minded boy. I could have loved him if I had let myself and if Redival had been out of the way. But I would never give my heart again to any young creature.

Out of Phars we had turned westward into Essur by deep passes through the mountains. This was a country of forests greater than I had yet seen and rushing rivers, with great plenty of birds, deer, and other game. The people I had with me were all young and took great pleasure in their travels, and the journey itself had by now linked us all together—all burned brown, and with a world of hopes, cares, jests, and knowledge, all sprung up since we left home, and shared among us. At first they had been in awe of me and had ridden in silence; now we were good friends. My own heart lifted. The eagles wheeled above us and the waterfalls roared.

From the mountains we came down into Essur and lay three nights in the King's house. He was, I think, not a bad sort of man, but too slavish-courteous to me; for Glome and Phars in alliance had made Essur change her tune. His queen was manifestly terrified by my veil and by the stories she had heard of me. And from that house I had meant to turn homewards, but we were told of a natural hot spring fifteen miles further to the west. I knew Ilerdia longed to see it, and I thought (between sadness and smiling) how the Fox would have scolded me if I had been so near any curious work of nature and not examined it. So I said we would go the day's journey further and turn then.

It was the calmest day—pure autumn—very hot, yet the sunlight on the stubble looked aged and gentle, not fierce like the summer heats. You would think the year was resting, its work done. And I whispered to myself that I too would begin to rest. When I was back at

Glome I would no longer pile task on task. I would let Bardia rest too (I had often thought he had begun to look tired) and we would let younger heads be busy, while we sat in the sun and talked of our old battles. What more was there for me to do? Why should I not be at peace? I thought this was the wisdom of old age beginning.

The hot spring (like all such rarities) was only food for stupid wonder. When we had seen it we went further down the warm, green valley in which it rose and found a good camping place between a stream and a wood. While my people were busied with the tents and the horses, I went a little way into the wood and sat there in the coolness. Before long I heard the ringing of a temple bell (all temples, nearly, have bells in Essur) from somewhere behind me. Thinking it would be pleasant to walk a little after so many hours on horseback, I rose and went slowly through the trees to find the temple, very idly, not caring whether I found it or not. But in a few minutes I came out into a mossy place free of trees, and there it was; no bigger than a peasant's hut but built of pure white stone, with fluted pillars in the Greek style. Behind it I could see a small thatched house where, no doubt, the priest lived.

The place itself was quiet enough, but inside the temple there was a far deeper silence and it was very cool. It was clean and empty and there were none of the common temple smells about it, so that I thought it must belong to one of those small peaceful gods who are content with flowers and fruit for sacrifice. Then I saw it must be a goddess, for there was on the altar the image of a woman about two feet high carved in wood, not badly done and all the fairer (to my mind) because there was no painting or gilding but only the natural pale colour of the wood. The thing that marred it was a band or scarf of some black stuff tied round the head of the image so as to hide its face—much like my own veil, but that mine was white.

I thought how much better all this was than the house of Ungit, and how unlike. Then I heard a step behind me and, turning, saw that a man in a black robe had come in. He was an old man with quiet eyes, perhaps a little simple.

"Does the Stranger want to make an offering to the goddess?" he asked.

I slipped a couple of coins into his hand and asked what goddess she was.

"Istra," he said.

The name is not so uncommon in Glome and the neighbouring lands that I had much cause to be startled; but I said I had never heard of a goddess called that.

"Oh, that is because she is a very young goddess. She has only just begun to be a goddess. For you must know that, like many other gods, she began by being a mortal."

"And how was she godded?"

"She is so lately godded that she is still a rather poor goddess, Stranger. Yet for one little silver piece I will tell you the sacred story. Thank you, kind Stranger, thank you. Istra will be your friend for this. Now I will tell you the sacred story. Once upon a time in a certain land there lived a king and a queen who had three daughters, and the youngest was the most beautiful princess in the whole world. . . ."

And so he went on, as such priests do, all in a sing-song voice, and using words which he clearly knew by heart. And to me it was as if the old man's voice, and the temple, and I myself and my journey, were all things in such a story; for he was telling the very history of our Istra, of Psyche herself—how Talapal (that's the Essurian Ungit) was jealous of her beauty and made her to be offered to a brute on a mountain, and how Talapal's son Ialim, the most beautiful of the gods, loved her and took her away to his secret palace. He even knew that Ialim had there visited her only in darkness and had forbidden her to see his face. But he had a childish reason for that: "You see, Stranger, he had to be very secret because of his mother Talapal. She would have been very angry with him if she had known he had married the woman she most hated in the world."

I thought to myself, "It's well for me I didn't hear this story fifteen years ago; yes, or even ten. It would have reawakened all my sleeping miseries. Now, it moves me hardly at all." Then, suddenly struck afresh with the queerness of the thing, I asked him, "Where did you learn all this?"

He stared at me as if he didn't well understand such a question. "It's the sacred story," he said. I saw that he was rather silly than cunning and that it would be useless to question him. As soon as I was silent he went on.

But now all the dreamlike feeling in me suddenly vanished. I was wide awake and I felt the blood rush into my face. He was telling it wrong—hideously and stupidly wrong. First of all, he made it that both Psyche's sisters had visited her in the secret palace of the god (to think of Redival going there!). "And so," he said, "when her two sisters had seen the beautiful palace and been feasted and given gifts, they—"

"They *saw* the palace?"

"Stranger, you are hindering the sacred story. Of course they saw the palace. They weren't blind. And then—"

It was as if the gods themselves had first laughed, and then spat, in my face. So this was the shape the story had taken. You may say, the shape the gods had given it. For it must be they who had put it into the old fool's mind or into the mind of some other dreamer from whom he'd learned it. How could any mortal have known of that palace at all? That much of the truth they had dropped into someone's mind, in a dream, or an oracle, or however they do such things. That much; and wiped clean out the very meaning, the pith, the central knot, of the whole tale. Do I not do well to write a book against them, telling what they have kept hidden? Never, sitting on my judgement seat, had I caught a false witness in a more cunning half-truth. For if the true story had been like their story, no riddle would have been set me; there would have been no guessing and no guessing wrong. More than that, it's a story belonging to a different world, a world in which the gods show themselves clearly and don't torment men with glimpses, nor unveil to one what they hide from another, nor ask you to believe what contradicts your eyes and ears and nose and tongue and fingers. In such a world (is there such? it's not ours, for certain) I would have walked aright. The gods themselves would have been able to find no fault in me. And now to tell my story as if I had had the very sight they had denied me . . . is it not as if you told a cripple's story and never said he was lame, or told how a man betrayed a secret but never said it was after twenty hours of torture? And I saw all in a moment how the false story would grow and spread and be told all over the earth; and I wondered how many of the other sacred stories are just such twisted falsities as this.

"And so," the priest was saying, "when these two wicked sisters had made their plan to ruin Istra, they brought her the lamp and—"

"But why did she—they—want to separate her from the god, if they had seen the palace?"

"They wanted to destroy her *because* they had seen her palace."

"But why?"

"Oh, because they were jealous. Her husband and her house were so much finer than theirs."

That moment I resolved to write this book. For years now my old quarrel with the gods had slept. I had come into Bardia's way of thinking; I no longer meddled with them. Often, though I had seen a god myself, I was near to believing that there are no such things. The memory of his voice and face was kept in one of those rooms of my soul that I didn't lightly unlock. Now, instantly, I knew I was facing them—I with no strength and they with all; I visible to them, they invisible to me; I easily wounded (already so wounded that all my life had been but a hiding and staunching of the wound), they invulnerable; I one, they many. In all these years they had only let me run away from them as far as the cat lets the mouse run. Now, snatch! and the claw on me again. Well, I could speak. I could set down the truth. What had never perhaps been done in the world before should be done now. The case against them should be written.

Jealousy! I jealous of Psyche? I sickened not only at the vileness of the lie but at its flatness. It seemed as if the gods had minds just like the lowest of the people. What came easiest to them, what seemed the likeliest and simplest reason to put in a story, was the dull, narrow passion of the beggars' streets, the temple-brothels, the slave, the child, the dog. Could they not lie, if lie they must, better than that?

". . . and wanders over the earth, weeping, weeping, always weeping." How long had the old man been going on? That one word rang in my ears as if he had repeated it a thousand times. I set my teeth and my soul stood on guard. A moment more and I should have begun to hear the sound myself again. She would have been weeping in that little wood outside the temple door.

"That's enough," I shouted. "Do you think I don't know a girl cries when her heart breaks? Go on, go on."

245

"Wanders, weeping, weeping, always weeping," he said. "And falls under the power of Talapal, who hates her. And of course Ialim can't protect her because Talapal is his mother and he's afraid of her. So Talapal torments Istra and sets her to all manner of hard labours, things that seem impossible. But when Istra has done them all, then at last Talapal releases her, and she is reunited to Ialim and becomes a goddess. Then we take off her black veil, and I change my black robe for a white one, and we offer—"

"You mean she will some day be reunited to the god; and you will take off her veil then? When is this to happen?"

"We take off the veil and I change my robe in the spring."

"Do you think I care what you do? Has the thing itself happened yet or not? Is Istra now wandering over the earth or has she already become a goddess?"

"But, Stranger, the sacred story is about the sacred things—the things we do in the temple. In spring, and all summer, she is a goddess. Then when harvest comes we bring a lamp into the temple in the night and the god flies away. Then we veil her. And all winter she is wandering and suffering; weeping, always weeping. . . ."

He knew nothing. The story and the worship were all one in his mind. He could not understand what I was asking.

"I've heard your story told otherwise, old man," said I. "I think the Sister—or the Sisters—might have more to say for themselves than you know."

246

"You may be sure that they would have plenty to say for themselves," he replied. "The jealous always have. Why, my own wife now—"

I saluted him and went out of that cold place into the warmth of the wood. I could see through the trees the red light of the fire my people had already kindled. The sun had set.

I hid all the things I was feeling—and indeed I did not know what they were, except that all the peace of that autumnal journey was shattered—so as not to spoil the pleasure of my people. Next day I understood more clearly. I could never be at peace again till I had written my charge against the gods. It burned me from within. It quickened; I was with book, as a woman is with child.

And so it comes about that I can tell nothing of our journey back to Glome. There were seven or eight days of it, and we passed many notable places in Essur; and in Glome, after we had crossed the border, we saw everywhere such good peace and plenty and such duty and, I think, love towards myself as ought to have gladdened me. But my eyes and ears were shut up. All day, and often all night too, I was recalling every passage of the true story, dragging up terrors, humiliations, struggles, and anguish that I had not thought of for years, letting Orual wake and speak, digging her almost out of a grave, out of the walled well. The more I remembered, the more still I could remember—often weeping beneath my veil as if I had never been Queen, yet never in so much sorrow that my burning indignation did not rise above it. I was in haste too. I must write it all quickly before

247

the gods found some way to silence me. Whenever, towards evening, Ilerdia pointed and said, "There, Queen, would be a good place for the tents," I said (before I had thought what I would say), "No, no. We can make three more miles tonight; or five." Every morning I woke earlier. At first I endured the waiting, fretting myself in the cold mist, listening to the deep-breathed sleep of those young sleepers. But soon my patience would serve me no longer. I took to waking them. I woke them earlier each morning. In the end we were travelling like those who fly from a victorious enemy. I became silent, and this struck the others silent too. I could see they were bewildered and all the comfort of their travels was gone. I suppose they whispered together about the Queen's moods.

When I reached home, even then I could not set about it as suddenly as I had hoped. All manner of petty work had piled up. And now, when I most needed help, word was sent me that Bardia was a little sick and kept his bed. I asked Arnom about Bardia's sickness, and Arnom said, "It's neither poison nor fever, Queen—a small matter for a strong man. But he'd best not rise. He's aging, you know." It would have given me a thrust of fear but that I already knew (and had seen growing signs of it lately) how that wife of his cockered and cosseted him, like a hen with one chicken—not, I'd swear, through any true fears, but to keep him at home and away from the palace.

Yet at last after infinite hindrances, I made my book and here it stands. Now, you who read, judge between the gods and me. They gave me nothing in the world to love but Psyche and then took her from me. But that was not enough. They then brought me to her at such a place and time that it hung on my word whether she should continue in bliss or be cast out into misery. They would not tell me whether she was the bride of a god, or mad, or a brute's or villain's spoil. They would give no clear sign, though I begged for it. I had to guess. And because I guessed wrong they punished me—what's worse, punished me through her. And even that was not enough; they have now sent out a lying story in which I was given no riddle to guess, but knew and saw that she was the god's bride, and of my own will destroyed her, and that for jealousy. As if I were another Redival. I say the gods deal very unrightly with us. For they will neither (which would be best of all) go away and leave us to live our own short days to ourselves, nor will they show themselves openly and tell us what they would have us do. For that too would be endurable. But to hint and hover, to draw near us in dreams and oracles, or in a waking vision that vanishes as soon as seen, to be dead silent when we question them and then glide back and whisper (words we cannot understand) in our ears when we most wish to be free of them, and to show to one what they hide from another; what is all this but cat-and-mouse play, blindman's buff, and mere jugglery? Why must holy places be dark places?

I say, therefore, that there is no creature (toad, scorpion, or serpent) so noxious to man as the gods. Let them answer my charge if they can. It may well be that, instead of answering, they'll strike me mad or leprous or turn me into beast, bird, or tree. But will not all the world then know (and the gods will know it knows) that this is because they have no answer?

ONE

Nor many days have passed since I wrote those
words *no answer*, but I must unroll my book
again. It would be better to rewrite it from the
beginning, but I think there's no time for that. Weakness
comes on me fast, and Arnom shakes his head and tells
me I must rest. They think I don't know they have sent
a message to Daaran.

Since I cannot mend the book, I must add to it. To
leave it as it was would be to die perjured; I know so
much more than I did about the woman who wrote it.
What began the change was the very writing itself. Let
no one lightly set about such a work. Memory, once
waked, will play the tyrant. I found I must set down
(for I was speaking as before judges and must not lie)
passions and thoughts of my own which I had clean forgotten. The past which I wrote down was not the past
that I thought I had (all these years) been remembering. I did not, even when I had finished the book, see
clearly many things that I see now. The change which
the writing wrought in me (and of which I did not
write) was only a beginning—only to prepare me for the

gods' surgery. They used my own pen to probe my wound.

Very early in the writing there came also a stroke from without. While I related my first years, when I wrote how Redival and I built mud houses in the garden, a thousand other things came back into my mind, all about those days when there was no Psyche and no Fox—only I and Redival. Catching tadpoles in the brook, hiding from Batta in the hay, waiting at the door of the hall when our father gave a feast and wheedling titbits out of the slaves as they went in and out. And I thought, how terribly she changed. This, all within my own mind. But then the stroke from without. On top of many other hindrances came word of an embassy from the Great King who lives to the South and East.

"Another plague," said I. And when the strangers came (and there must be hours of talk, and a feast for them afterwards) I liked them none the better for finding that their chief man was a eunuch. Eunuchs are very great men at that court. This one was the fattest man I ever saw, so fat his eyes could hardly see over his cheeks, all shining and reeking with oil, and tricked out with as much doll-finery as one of Ungit's girls. But as he talked and talked I began to think there was a faint likeness in him to someone I had seen long ago. And, as we do, I chased it and gave it up, and chased it and gave it up again, till suddenly, when I least thought of it, the truth started into my mind and I shouted out, "Tarin!"

"Oh yes, Queen, oh yes," said he, spiteful-pleased (I thought) and leering. "Oh yes, I was him you called

Tarin. Your father did not love me, Queen, did he? But
. . . te-hee, te-hee . . . he made my fortune. Oh yes,
he set me on the right road. With two cuts of a razor.
But for him I should not have been the great man I am
now."

I wished him joy of his advancement.

"Thank you, Queen, thank you. It is very good. And
to think . . . te-hee . . . that but for your father's
temper I might have gone on carrying a shield in the
guard of a little barbarous king whose whole kingdom
could be put into one corner of my master's hunting park
and never be noticed! You will not be angry, no?"

I said I had always heard that the Great King had
an admirable park.

"And your sister, Queen?" said the eunuch. "Ah, she
was a pretty little girl . . . though, te-hee, te-hee, I've
had finer women through my hands since . . . is she
still alive?"

"She is the Queen of Phars," said I.

"Ah, so. Phars. I remember. One forgets the names
of all these little countries. Yes . . . a pretty little girl.
I took pity on her. She was lonely."

"Lonely?" said I.

"Oh yes, yes, very lonely. After the other princess,
the baby, came. She used to say, 'First of all Orual loved
me much; then the Fox came and she loved me little;
then the baby came and she loved me not at all.' So she
was lonely. I was sorry for her . . . te-hee-hee . . .
oh, I was a fine young fellow then. Half the girls in

Glome were in love with me." I led him back to our affairs of state.

This was only the first stroke, a light one; the first snowflake of the winter that I was entering, regarded only because it tells us what's to come. I was by no means sure that Tarin spoke truly. I am sure still that Redival was false and a fool. And for her folly the gods themselves cannot blame me; she had that from her father. But one thing was certain: I had never thought at all how it might be with her when I turned first to the Fox and then to Psyche. For it had been somehow settled in my mind from the very beginning that I was the pitiable and ill-used one. She had her gold curls, hadn't she?

So back to my writing. And the continual labour of mind to which it put me began to overflow into my sleep. It was a labour of sifting and sorting, separating motive from motive and both from pretext; and this same sorting went on every night in my dreams, but in a changed fashion. I thought I had before me a huge, hopeless pile of seeds, wheat, barley, poppy, rye, millet, what not? and I must sort them out and make separate piles, each all of one kind. Why I must do it, I did not know; but infinite punishment would fall upon me if I rested a moment from my labour or if, when all was done, a single seed were in the wrong pile. In waking life a man would know the task impossible. The torment of the dream was that, there, it could conceivably be done. There was one chance in ten thousand of finishing the labour in time, and one in a hundred thousand of making no mistake. It was all but certain I should fail, and be punished—but not certain. And so to it: searching, peering, picking up each seed between finger and thumb. Yet not always finger and thumb. For in some dreams, more madly still, I became a little ant, and the seeds were as big as millstones; and labouring with all my might, till my six legs cracked, I carried them to their places—holding them in front of me as ants do, loads bigger than myself.

One thing that shows how wholly the gods kept me to my two labours, the day's and the night's, is that all this time I hardly gave Bardia a thought, save to grumble at his absence because it meant that I was more hindered in my writing. While the rage of it lasted nothing seemed to matter a straw except finishing my book. Of Bardia I only said (once and again), "Does he mean to slug abed for the rest of his life?" or, "It's that wife of his."

Then there came a day when that last line of the book (*they have no answer*) was still wet, and I found myself listening to Arnom and understanding, as if for the first time, what his looks and voice meant. "Do you mean," I cried, "that the Lord Bardia is in danger?"

"He's very weak, Queen," said the priest. "I wish the Fox were with us. We are bunglers, we of Glome. It seems to me that Bardia has no strength or spirit to fight the sickness."

"Good gods," said I, "why did you not make me understand this before? Ho! Slave! My horse. I will go and see him."

Arnom was an old and trusted counsellor now. He

laid his hand on my arm. "Queen," he said gently and very gravely, "it would make him the less likely to recover if you now went to him."

"Do I carry such an infection about me?" said I. "Is there death in my aspect, even through a veil?"

"Bardia is your most loyal and most loving subject," said Arnom. "To see you would call up all his powers—perhaps crack them. He'd rouse himself to his duty and courtesy. A hundred affairs of state on which he meant to speak to you would crowd into his mind. He'd rack his brains to remember things he has forgotten for these last nine days. It might kill him. Leave him to drowse and dream. It's his best chance now."

It was as bitter a truth as I'd ever tasted, but I drank it. Would I not have crouched silent in my own dungeons as long as Arnom bade me if it would add one featherweight to Bardia's chance of life? Three days I bore it (I, the old fool, with hanging dugs and shrivelled flanks). On the fourth I said, "I can bear it no longer." On the fifth Arnom came to me, himself weeping, and I knew his tidings without words. And this is a strange folly, that what seemed to me worst of all was that Bardia had died without ever hearing what it would have shamed him to hear. It seemed to me that all would be bearable if, once only, I could have gone to him and whispered in his ear, "Bardia, I loved you."

When they laid him on the pyre I could only stand by to honour him. Because I was neither his wife nor kin, I might not wail nor beat the breast for him. Ah, if

I could have beaten the breast, I would have put on steel gloves or hedgehog skins to do it.

I waited three days, as the custom is, and then went to comfort (so they call it) his widow. It was not only duty and usage that drove me. Because he had loved her she was, in a way, surely enough the enemy; yet who else in the whole world could now talk to me?

They brought me into the upper room in her house where she sat at her spinning—very pale, but very calm. Calmer than I. Once I had been surprised that she was so much less beautiful than report had made her. Now, in her later years, she had won a new kind of beauty; it was a proud, still sort of face.

"Lady—Ansit," I said, taking both her hands (she had not time to get them away from me), "what shall I say to you? How can I speak of him and not say that your loss is indeed without measure? And that's no comfort. Unless you can think even now that it is better to have had and lost such a husband than to enjoy any man else in the world forever."

"The Queen does me great honour," said Ansit, pulling her hands out of mine so as to stand with them crossed on her breast, her eyes cast down, in the court fashion.

"Oh, dear Lady, un-queen me a little, I beseech you. Is it as if you and I had never met till yesterday? After yours (never think I'd compare them) my loss is greatest. I pray you, your seat again. And your distaff. We shall talk better to that movement. And you will let me sit here beside you?"

She sat down and resumed her spinning; her face at rest and her lips a little pursed, very housewifely. She would give me no help.

"It was very unlooked for," said I. "Did you at first see any danger in this sickness?"

"Yes."

"Did you so? To me Arnom said it ought to have been a light matter."

"He said that to me, Queen. He said it would be a light matter for a man who had all his strength to fight it."

"Strength? But the Lord Bardia was a strong man."

"Yes—as a tree that is eaten away within."

"Eaten away? And with what? I never knew this."

"I suppose not, Queen. He was tired. He had worked himself out—or been worked. Ten years ago he should have given over and lived as old men do. He was not made of iron or brass, but flesh."

"He never looked nor spoke like an old man."

"Perhaps you never saw him, Queen, at the times when a man shows his weariness. You never saw his haggard face in early morning. Nor heard his groan when you (because you had sworn to do it) must shake him and force him to rise. You never saw him come home late from the palace, hungry, yet too tired to eat. How should you, Queen? I was only his wife. He was too well-mannered, you know, to nod and yawn in a Queen's house."

"You mean that his work—?"

"Five wars, thirty-one battles, nineteen embassies,

taking thought for this and thought for that, speaking a word in one ear, and another, and another, soothing this man and scaring that and flattering a third, devising, consulting, remembering, guessing, forecasting . . . and the Pillar Room and the Pillar Room. The mines are not the only place where a man can be worked to death."

This was worse than the worst I had looked for. A flash of anger passed through me, then a horror of misgiving; could it (but that was fantastical) be true? But the misery of that mere suspicion made my own voice almost humble.

"You speak in your sorrow, Lady. But (forgive me) this is mere fantasy. I never spared myself more than him. Do you tell me a strong man'd break under the burden a woman's bearing still?"

"Who that knows men would doubt it? They're harder, but we're tougher. They do not live longer than we. They do not weather a sickness better. Men are brittle. And you, Queen, were the younger."

My heart shrivelled up cold and abject within me. "If this is true," said I, "I've been deceived. If he had dropped but a word of it, I'd have taken every burden from him, sent him home forever, loaded with every honour I could give."

"You know him little, Queen, if you think he'd ever have spoken that word. Oh, you have been a fortunate queen; no prince ever had more loving servants."

"I know I have had loving servants. Do you grudge me that? Even now, in your grief, will your heart serve

261

you to grudge me that? Do you mock me because that is the only sort of love I ever had or could have? No husband; no child. And you—you who have had all—"

"All you left me, Queen."

"Left you, fool? What mad thought is in your mind?"

"Oh, I know well enough that you were not lovers. You left me that. The divine blood will not mix with subjects', they say. You left me my share. When you had used him, you would let him steal home to me; until you needed him again. After weeks and months at the wars—you and he night and day together, sharing the councils, the dangers, the victories, the soldiers' bread, the very jokes—he could come back to me, each time a little thinner and greyer and with a few more scars, and fall asleep before his supper was down, and cry out in his dream, 'Quick, on the right there. The Queen's in danger.' And next morning—the Queen's a wonderful early riser in Glome—the Pillar Room again. I'll not deny it; I had what you left of him."

Her look and voice now were such as no woman could mistake.

"What?" I cried. "Is it possible you're jealous?"

She said nothing.

I sprang to my feet and pulled aside my veil. "Look, look, you fool!" I cried. "Are you jealous of this?"

She started back from me, gazing, so that for a moment I wondered if my face were a terror to her. But it was not fear that moved her. For the first time that prim mouth of hers twitched. The tears began to gather

in her eyes. "Oh," she gasped, "Oh. I never knew . . .
you also . . . ?"

"What?"

"You loved him. You've suffered, too. We both . . ."

She was weeping; and I. Next moment we were in
each other's arms. It was the strangest thing that our
hatred should die out at the very moment she first knew
her husband was the man I loved. It would have been far
otherwise if he were still alive; but on that desolate
island (our blank, un-Bardia'd life) we were the only
two castaways. We spoke a language, so to call it, which
no one else in the huge heedless world could understand.
Yet it was a language only of sobs. We could not even
begin to speak of him in words; that would have un-
sheathed both daggers at once.

The softness did not last. I have seen something like
this happen in a battle. A man was coming at me, I at
him, to kill. Then came a sudden great gust of wind
that wrapped our cloaks over our swords and almost
over our eyes, so that we could do nothing to one another
but must fight the wind itself. And that ridiculous con-
tention, so foreign to the business we were on, set us both
laughing, face to face—friends for a moment—and then
at once enemies again and forever. So here.

Presently (I have no memory how it came about) we
were apart again; I now resuming my veil, her face hard
and cold.

"Well!" I was saying. "You have made me little better than the Lord Bardia's murderer. It was your aim to
torture me. And you chose your torture well. Be con-

tent; you are avenged. But tell me this. Did you speak only to wound, or did you believe what you said?"

"Believe? I do not believe, I know, that your queenship drank up his blood year by year and ate out his life."

"Then why did you not tell me? A word from you would have sufficed. Or are you like the gods who will speak only when it is too late?"

"Tell you?" she said, looking at me with a sort of proud wonder. "Tell you? And so take away from him his work, which was his life (for what's any woman to a man and a soldier in the end?) and all his glory and his great deeds? Make a child and a dotard of him? Keep him to myself at that cost? Make him so mine that he was no longer his?"

"And yet—he would have been yours."

"But I would be his. I was his wife, not his doxy. He was my husband, not my house-dog. He was to live the life he thought best and fittest for a great man—not that which would most pleasure me. You have taken Ilerdia now too. He will turn his back on his mother's house more and more; he will seek strange lands, and be occupied with matters I don't understand, and go where I can't follow, and be daily less mine—more his own and the world's. Do you think I'd lift up my little finger if lifting it would stop it?"

"And you could—and you can—bear that?"

"You ask that? Oh, Queen Orual, I begin to think you know nothing of love. Or no; I'll not say that. Yours is Queen's love, not commoners'. Perhaps you who

264

spring from the gods love like the gods. Like the Shadowbrute. They say the loving and the devouring are all one, don't they?"

"Woman," said I, "I saved his life. Thankless fool! You'd have been widowed many a year sooner if I'd not been there one day on the field of Ingarn—and got that wound which still aches at every change of weather. Where are *your* scars?"

"Where a woman's are when she has borne eight children. Yes. Saved his life. Why, you had use for it. Thrift, Queen Orual. Too good a sword to throw away. Faugh! You're full fed. Gorged with other men's lives, women's too: Bardia's, mine, the Fox's, your sister's— both your sisters'."

"It's enough," I cried. The air in her room was shot with crimson. It came horribly in my mind that if I ordered her to torture and death no one could save her. Arnom would murmur. Ilerdia would turn rebel. But she'd be twisting (cockchafer-like) on a sharp stake before anyone could help her.

Something (if it was the gods, I bless their name) made me unable to do this. I got somehow to the door. Then I turned and said to her,

"If you had spoken thus to my father, he'd have had your tongue cut out."

"What? Afraid of it?" said she.

As I rode homeward I said to myself, "She shall have her Ilerdia back. He can go and live on his lands. Turn oaf. Grow fat and mumble between his belches about the price of bullocks. I would have made him a great man. Now he shall be nothing. He may thank his mother. She'll not have need to say again that I devour her men-folk."

But I did none of these things to Ilerdia.

And now those divine Surgeons had me tied down and were at work. My anger protected me only for a short time; anger wearies itself out and truth comes in. For it was all true—truer than Ansit could know. I had rejoiced when there was a press of work, had heaped up needless work to keep him late at the palace, plied him with questions for the mere pleasure of hearing his voice. Anything to put off the moment when he would go and leave me to my emptiness. And I had hated him for going. Punished him too. Men have a hundred ways of mocking a man who's thought to love his wife too well, and Bardia was defenceless; everyone knew he'd married an undowered girl, and Ansit boasted that she'd no need (like most) to seek out the ugliest girls in the slave-market for her household. I never mocked him myself; but I had endless sleights and contrivances (behind my veil) for pushing the talk in such directions as, I knew, would make others mock him. I hated them for doing it, but I had a bittersweet pleasure at his clouded face. Did I hate him, then? Indeed, I believe so. A love like that can grow to be nine-tenths hatred and still call itself love. One thing's certain; in my mad midnight fantasies (Ansit dead, or, better still, proved whore, witch, or traitress) when he was at last to be seeking my love, I always had him begin by imploring my forgiveness. Sometimes he had hard work to get it. I would bring him within an ace of killing himself first.

But the result, when all those bitter hours were over, was a strange one. The craving for Bardia was ended. No one will believe this who has not lived long and looked hard, so that he knows how suddenly a passion which has for years been wrapped round the whole heart will dry up and wither. Perhaps in the soul, as in the soil, those growths that show the brightest colours and put forth the most overpowering smell have not always the deepest root. Or perhaps it's age that does it. But most of all, I think, it was this. My love for Bardia (not Bardia himself) had become to me a sickening thing. I had been dragged up and out onto such heights and precipices of truth, that I came into an air where it could not live. It stank; a gnawing greed for one to whom I could give nothing, of whom I craved all. Heaven knows how we had tormented him, Ansit and I. For it needs no Oedipus to guess that, many and many a night, her jealousy of me had welcomed him home, late from the palace, to a bitter hearth.

But when the craving went, nearly all that I called myself went with it. It was as if my whole soul had been one tooth and now that tooth was drawn. I was a gap. And now I thought I had come to the very bottom and that the gods could tell me no worse.

TWO

A FEW days after I had been with Ansit came the rite of the Year's birth. This is when the Priest is shut up in the house of Ungit from sunset, and on the following noon fights his way out and is said to be born. But of course, like all these sacred matters, it is and it is not (so that it was easy for the Fox to show its manifold contradictions). For the fight is with wooden swords, and instead of blood wine is poured over the combatants, and though they say he is shut into the house, it's only the great door to the city and the west that is shut, and the two smaller doors at the other end are open and common worshippers go in and out at will.

When there is a King in Glome he has to go in with the Priest at sunset and remain in the house till the Birth. But it is unlawful for a virgin to be present at the things which are done in the house that night; so I go in, by the north door, only an hour before the Birth. (The others who have to be there are one of the nobles, and one of the elders, and one of the people, chosen in a sacred manner which I am not allowed to write.)

That year it was a fresh morning, very sweet, with a light wind from the south; and because of that freshness out of doors, I felt it more than ever a horrible thing to go into the dark holiness of Ungit's house. I have (I think) said before that Arnom had made it a little lighter and cleaner. But it was still an imprisoning, smothering sort of place; and especially on the morning of the Birth, when there had been censing and slaughtering, and pouring of wine and pouring of blood, and dancing and feasting and towsing of girls, and burning of fat, all night long. There was as much taint of sweat and foul air as (in a mortal's house) would have set the laziest slut to opening windows, scouring and sweeping.

I came and sat on the flat stone which is my place, opposite the sacred stone which is Ungit herself; the new, woman-shaped image a little on my left. Arnom's seat was on my right. He was in his mask, of course, nodding with weariness. They were beating the drums, but not loud, and otherwise there was silence.

I saw the terrible girls sitting in rows down both sides of the house, each cross-legged at the door of her cell. Thus they sat year after year (and usually barren after a few seasons) till they turned into the toothless crones who were hobbling about the floor, tending fires and sweeping—sometimes, after a swift glance round, stooping as suddenly as a bird to pick up a coin or a half-gnawed bone and hide it in their gowns. And I thought how the seed of men that might have gone to make hardy boys and fruitful girls was drained into that house, and nothing given back; and how the silver that

269

men had earned hard and needed was also drained in there, and nothing given back; and how the girls themselves were devoured and were given nothing back.

Then I looked at Ungit herself. She had not, like most sacred stones, fallen from the sky. The story was that at the very beginning she had pushed her way up out of the earth—a foretaste of, or an ambassador from, whatever things may live and work down there one below the other all the way down under the dark and weight and heat. I have said she had no face; but that meant she had a thousand faces. For she was very uneven, lumpy and furrowed, so that, as when we gaze into a fire, you could always see some face or other. She was now more rugged than ever because of all the blood they had poured over her in the night. In the little clots and chains of it I made out a face; a fancy at one moment, but then, once you had seen it, not to be evaded. A face such as you might see in a loaf, swollen, brooding, infinitely female. It was a little like Batta as I remembered her in certain of her moods. Batta, when we were very small, had her loving moods, even to me. I have run out into the garden to get free—and to get, as it were, freshened and cleansed—from her huge, hot, strong yet flabby-soft embraces, the smothering, engulfing tenacity of her.

"Yes," I thought, "Ungit is very like Batta today."

"Arnom," said I, whispering, "who is Ungit?"

"I think, Queen," said he (his voice strange out of the mask), "she signifies the earth, which is the womb and mother of all living things." This was the new way

270

of talking about the gods which Arnom, and others, had learned from the Fox.

"If she is the mother of all things," said I, "in what way more is she the mother of the god of the Mountain?"

"He is the air and the sky, for we see the clouds coming up from the earth in mists and exhalations."

"Then why do the stories sometimes say he's her husband, too?"

"That means that the sky by its showers makes the earth fruitful."

"If that's all they mean, why do they wrap it up in so strange a fashion?"

"Doubtless," said Arnom (and I could tell that he was yawning inside the mask, being worn out with his vigil), "doubtless to hide it from the vulgar."

I would torment him no more, but I said to myself, "It's very strange that our fathers should first think it worth telling us that rain falls out of the sky, and then, for fear such a notable secret should get out (why not hold their tongues?) wrap it up in a filthy tale so that no one could understand the telling."

The drums went on. My back began to ache. Presently the little door on my right opened and a woman, a peasant, came in. You could see she had not come for the Birth feast, but on some more pressing matter of her own. She had done nothing (as even the poorest contrive for that feast) to make herself gay, and the tears were wet on her cheeks. She looked as if she had cried all night, and in her hands she held a live pigeon. One of the lesser priests came forward at once, took the tiny offering from her, slit it open with his stone knife, splashed the little shower of blood over Ungit (where it became like dribble from the mouth of the face I saw in her) and gave the body to one of the temple slaves. The peasant woman sank down on her face at Ungit's feet. She lay there a very long time, so shaking that anyone could tell how bitterly she wept. But the weeping ceased. She rose up on her knees and put back her hair from her face and took a long breath. Then she rose to go, and as she turned I could look straight into her eyes. She was grave enough; and yet (I was very close to her and could not doubt it) it was as if a sponge had been passed over her. The trouble was soothed. She was calm, patient, able for whatever she had to do.

"Has Ungit comforted you, child?" I asked.

"Oh yes, Queen," said the woman, her face almost brightening, "Oh yes. Ungit has given me great comfort. There's no goddess like Ungit."

"Do you always pray to *that* Ungit," said I (nodding toward the shapeless stone), "and not to *that?*" Here I nodded towards our new image, standing tall and straight in her robes and (whatever the Fox might say of it) the loveliest thing our land has ever seen.

"Oh, always this, Queen," said she. "That other, the Greek Ungit, she wouldn't understand my speech. She's only for nobles and learned men. There's no comfort in her."

Soon after that it was noon and the sham fight at the

western door had to be done and we all came out into the daylight, after Arnom. I had seen often enough before what met us there: the great mob, shouting, "He is born! He is born!" and whirling their rattles, and throwing wheat-seed into the air, all sweaty and struggling and climbing on one another's backs to get a sight of Arnom and the rest of us. Today it struck me in a new way. It was the joy of the people that amazed me. There they stood where they had waited for hours, so pressed together they could hardly breathe, each doubtless with a dozen cares and sorrows upon him (who has not?), yet every man and woman and the very children looking as if all the world was well because a man dressed up as a bird had walked out of a door after striking a few blows with a wooden sword. Even those who were knocked down in the press to see us made light of it and indeed laughed louder than the others. I saw two farmers whom I well knew for bitterest enemies (they'd wasted more of my time when I sat in judgement than half the remainder of my people put together) clap hands and cry, "He's born!" brothers for the moment.

I went home and into my own chamber to rest, for now that I am old that sitting on the flat stone wearies me cruelly. I sank into deep thought.

"Get up, girl," said a voice. I opened my eyes. My father stood beside me. And instantly all the long years of my queenship shrank up small like a dream. How could I have believed in them? How could I ever have thought I should escape from the King? I got up from

273

my bed obediently and stood before him. When I made to put on my veil, he said, "None of that folly, do you hear?" and I laid it obediently aside.

"Come with me to the Pillar Room," he said.

I followed him down the stair (the whole palace was empty) and we went into the Pillar Room. He looked all round him, and I became very afraid because I felt sure he was looking for that mirror of his. But I had given it to Redival when she became Queen of Phars; and what would he do to me when he learned that I had stolen his favourite treasure? But he went to one corner of the room and found there (which were strange things to find in such a place) two pickaxes and a crowbar. "To your work, goblin," he said, and made me take one of the picks. He began to break up the paved floor in the center of the room, and I helped him. It was very hard labour because of the pain in my back. When we had lifted four or five of the big stone flags we found a dark hole, like a wide well, beneath them.

"Throw yourself down," said the King, seizing me by the hand. And however I struggled, I could not free myself, and we both jumped together. When we had fallen a long way we alighted on our feet, nothing hurt by our fall. It was warmer down here and the air was hard to breathe, but it was not so dark that I could not see the place we were in. It was another Pillar Room, exactly like the one we had left, except that it was smaller and all made (floor, walls, and pillars) of raw earth. And here also my father looked about him, and once again I was afraid he would ask what I had done with his mirror. But instead, he went into a corner of the earthen room and there found two spades and put one into my hand and said, "Now, work. Do you mean to slug abed all your life?" So then we had to dig a hole in the center of the room. And this time the labour was worse than before, for what we dug was all tough, clinging clay, so that you had rather to cut it out in squares with the spade than to dig it. And the place was stifling. But at last we had done so much that another black hole opened beneath us. This time I knew what he meant to do to me, so I tried to keep my hand from his. But he caught it and said,

"Do you begin to set your wits against mine? Throw yourself down."

"Oh no, no, no; no further down; mercy!" said I.

"There's no Fox to help you here," said my father. "We're far below any dens that foxes can dig. There's hundreds of tons of earth between you and the deepest of them." Then we leaped down into the hole, and fell further than before, but again alighted unhurt. It was far darker here, yet I could see that we were in yet another Pillar Room; but this was of living rock, and water trickled down the walls of it. Though it was so like the two shallower rooms, this was far the smallest. And as I looked I could see that it was getting smaller still. The roof was closing in on us. I tried to cry out to him, "If you're not quick, we shall be buried," but I was smothering and no voice came from me. Then I thought, "He doesn't care. It's nothing for him to be buried, for he's dead already."

275

"Who is Ungit?" said he, still holding my hand.

Then he led me across the floor; and, a long way off before we came to it, I saw that mirror on the wall, just where it always had been. At the sight of it my terror increased, and I fought with all my strength not to go on. But his hand had grown very big now and it was as soft and clinging as Batta's arms, or as the tough clay we had been digging, or as the dough of a huge loaf. I was not so much dragged as sucked along till we stood right in front of the mirror. And in it I saw him, looking as he had looked that other day when he led me to the mirror long ago.

But my face was the face of Ungit as I had seen it that day in her house.

"Who is Ungit?" asked the King.

"I am Ungit." My voice came wailing out of me and I found that I was in the cool daylight and in my own chamber. So it had been what we call a dream. But I must give warning that from this time onward they so drenched me with seeings that I cannot well discern dream from waking nor tell which is the truer. This vision, anyway, allowed no denial. Without question it was true. It was I who was Ungit. That ruinous face was mine. I was that Batta-thing, that all-devouring womblike, yet barren, thing. Glome was a web—I the swollen spider, squat at its center, gorged with men's stolen lives.

"I will not be Ungit," said I. I got up, shivering as with fever, from my bed and bolted the door. I took down my old sword, the very same that Bardia had taught me to use, and drew it. It looked such a happy thing (and it was indeed a most true, perfect, fortunate blade) that tears came into my eyes. "Sword," said I, "you have had a happy life. You killed Argan. You saved Bardia. Now, for your masterpiece."

It was all foolishness, though. The sword was too heavy for me now. My grip—think of a veined, claw-like hand, skinny knuckles—was childish. I would never be able to strike home; and I had seen enough of wars to know what a feeble thrust would do. This way of ceasing to be Ungit was now too hard for me. I sat down—the cold, small, helpless thing I was—on the edge of my bed and thought again.

There must, whether the gods see it or not, be something great in the mortal soul. For suffering, it seems, is infinite, and our capacity without limit.

Of the things that followed I cannot at all say whether they were what men call real or what men call dream. And for all I can tell, the only difference is that what many see we call a real thing, and what only one sees we call a dream. But things that many see may have no taste or moment in them at all, and things that are shown only to one may be spears and water-spouts of truth from the very depth of truth.

The day passed somehow. All days pass, and that's great comfort; unless there should be some terrible region in the deadlands where the day never passes. But when the house slept I wrapped myself in a dark cloak and took a stick to lean on; for I think the bodily weakness, which I die of now, must have begun about

277

that time. Then a new thought came to me. My veil was no longer a means to be unknown. It revealed me; all men knew the veiled Queen. My disguise now would be to go bareface; there was hardly anyone who had seen me unveiled. So, for the first time in many years, I went out bareface; showed that face which many had said, more truly than they could know, was too dreadful to be seen. It would have shamed me no more to go buff-naked. For I thought I would look as like Ungit to them as I had seen myself to be in that mirror beneath the earth. As like Ungit? I *was* Ungit; I in her and she in me. Perhaps if any saw me, they would worship me. I had become what the people, and the old Priest, called holy.

I went out, as often before, by the little eastern doorway that opens on the herb-garden. And thence, with endless weariness, through the sleeping city. I thought they would not sleep so sound if they knew what dark thing hobbled past their windows. Once I heard a child cry; perhaps it had dreamed of me. "If the Shadowbrute begins coming down into the City, the people will be greatly afraid," said the old Priest. If I were Ungit, I might be the Shadowbrute also. For the gods work in and out of one another as of us.

So at last, fainting with weariness, out beyond the city and down to the river; I myself had made it deep. The old Shennit, as she was before my works, would not, save in spate, have drowned even a crone.

I had to go a little way along the river to a place where I knew that the bank was high, so that I could fling myself down; for I doubted my courage to wade in and feel death first up to my knee, and then to my belly, and then to my neck, and still to go on. When I came to the high bank I took my girdle and tied my ankles together with it lest even in my old age I might save my life, or lengthen my death, by swimming. Then I straightened myself, panting from the labour, and stood footfast like a prisoner.

I hopped—what blending of misery and buffoonery it would have looked if I could have seen it!—hopped with my strapped feet a little nearer to the edge.

A voice came from beyond the river: "Do not do it."

Instantly—I had been freezing cold till now—a wave of fire passed over me, even down to my numb feet. It was the voice of a god. Who should know better than I? A god's voice had once shattered my whole life. They are not to be mistaken. It may well be that by trickery of priests men have sometimes taken a mortal's voice for a god's. But it will not work the other way. No one who hears a god's voice takes it for a mortal's.

"Lord, who are you?" said I.

"Do not do it," said the god. "You cannot escape Ungit by going to the deadlands, for she is there also. Die before you die. There is no chance after."

"Lord, I am Ungit."

But there was no answer. And that is another thing about the voices of the gods; when once they have ceased, though it is only a heart-beat ago and the bright hard syllables, the heavy bars or mighty obelisks of sound, are still master in your ears, it is as if they had ceased a thousand years before, and to expect further utterance is like asking for an apple from a tree that fruited the day the world was made.

The voice of the god had not changed in all those years, but I had. There was no rebel in me now. I must not drown and doubtless should not be able to.

I crawled home, troubling the quiet city once more with my dark witch-shape and my tapping stick. And when I laid my head on my pillow it seemed but a moment before my women came to wake me, whether because the whole journey had been a dream or because my weariness (which would be no wonder) had thrown me into a very fast sleep.

THREE

THEN the gods left me for some days to chew the strange bread they had given me. I was Ungit. What did it mean? Do the gods flow in and out of us as they flow in and out of each other? And again, they would not let me die till I had died. I knew there were certain initiations, far away at Eleusis in the Greeklands, whereby a man was said to die and live again before the soul left the body. But how could I go there? Then I remembered that conversation which his friends had with Socrates before he drank the hemlock, and how he said that true wisdom is the skill and practice of death. And I thought Socrates understood such matters better than the Fox, for in the same book he has said how the soul "is dragged back through the fear of the invisible"; so that I even wondered if he had not himself tasted this horror as I had tasted it in Psyche's valley. But by the death which is wisdom I supposed he meant the death of our passions and desires and vain opinions. And immediately (it is terrible to be a fool) I thought I saw my way clear and not impossible. To say that I was Ungit meant that I was as ugly in soul as she; greedy, blood-gorged. But if I practiced true philosophy, as Socrates meant it, I should change my ugly soul into a fair one. And this, the gods helping me, I would do. I would set about it at once.

The gods helping . . . but would they help? Nevertheless I must begin. And it seemed to me they would not help. I would set out boldly each morning to be just and calm and wise in all my thoughts and acts; but before they had finished dressing me I would find that I was back (and knew not how long I had been back) in some old rage, resentment, gnawing fantasy, or sullen bitterness. I could not hold out half an hour. And a horrible memory crept into my mind of those days when I had tried to mend the ugliness of my body with new devices in the way I did my hair or the colours I wore. I'd a cold fear that I was at the same work again. I could mend my soul no more than my face. Unless the gods helped. And why did the gods not help?

Babai! A terrible sheer thought, huge as a cliff, towered up before me, infinitely likely to be true. No man will love you, though you gave your life for him, unless you have a pretty face. So (might it not be?), the gods will not love you (however you try to pleasure them, and whatever you suffer) unless you have that beauty of soul. In either race, for the love of men or the love of a god, the winners and losers are marked out from birth. We bring our ugliness, in both kinds, with us into the world, with it our destiny. How bitter this was, every ill-favoured woman will know. We have all had our dream of some other land, some other world, some other way of giving the prizes which would bring us in as the conquerors; leave the smooth, rounded limbs, and the little pink and white faces, and the hair like burnished gold, far behind; their day ended, and ours come. But how if it's not so at all? How if we were made to be dregs and refuse everywhere and everyway?

About this time there came (if you call it so) another dream. But it was not like a dream, for I went into my chamber an hour after noon (none of my women being there) and without lying down, or even sitting down, walked straight into the vision by merely opening the door. I found myself standing on the bank of a bright and great river. And on the further bank I saw a flock —of sheep, I thought. Then I considered them more closely, and I saw that they were all rams, high as horses, mightily horned, and their fleeces such bright gold that I could not look steadily at them. (There was deep, blue sky above them, and the grass was a luminous green like emerald, and there was a pool of very dark shadow, clear-edged, under every tree. The air of that country was sweet as music.) "Now those," thought I, "are the rams of the gods. If I can steal but one golden flock off their sides, I shall have beauty. Redival's ringlets were nothing to that wool." And in my vision I was able to do what I had feared to do at the Shennit; for I went into the cold water, up to my knee, up to my belly, up to my neck, and then lost the bottom and swam and found the bottom again and came up out of the river into the pastures of the gods. And I walked forward over that holy turf with a good and glad heart. But all the golden

283

rams came at me. They drew closer to one another as their onrush brought them closer to me, till it was a solid wall of living gold. And with terrible force their curled horns struck me and knocked me flat and their hoofs trampled me. They were not doing it in anger. They rushed over me in their joy—perhaps they did not see me—certainly I was nothing in their minds. I understood it well. They butted and trampled me because their gladness led them on; the Divine Nature wounds and perhaps destroys us merely by being what it is. We call it the wrath of the gods; as if the great cataract in Phars were angry with every fly it sweeps down in its green thunder.

Yet they did not kill me. When they had gone over me, I lived and knew myself, and presently could stand on my feet. Then I saw that there was another mortal woman with me in the field. She did not seem to see me. She was walking slowly, carefully, along the hedge which bordered that grassland, scanning it like a gleaner, picking something out of it. Then I saw what. Bright gold hung in flecks upon the thorns. Of course! The rams had left some of their golden wool on them as they raced past. This she was gleaning, handful after handful, a rich harvest. What I had sought in vain by meeting the joyous and terrible brutes, she took at her leisure. She won without effort what utmost effort would not win for me.

I now despaired of ever ceasing to be Ungit. Though it was spring without, in me a winter which, I thought, must be everlasting, locked up all my powers. It was as if I were dead already, but not as the god, or Socrates, bade me die. Yet all the time I was able to go about my work, doing and saying whatever was needful, and no one knew that there was anything amiss. Indeed the dooms I gave, sitting on my judgement seat, about this time, were thought to be even wiser and more just than before; it was work on which I spent much pains and I know I did it well. But the prisoners and plaintiffs and witnesses and the rest now seemed to me more like shadows than real men. I did not care a straw (though I still laboured to discern) who had a right to the little field or who had stolen the cheeses.

I had only one comfort left me. However I might have devoured Bardia, I had at least loved Psyche truly. There, if nowhere else, I had the right of it and the gods were in the wrong. And as a prisoner in a dungeon or a sick man on his bed makes much of any little shred of pleasure he still has, so I made much of this. And one day, when my work had been very wearisome, I took this book, as soon as I was free, and went out into the garden to comfort myself, and gorge myself with comfort, by reading over how I had cared for Psyche and taught her and tried to save her and wounded myself for her sake.

What followed was certainly vision and no dream. For it came upon me before I had sat down or unrolled the book. I walked into the vision with my bodily eyes wide open.

I was walking over burning sands, carrying an empty bowl. I knew well what I had to do. I must find the spring that rises from the river that flows in the dead-lands, and fill it with the water of death and bring it back without spilling a drop and give it to Ungit. For in this vision it was not I who was Ungit; I was Ungit's slave or prisoner, and if I did all the tasks she set me perhaps she would let me go free. So I walked in the dry sand up to my ankles, white with sand to my middle, my throat rough with sand—unmitigated noon above me, and the sun so high that I had no shadow. And I longed for the water of death; for however bitter it was, it must surely be cold, coming from the sunless country. I walked for a hundred years. But at last the desert ended at the foot of some great mountains, crags and pin-nacles and rotting cliffs that no one could climb. Rocks were loosened and fell from the heights all the time; their booming and clanging as they bounced from one jag to another and the thud when they fell on the sand, were the only sounds there. Looking at the waste of rock, I first thought it empty, and that what flickered over its hot surface was the shadows of clouds. But there were no clouds. Then I saw what it really was. Those mountains were alive with innumerable serpents and scorpions that scuttled and slithered over them contin-ually. The place was a huge torture chamber, but the instruments were all living. And I knew that the well I was looking for rose in the very heart of these moun-tains.

"I can never get up," said I.

I sat upon the sand gazing up at them, till I felt as if the flesh would be burned off my bones. Then at last there came a shadow. Oh, mercy of the gods, could it be a cloud? I looked up at the sky and was nearly blinded, for the sun was still straight above my head; I had come, it seemed, into that country where the day never passes. Yet at last, though the terrible light seemed to bore through my eyeballs into my brain, I saw something—black against the blue, but far too small for a cloud. Then by its circlings I knew it to be a bird. Then it wheeled and came lower and at last was plainly an eagle, but an eagle from the gods, far greater than those of the highlands in Phars. It lighted on the sand and looked at me. Its face was a little like the old Priest's, but it was not he; it was a divine creature.

"Woman," it said, "who are you?"

"Orual, Queen of Glome," said I.

"Then it is not you that I was sent to help. What is that roll you carry in your hands?"

I now saw, with great dismay, that what I had been carrying all this time was not a bowl but a book. This ruined everything.

"It is my complaint against the gods," said I.

The eagle clapped his wings and lifted his head and cried out with a loud voice, "She's come at last. Here is the woman who has a complaint against the gods."

Immediately a hundred echoes roared from the face of the mountain, "Here is the woman . . . a complaint against the gods . . . plaint against the gods."

"Come," said the eagle.

"Where?" said I.

"Come into court. Your case is to be heard." And

he called aloud once more, "She's come. She's come." Then from every crack and hole in the mountains there came out dark things like men, so that there was a crowd of them all round me before I could fly. They seized on me and hustled me and passed me on from one to another, each shouting towards the mountain-face, "Here she comes. Here is the woman." And voices (as it seemed) from within the mountain answered them, "Bring her in. Bring her into court. Her case is to be heard." I was dragged and pushed and sometimes lifted, up among the rocks, till at last a great black hole yawned before me. "Bring her in. The court waits," came the voices. And with a sudden shock of cold I was hurried in out of the burning sunlight into the dark inwards of the mountain, and then further and further in, always in haste, always passed from hand to hand, and always with that din of shouts: "Here she is— She's come at last— To the judge, to the judge." Then the voices changed and grew quieter; and now it was, "Let her go. Make her stand up. Silence in the court. Silence for her complaint."

I was free now from all their hands, alone (as I thought) in silent darkness. Then a sort of grey light came. I stood on a platform or pillar of rock in a cave so great that I could see neither the sides nor the roof of it. All round me, below me, up to the very edges of the stone I stood on, there surged a sort of unquiet darkness. But soon my eyes grew able to see things in that half light. The darkness was alive. It was a great assembly, all staring upon me, and I uplifted on my perch above their heads. Never in peace or war have I seen so vast a concourse. There were tens of thousands of them, all silent, every face watching me. Among them I saw Batta and the King my father and the Fox and Argan. They were all ghosts. In my foolishness I had not thought before how many dead there must be. The faces, one above the other (for the place was shaped that way) rose and rose and receded in the greyness till the very thought of counting—not the faces, that would be madness—but the mere ranks of them, was tormenting. The endless place was packed full as it could hold. The court had met.

But on the same level with me, though far away, sat the judge. Male or female, who could say? Its face was veiled. It was covered from crown to toe in sweepy black.

"Uncover her," said the judge.

Hands came from behind me and tore off my veil—after it, every rag I had on. The old crone with her Ungit face stood naked before those countless gazers. No thread to cover me, no bowl in my hand to hold the water of death; only my book.

"Read your complaint," said the judge.

I looked at the roll in my hand and saw at once that it was not the book I had written. It couldn't be; it was far too small. And too old—a little, shabby, crumpled thing, nothing like my great book that I had worked on all day, day after day, while Bardia was dying. I thought I would fling it down and trample on it. I'd tell them someone had stolen my complaint and slipped this thing into my hand instead. Yet I found myself unrolling it. It was written all over inside, but the hand was not like mine. It was all a vile scribble—each stroke mean and yet savage, like the snarl in my father's voice, like the ruinous faces one could make out in the Ungit stone. A great terror and loathing came over me. I said to myself, "Whatever they do to me, I will never read out this stuff. Give me back my Book." But already I heard myself reading it. And what I read out was like this:

"I know what you'll say. You will say the real gods are not at all like Ungit, and that I was shown a real god and the house of a real god and ought to know it. Hypocrites! I do know it. As if that would heal my wounds! I could have endured it if you were things like Ungit and the Shadowbrute. You know well that I never really began to hate you until Psyche began talking of her palace and her lover and her husband. Why did you lie to me? You said a brute would devour her. Well, why didn't it? I'd have wept for her and buried what was left and built her a tomb and . . . and. . . . But to steal her love from me! Can it be that you really don't understand? Do you think we mortals will find you gods easier to bear if you're beautiful? I tell you that if that's true we'll find you a thousand times worse. For then (I know what beauty does) you'll lure and entice. You'll leave us nothing; nothing that's worth our keeping or your taking. Those we love best—whoever's most worth loving—those are the very ones you'll pick out. Oh, I can see it happening, age after age, and growing worse and worse the more you reveal your beauty: the son turning his back on the mother and the bride on her groom, stolen away by this everlasting calling, calling, calling of the gods. Taken where we can't follow. It would be far better for us if you were foul and ravening. We'd rather you drank their blood than stole their hearts. We'd rather they were ours and dead than yours and made immortal. But to steal her love from me, to make her see things I couldn't see . . . oh, you'll say (you've been whispering it to me these forty years) that I'd signs enough her palace was real, could have known the truth if I'd wanted. But how could I want to know it? Tell me that. The girl was mine. What right had you to steal her away into your dreadful heights? You'll say I was jealous. Jealous of Psyche? Not while she was mine. If you'd gone the other way to work—if it was my eyes you had opened—you'd soon have seen how I would have shown her and told her and taught her and led her up to my level. But to hear a chit of a girl who had (or ought to have had) no thought in her head that I'd not put there, setting up for a seer and a prophetess and next thing to a goddess . . . how could anyone endure it? That's why I say it makes no difference whether you're fair or foul. That there should be gods at all, there's our misery and bitter wrong. There's no room for you and us in the same world. You're a tree in whose shadow we can't thrive. We want to be our own. I was my own and Psyche was mine and no one else had any right to her. Oh, you'll say you took her away into bliss and joy such as I could never have given her, and I ought to have been glad of it for her sake. Why? What should I care for some horrible, new happiness which I hadn't given her and which separated her from me? Do you think I wanted her to be happy, that way? It would have been better if I'd seen the Brute tear her in pieces before my eyes. You stole her to make her happy, did you? Why, every wheedling, smiling, cat-foot rogue who lures away another man's wife or slave or dog might say the same. Dog, now. That's very much to the purpose. I'll thank you to let me feed my own; it needed no titbits from your table. Did you ever remember whose the girl was? She was mine. *Mine.* Do you not know what the word means? Mine! You're thieves, seducers. That's my wrong. I'll not complain (not now) that you're blood-drinkers and man-eaters. I'm past that. . . ."

"Enough," said the judge.

There was utter silence all round me. And now for the first time I knew what I had been doing. While I was reading, it had, once and again, seemed strange to me that the reading took so long; for the book was a small one. Now I knew that I had been reading it over and over—perhaps a dozen times. I would have read it for-ever, quick as I could, starting the first word again almost before the last was out of my mouth, if the judge had not stopped me. And the voice I read it in was strange to my ears. There was given to me a certainty that this, at last, was my real voice.

There was silence in the dark assembly long enough for me to have read my book out yet again. At last the judge spoke.

"Are you answered?" he said.

"Yes," said I.

FOUR

THE complaint was the answer. To have heard myself making it was to be answered. Lightly men talk of saying what they mean. Often when he was teaching me to write in Greek the Fox would say, "Child, to say the very thing you really mean, the whole of it, nothing more or less or other than what you really mean; that's the whole art and joy of words." A glib saying. When the time comes to you at which you will be forced at last to utter the speech which has lain at the center of your soul for years, which you have, all that time, idiot-like, been saying over and over, you'll not talk about joy of words. I saw well why the gods do not speak to us openly, nor let us answer. Till that word can be dug out of us, why should they hear the babble that we think we mean? How can they meet us face to face till we have faces?

"Best leave the girl to me," said a well-known voice. "I'll lesson her." It was the spectre which had been my father.

Then a new voice spoke from beneath me. It was the Fox's. I thought he too was going to give some terrible evidence against me. But he said, "Oh, Minos, or Rhadamanthus, or Persephone, or by whatever name you are called, I am to blame for most of this, and I should bear the punishment. I taught her, as men teach a parrot, to say, 'Lies of poets,' and 'Ungit's a false image.' I made her think that ended the question. I never said, Too true an image of the demon within. And then the other face of Ungit (she has a thousand) . . . something live anyway. And the real gods more alive. Neither they nor Ungit mere thoughts or words. I never told her why the old Priest got something from the dark House that I never got from my trim sentences. She never asked me (I was content she shouldn't ask) why the people got something from the shapeless stone which no one ever got from that painted doll of Arnom's. Of course, I didn't know; but I never told her I didn't know. I don't know now. Only that the way to the true gods is more like the house of Ungit . . . oh, it's unlike too, more unlike than we yet dream, but that's the easy knowledge, the first lesson; only a fool would stay there, posturing and repeating it. The Priest knew at least that there must be sacrifices. They will have sacrifice—will have man. Yes, and the very heart, center, ground, roots of a man; dark and strong and costly as blood. Send me away, Minos, even to Tartarus, if Tartarus can cure glibness. I made her think that a prattle of maxims would do, all thin and clear as water. For of course water's good; and it didn't cost much, not where I grew up. So I fed her on words."

I wanted to cry out that it was false, that he had fed

me not on words but on love, that he had given, if not to the gods, yet to me, all that was costliest. But I had not time. The trial, it seemed, was over.

"Peace," said the judge. "The woman is a plaintiff, not a prisoner. It is the gods who have been accused. They have answered her. If they in turn accuse her, a greater judge and a more excellent court must try the case. Let her go."

Which way should I turn, set up on that pillar of rock? I looked on every side. Then, to end it, I flung myself down into the black sea of spectres. But before I reached the floor of the cavern one rushed forward and caught me in strong arms. It was the Fox.

"Grandfather!" I cried. "But you're real and warm. Homer said one could not embrace the dead . . . they were only shadows."

"My child, my beloved," said the Fox, kissing my eyes and head in the old way. "One thing that I told you was true. The poets are often wrong. But for all the rest—ah, you'll forgive me?"

"I to forgive you, Grandfather? No, no, I must speak. I knew at the time that all those good reasons you gave for staying in Glome after you were a freeman were only disguises for your love. I knew you stayed only in pity and love for me. I knew you were breaking your heart for the Greeklands. I ought to have sent you away. I lapped up all you gave me like a thirsty animal. Oh, Grandfather, Ansit's right. I've battened on the lives of men. It's true. Isn't it true?"

"Why, child, it is. I could almost be glad; it gives me

something to forgive. But I'm not your judge. We must go to your true judges now. I am to bring you there."

"My judges?"

"Why, yes, child. The gods have been accused by you. Now's their turn."

"I cannot hope for mercy."

"Infinite hopes—and fears—may both be yours. Be sure that, whatever else you get, you will not get justice."

"Are the gods not just?"

"Oh no, child. What would become of us if they were? But come and see."

He was leading me somewhere and the light was strengthening as we went. It was a greenish, summery light. In the end it was sunshine falling through vine leaves. We were in a cool chamber, walls on three sides of us, but on the fourth side only pillars and arches with a vine growing over them on the outside. Beyond and between the light pillars and the soft leaves I saw level grass and shining water.

"We must wait here till you are sent for," said the Fox. "But there is plenty here that's worth studying."

I now saw that the walls of the place were all painted with stories. We have little skill with painting in Glome, so that it's small praise to say they seemed wonderful to me. But I think all mortals would have wondered at these.

"They begin here," said the Fox, taking me by the hand and leading me to part of the wall. For an instant I was afraid that he was leading me to a mirror as my father had twice done. But before we came near enough to the picture to understand it, the mere beauty of the coloured wall put that out of my head.

Now we were before it and I could see the story it told. I saw a woman coming to the river bank. I mean that by her painted posture I could see it was a picture of one walking. That at first. But no sooner had I understood this than it became alive, and the ripples of the water were moving and the reeds stirred with the water and the grass stirred with the breeze, and the woman moved on and came to the river's edge. There she stood and stooped down and seemed to be doing something —I could not at first tell what—with her feet. She was tying her ankles together with her girdle. I looked closer at her. She was not I. She was Psyche.

I am too old, and I have no time, to begin to write all over again of her beauty. But nothing less would serve, and no words I have would serve even then, to tell you how beautiful she was. It was as though I had never seen her before. Or had I forgotten . . . no, I could never have forgotten her beauty, by day or by night, for one heart-beat. But all this was a flash of thought, swallowed up at once in my horror of the thing she had come to that river to do.

"Do not do it. Do not do it," I cried out, madly, as if she could hear me. Nevertheless she stopped, and untied her ankles and went away. The Fox led me to the next picture. And it too came alive, and there in some dark place, cavern or dungeon, when I looked hard into the murk I could see that what was moving in it was

Psyche—Psyche in rags and iron fetters—sorting out the seeds into their proper heaps. But the strangest thing was that I saw in her face no such anguish as I looked for. She was grave, her brow knitted as I have seen it knitted over a hard lesson when she was a child (and that look became her well; what look did not?). Yet I thought there was no despair in it. Then of course I saw why. Ants were helping her. The floor was black with them.

"Grandfather," said I, "did—"

"Hush," said the Fox, laying his thick old finger (the very feel of that finger again, after so many years!) on my lips. He led me to the next.

Here we were back in the pasture of the gods. I saw Psyche creeping, cautious as a cat, along the hedgerow; then standing, her finger at her lip, wondering how she could ever get one curl of their golden wool. Yet now again, only more than last time, I marvelled at her face. For though she looked puzzled, it was only as if she were puzzled at some game; as she and I had both been puzzled over the game Poobi used to play with her beads. It was even as if she laughed inwardly a little at her own bewilderment. (And that too I'd seen in her before, when she blundered over her tasks as a child; she was never out of patience with herself, no more than with her teacher.) But she did not puzzle long. For the rams scented some intruder and turned their tails to Psyche and all lifted their terrible heads, and then lowered them again for battle, and all charged away together to the other end of the meadow, drawing

299

nearer to each other as they came nearer to their enemy, so that an unbroken wave or wall of gold overwhelmed her. Then Psyche laughed and clapped her hands and gathered her bright harvest off the hedge at ease.

In the next picture I saw both Psyche and myself, but I was only a shadow. We toiled together over those burning sands, she with her empty bowl, I with the book full of my poison. She did not see me. And though her face was pale with the heat and her lips cracked with thirst, she was no more pitiable than when I have seen her, often, pale with heat and thirsty, come back with the Fox and me from a summer day's ramble on the old hills. She was merry and in good heart. I believe, from the way her lips moved, she was singing. When she came to the foot of the precipices I vanished away. But the eagle came to her, and took her bowl, and brought it back to her brim-full of the water of death.

We had now travelled round two of the three walls and the third remained.

"Child," said the Fox, "have you understood?"

"But are these pictures true?"

"All here's true."

"But how could she—did she really—do such things and go to such places—and not . . . ? Grandfather, she was all but unscathed. She was almost happy."

"Another bore nearly all the anguish."

"I? Is it possible?"

"That was one of the true things I used to say to you. Don't you remember? We're all limbs and parts of one

Whole. Hence, of each other. Men, and gods, flow in and out and mingle."

"Oh, I give thanks. I bless the gods. Then it was really I—"

"Who bore the anguish. But she achieved the tasks. Would you rather have had justice?"

"Would you mock me, Grandfather? Justice? Oh, I've been a queen and I know the people's cry for justice must be heard. But not my cry. A Batta's muttering, a Redival's whining: 'Why can't I?' 'Why should she?' 'It's not fair.' And over and over. Faugh!"

"That's well, daughter. But now, be strong and look upon the third wall."

We looked and saw Psyche walking alone in a wide way under the earth—a gentle slope, but downwards, always downwards.

"This is the last of the tasks that Ungit has set her. She must—"

"Then there is a real Ungit?"

"All, even Psyche, are born into the house of Ungit. And all must get free from her. Or say that Ungit in each must bear Ungit's son and die in childbed—or change. And now Psyche must go down into the deadlands to get beauty in a casket from the Queen of the Deadlands, from death herself; and bring it back to give it to Ungit so that Ungit will become beautiful. But this is the law for her journey. If, for any fear or favour or love or pity, she speaks to anyone on the way, then she will never come back to the sunlit lands again. She must keep straight on, in silence, till she stands before the throne of the Queen of Shadows. All's at stake. Now watch."

He needed not to tell me that. We both watched. Psyche went on and on, deeper into the earth, colder, deeper, darker. But at last there came a chilly light on one side of her way, and there (I think) the great tunnel or gallery in which she journeyed opened out. For there, in that cold light, stood a great crowd of rabble. Their speech and clothes showed me at once that they were people of Glome. I saw the faces of some I knew.

"Istra! Princess! Ungit!" they called out, stretching their hands towards her. "Stay with us. Be our goddess. Rule us. Speak oracles to us. Receive our sacrifices. Be our goddess."

Psyche walked on and never looked at them.

"Whoever the enemy is," said I, "he's not very clever if he thinks she would falter for that."

"Wait," said the Fox.

Psyche, her eyes fixed straight ahead, went further on and further down, and again, on the left side of her road, there came a light. One figure rose up in it. I was startled at this one, and looked to my side. The Fox was with me still; but he who rose up in the cold light to meet Psyche by the wayside was also the Fox—but older, greyer, paler than the Fox who was with me.

"O Psyche, Psyche," said the Fox in the picture (say, in that other world; it was no painted thing), "what folly is this? What are you doing, wandering through a tunnel beneath the earth? What? You think it is the way to the Deadlands? You think the gods have sent

302

you there? All lies of priests and poets, child. It is only a cave or a disused mine. There are no deadlands such as you dream of, and no such gods. Has all my teaching taught you no more than this? The god within you is the god you should obey: reason, calmness, self-discipline. Fie, child, do you want to be a barbarian all your days? I would have given you a clear, Greek, full-grown soul. But there's still time. Come to me and I'll lead you out of all this darkness; back to the grass plot behind the pear trees, where all was clear, hard, limited, and simple."

But Psyche walked on and never looked at him. And presently she came to a third place where there was a little light on the left of the dark road. Amid that light something like a woman rose up; its face was unknown to me. When I looked at it I felt a pity that nearly killed my heart. It was not weeping, but you could see from its eyes that it had already wept them dry. Despair, humiliation, entreaty, endless reproach—all these were in it. And now I trembled for Psyche. I knew the thing was there only to entrap her and turn her from her path. But did she know it? And if she did, could she, so loving and so full of pity, pass it by? It was too hard a test. Her eyes looked straight forward; but of course she had seen it out of the corner of her eye. A quiver ran through her. Her lip twitched, threatened with sobbing. She set her teeth in the lip to keep it straight. "O great gods, defend her," I said to myself. "Hurry, hurry her past."

The woman held out her hands to Psyche, and I saw

that her left arm dripped with blood. Then came her voice, and what a voice it was! So deep, yet so woman-like, so full of passion, it would have moved you even if it spoke happy or careless things. But now (who could resist it?) it would have broken a heart of iron.

"Oh Psyche," it wailed. "Oh my own child, my only love. Come back. Come back. Back to the old world where we were happy together. Come back to Maia."

Psyche bit her lip till the blood came and wept bitterly. I thought she felt more grief than that wailing Orual. But that Orual had only to suffer; Psyche had to keep on her way as well. She kept on, went on out of sight, journeying always further into death. That was the last of the pictures.

The Fox and I were alone again.

"Did we really do these things to her?" I asked.

"Yes. All here's true."

"And we said we loved her."

"And we did. She had no more dangerous enemies than us. And in that far distant day when the gods become wholly beautiful, or we at last are shown how beautiful they always were, this will happen more and more. For mortals, as you said, will become more and more jealous. And mother and wife and child and friend will all be in league to keep a soul from being united with the Divine Nature."

"And Psyche, in that old terrible time when I thought her cruel . . . she suffered more than I, perhaps?"

"She bore much for you then. You have borne something for her since."

304

"And will the gods one day grow thus beautiful, Grandfather?"

"They say . . . but even I, who am dead, do not yet understand more than a few broken words of their language. Only this I know. This age of ours will one day be the distant past. And the Divine Nature can change the past. Nothing is yet in its true form."

But as he said this many voices from without, sweet and to be feared, took up the cry, "She comes. Our lady returns to her house; the goddess Psyche, back from the lands of the dead, bringing the casket of beauty from the Queen of Shadows."

"Come," said the Fox. I think I had no will in me at all. He took my hand and led me out between the pillars (the vine leaves brushed my hair) into the warm sunlight. We stood in a fair, grassy court, with blue, fresh sky above us; mountain sky. In the center of the court was a bath of clear water in which many could have swum and sported together. Then there was a moving and rustling of invisible people, and more voices (now somewhat hushed). Next moment I was flat on my face; for Psyche had come and I was kissing her feet.

"Oh Psyche, oh goddess," I said. "Never again will I call you mine; but all there is of me shall be yours. Alas, you know now what it's worth. I never wished you well, never had one selfless thought of you. I was a craver."

She bent over me to lift me up. Then, when I would not rise, she said, "But Maia, dear Maia, you must stand up. I have not given you the casket. You know I went a long journey to fetch the beauty that will make Ungit beautiful."

I stood up then; all wet with a kind of tears that do not flow in this country. She stood before me, holding out something for me to take. Now I knew that she was a goddess indeed. Her hands burned me (a painless burning) when they met mine. The air that came from her clothes and limbs and hair was wild and sweet; youth seemed to come into my breast as I breathed it. And yet (this is hard to say) with all this, even because of all this, she was the old Psyche still; a thousand times more her very self than she had been before the Offering. For all that had then but flashed out in a glance or a gesture, all that one meant most when one spoke her name, was now wholly present, not to be gathered up from hints nor in shreds, not some of it in one moment and some in another. Goddess? I had never seen a real woman before.

"Did I not tell you, Maia," she said, "that a day was coming when you and I would meet in my house and no cloud between us?"

Joy silenced me. And I thought I had now come to the highest, and to the utmost fullness of being which the human soul can contain. But now, what was this? You have seen the torches grow pale when men open the shutters and broad summer morning shines in on the feasting hall? So now. Suddenly, from a strange look in Psyche's face (I could see she knew something she had not spoken of), or from a glorious and awful deepening of the blue sky above us, or from a deep breath like a sigh uttered all round us by invisible lips, or from a deep, doubtful, quaking and surmise in my own heart, I knew that all this had been only a preparation. Some far greater matter was upon us. The voices spoke again; but not loud this time. They were awed and trembled. "He is coming," they said. "The god is coming into his house. The god comes to judge Orual."

If Psyche had not held me by the hand I should have sunk down. She had brought me now to the very edge of the pool. The air was growing brighter and brighter about us; as if something had set it on fire. Each breath I drew let into me new terror, joy, overpowering sweetness. I was pierced through and through with the arrows of it. I was being unmade. I was no one. But that's little to say; rather, Psyche herself was, in a manner, no one. I loved her as I would once have thought it impossible to love, would have died any death for her. And yet, it was not, not now, she that really counted. Or if she counted (and oh, gloriously she did) it was for another's sake. The earth and stars and sun, all that was or will be, existed for his sake. And he was coming. The most dreadful, the most beautiful, the only dread and beauty there is, was coming. The pillars on the far side of the pool flushed with his approach. I cast down my eyes.

Two figures, reflections, their feet to Psyche's feet and mine, stood head downward in the water. But whose were they? Two Psyches, the one clothed, the other naked? Yes, both Psyches, both beautiful (if that mattered now) beyond all imagining, yet not exactly the same.

"You also are Psyche," came a great voice. I looked up then, and it's strange that I dared. But I saw no god, no pillared court. I was in the palace gardens, my foolish book in my hand. The vision to the eye had, I think, faded one moment before the oracle to the ear. For the words were still sounding.

That was four days ago. They found me lying on the grass, and I had no speech for many hours. The old body will not stand many more such seeings; perhaps (but who can tell?) the soul will not need them. I have got the truth out of Arnom; he thinks I am very near my death now. It's strange he should weep, and my women too. What have I ever done to please them? I ought to have had Daaran here and learned to love him and taught him, if I could, to love them.

I ended my first book with the words *no answer*. I know now, Lord, why you utter no answer. You are yourself the answer. Before your face questions die away. What other answer would suffice? Only words, words; to be led out to battle against other words. Long did I hate you, long did I fear you. I might—

(*I, Arnom, priest of Aphrodite, saved this roll and put it in the temple. From the markings after the word* might, *we think the Queen's head must have fallen forward on them as she died and we cannot read them. This book was all written by Queen Orual of Glome, who was the most wise, just, valiant, fortunate and mer-*

ciful of all the princes known in our parts of the world. If any stranger who intends the journey to Greece finds this book let him take it to Greece with him, for that is what she seems mostly to have desired. The Priest who comes after me has it in charge to give up the book to any stranger who will take an oath to bring it into Greece.)

NOTE

The story of Cupid and Psyche first occurs in one of the few surviving Latin novels, the *Metamorphoses* (sometimes called *The Golden Ass*) of Lucius Apuleius Platonicus, who was born about 125 A.D. The relevant parts are as follows:

A king and queen had three daughters of whom the youngest was so beautiful that men worshipped her as a goddess and neglected the worship of Venus for her sake. One result was that Psyche (as the youngest was called) had no suitors; men reverenced her supposed deity too much to aspire to her hand. When her father consulted the oracle of Apollo about her marriage he received the answer: "Hope for no human son-in-law. You must expose Psyche on a mountain to be the prey of a dragon." This he obediently did.

But Venus, jealous of Psyche's beauty, had already devised a different punishment for her; she had ordered her son Cupid to afflict the girl with an irresistible passion for the basest of men. Cupid set off to do so but, on seeing Psyche, fell in love with her himself. As soon as she was left on the mountain he therefore had her carried off by the West-Wind (Zephyrus) to a secret place where he had prepared a stately palace. Here he visited her by night and enjoyed her love; but he forbade her to see his face. Presently she begged that she might receive a visit from her two sisters. The god reluctantly consented and wafted them to her palace. Here they were royally feasted and expressed great delight at all the splendours

311

they saw. But inwardly they were devoured with envy, for their husbands were not gods and their houses not so fine as hers.

They therefore plotted to destroy her happiness. At their next visit they persuaded her that her mysterious husband must really be a monstrous serpent. "You must take into your bedroom to-night," they said, "a lamp covered with a cloak and a sharp knife. When he sleeps uncover the lamp—see the horror that is lying in your bed— and stab it to death." All this the gullible Psyche promised to do.

When she uncovered the lamp and saw the sleeping god she gazed on him with insatiable love, till a drop of hot oil from her lamp fell on his shoulder and woke him. Starting up, he spread his shining wings, rebuked her, and vanished from her sight.

The two sisters did not long enjoy their malice, for Cupid took such measures as led both to their death. Psyche meanwhile wandered away, wretched and desolate, and attempted to drown herself in the first river she came to; but the god Pan frustrated her attempt and warned her never to repeat it. After many miseries she fell into the hands of her bitterest enemy, Venus, who seized her for a slave, beat her, and set her what were meant to be impossible tasks. The first, that of sorting out seeds into separate heaps, she did by the help of some friendly ants. Next, she had to get a hank of golden wool from some man-killing sheep; a reed by a river bank whispered to her that this could be achieved by plucking the wool off the bushes. After that, she had to fetch a cupful of the water of the Styx, which could be reached only by climbing certain impracticable mountains, but an eagle met her, took the cup from her hand, and returned with it full of the water. Finally she was sent down to the lower world to bring back to Venus, in a box, the beauty of Persephone, the Queen of the Dead. A mysterious voice told her how she could reach Persephone and yet return to our world; on the way she would be asked for help by various people who seemed to deserve her pity, but she must refuse them all. And when Persephone gave her the box (full of beauty) she must on no account open the lid to look inside. Psyche obeyed all this and returned to the upper world with the box; but then at last curiosity overcame her and she looked into it. She immediately lost consciousness.

Cupid now came to her again, but this time he forgave her. He interceded with Jupiter, who agreed to permit his marriage and make Psyche a goddess. Venus was reconciled and they all lived happily ever after.

The central alteration in my own version consists in making Psyche's palace invisible to normal, mortal eyes—if "making" is not the wrong word for something which forced itself upon me, almost at my first reading of the story, as the way the thing must have been. This change of course brings with it a more ambivalent motive and a different character for my heroine and finally modifies the whole quality of the tale. I felt quite free to go behind Apuleius, whom I suppose to have been its transmitter, not its inventor. Nothing was further from my aim than to recapture the peculiar quality of the *Metamorphoses*—that strange compound of picaresque novel, horror comic, mystagogue's tract, pornography, and stylistic experiment. Apuleius was of course a man of genius: but in relation to my work he is a "source," not an "influence" nor a "model."

His version has been followed pretty closely by William Morris (in *The Earthly Paradise*) and by Robert Bridges (*Eros and Psyche*). Neither poem, in my opinion, shows its author at his best. The whole *Metamorphoses* was last translated by Mr. Robert Graves (*Penguin Books*, 1950).

C. S. L.

313

Books by C. S. Lewis
available from Harcourt Brace & Company
in Harvest paperback editions

All My Road Before Me: The Diary of C. S. Lewis, 1922–1927
The Business of Heaven: Daily Readings from C. S. Lewis
The Dark Tower and Other Stories
The Four Loves
Letters of C. S. Lewis
Letters to Malcolm: Chiefly on Prayer
A Mind Awake: An Anthology of C. S. Lewis
Narrative Poems
Of Other Worlds: Essays and Stories
On Stories: And Other Essays on Literature
Poems
Present Concerns
Reflections on the Psalms
Spirits in Bondage: A Cycle of Lyrics
Surprised by Joy: The Shape of My Early Life
Till We Have Faces: A Myth Retold
The World's Last Night and Other Essays